"What the blazes! Ol

"Who else would it be? Unless you presented some other woman with your pretend proposal and left her sleepless with the ridiculousness of it all."

She scraped her hands across her face, spreading her hair to the right and left so that she could see.

Oh dear, that was a mistake. It would be better to be blinded than look at Joseph Billings's bare chest.

Any gentleman would have buttoned his shirt to answer a knock on his front door.

The man was not decent. If he wished for the dreaded Hortencia not to seduce him, he would have to do better than this.

"Come in before you blow away." He caught her arm against a gust that had enough force to tip her. "It is nearly midnight. What were you thinking, coming out in this weather?"

How Olive wished she had not come...nearly wished it.

But... "I have questions." And she would not sleep a wink until she had the answers.

Author Note

You are the best. Without you I would have no one to share my fictional friends with. Thank you so much for choosing to spend some time with Olive and Joseph. I hope you enjoy their story.

Have you ever found yourself in a spot where doing the best thing for someone else is not quite what you really want to do?

It happens to our Olive. "Oh what a tangled web we weave when first we practice to deceive" is her life's motto. Sadly for Olive, one thing leads to another and she finds herself becoming ever more entangled in the web. One good thing, though, is that she's not entangled alone. Her new neighbor, the handsome heir to a viscount, is ensnared as tight as she is.

Together they build a pillar of lies...all with the best of intentions, of course. You must guess that it does not take long for sparks to fly between them.

But what will happen when the pillar tumbles? Will their love survive having the truth exposed?

As you know, in the world of romance love conquers all. Thank you so much for taking the journey with Olive and Joseph and discovering how they manage it.

Marriage Charade with the Heir

CAROL ARENS

ISBN-13: 978-1-335-59611-6

Marriage Charade with the Heir

For questions and comments about the quality of this book, please contact us at CustomerService@Harlequin.com.

TM and ® are trademarks of Harlequin Enterprises ULC.

Harlequin Enterprises ULC
22 Adelaide St. West, 41st Floor
Toronto, Ontario M5H 4E3, Canada
www.Harlequin.com

Printed in U.S.A.

Carol Arens delights in tossing fictional characters into hot water, watching them steam and then giving them a happily-ever-after. When she is not writing, she enjoys spending time with her family, beach camping or lounging about a mountain cabin. At home, she enjoys playing with her grandchildren and gardening. During rare spare moments, you will find her snuggled up with a good book. Carol enjoys hearing from readers at carolarens@yahoo.com or on Facebook.

Books by Carol Arens

Harlequin Historical

The Cowboy's Cinderella
"A Kiss from the Cowboy"
in *Western Christmas Brides*
The Rancher's Inconvenient Bride
A Ranch to Call Home
A Texas Christmas Reunion
The Earl's American Heiress
Rescued by the Viscount's Ring
The Making of Baron Haversmere
The Viscount's Yuletide Bride
To Wed a Wallflower
"A Kiss Under the Mistletoe"
in *A Victorian Family Christmas*
The Viscount's Christmas Proposal
Meeting Her Promised Viscount
The Gentleman's Cinderella Bride

The Rivenhall Weddings

Inherited as the Gentleman's Bride
In Search of a Viscountess
A Family for the Reclusive Baron

Visit the Author Profile page
at Harlequin.com for more titles.

Dedicated to the memory of Joseph De Cuir.
You are always in our hearts.
Love cannot be separated.

Chapter One

Fallen Leaf, North Yorkshire, 1871

'Oh what a tangled web we weave when first we practice to deceive.'

Olive Augustmore recited the motto she held dear while yanking the handle of her trunk and dragging it from its hiding place under a tool cupboard.

The screech it made scraping across the stones of the stable floor caught the attention of Gilroy, a highly curious goat. He uttered a bleat, sending her an inquisitive stare.

Many people would not recognize the stare as inquisitive, but Olive did. Gilroy was the father of most of her goat herd. She had raised him from the time he took his first leap.

'I do not know why you should be so curious, my boy. This is not the first time you have seen me drag out this trunk in the deep, dark dead of night.' She arched a brow at the goat. 'You would not guess it by what I am about to do, but I am an honest person. Scrupulously so. Until recently.'

For some reason, Olive found it comforting to speak to the animals.

Rain pattered on the roof, curse it. Haunting the road was easier in dry weather when moonlight shone bright on the path.

Ordinarily, Olive would not stoop to deception. As she had just explained to Gilroy, she was the very beacon of honesty. But in this case, what could not be helped, could not be helped.

Olive dug deep, then dragged out yards of gauzy fabric hidden at the bottom of the trunk. Sitting back on her heels, she unfolded it, then rose and carried it to one of two horse stalls.

'Don't you dare nibble it, Star,' she said to the horse while she spread the filmy fabric across a wooden rail.

Going back to the trunk, she withdrew the dark, fearsome-looking costume which had taken hours upon hours of sewing in the wee private hours of night to create.

It had turned out quite well, and she did not consider it vain to admire the garment. Honest appraisal of her handiwork was all it was. She might as well be honest in something.

'I make a right proper highwayman, Star, and you a right proper ghoul.' Olive glanced at Gilroy peeking out from his pen slats. 'We are a fearsome pair, you must agree.'

She untied her apron, then unbuttoned her dress to change. She was halfway shed of her petticoats when her sister rushed inside the stable, dripping rain and sobbing her poor heart out.

Olive opened her arms. Eliza rushed in. She wrapped her sister up even though the hug was wet and cold.

'Is Laura well?' Olive asked.

'She clung to me and cried when I left. I think she senses I am her mother. I cannot bear it any longer...truly, sister, I cannot.'

When Eliza's sobs evened to a sniffle, she glanced up,

seeming to be aware for the first time that Olive was standing in her shift.

'Is Father drinking?' her sister asked, her eyes taking on a round, horrified expression. 'Is he set on going to the tavern again?'

'It is what he intends. He is looking for his coat, so we must hurry. He is better at finding it than he used to be. Place Star's costume over her while I get into this.' She snatched the highwayman's trousers from the stable stones and stepped into them. Oh, but they were cold.

When her sister seemed about to dissolve into another bout of tears, she said, 'Hurry, Eliza. I must get into place before Father comes out, or everything will be ruined.'

'I will be, at any rate.'

Yes, Eliza would be, and no other way about it. Bearing a child out of wedlock was a shame which could bring a lass down quicker than anything else.

Urgency was the word of the moment. Olive must take to the road and scare Father away from the pub. If he managed to get there, he was sure to drink even more than he already had and speak of things he needed to keep quiet about. It was his way to blather indiscreetly when he was in his cups.

Such a disaster must be prevented at all costs. As far as Olive was concerned, Eliza was only ruined if the 'crime' was discovered.

Her sister was a kind, tenderhearted woman who had suffered a brief lack of judgement and was paying a heart-wrenching price for it.

'I am so sorry, Olive.' Tears spurted from Eliza's eyes again. 'You should not have to do this. I am the guilty one.'

'Sister, you are hardly the first girl to be led astray by

a sweet-talking snake in the grass, and you are unlikely to be the last.'

'You have never been led astray.'

'I am not as trusting as you are. And to be fair, he was the proverbial wolf in sheep's clothing. He did present himself rather respectably for a low-down cad.'

Laura's sire was a wandering poet and singer. Far more charming than an honest man had any right to be. From what Eliza had wailed against Olive's shoulder that night nearly two years ago, her deflowering had taken a shockingly short time…moments only.

Olive had no experience in the human act, but that did seem rather quick for much pleasure to be involved. She believed Gilroy gave more time and thought to the matter.

What she wondered, but did not say to her sister, is how many other young women the villain had seduced during his brief stay in Fallen Leaf.

As far as she knew, Eliza was the only one to pay the piper for her indiscretion.

But, of course, her niece was the sweetest child, and her existence could not be regretted in the least.

However, the price her sister had paid for the circumstance of her child's birth was wretched. Continuing to pretend that Laura was their neighbours' child instead of her own was tearing Eliza up.

'Thank the Good Lord for Mary and Harlow,' Olive said. 'They are the best people we know.'

The Stricklands had taken in Laura just days after she was born to raise along with their own baby girl, who was born the same week.

No doubt there was a special paradise in store for those good souls one day.

'Chin up, sister. No more tears. Laura is living close by. And our secret is safe. We cannot know the future. One day this situation might turn around.'

She could only pray it would. Although the road this far from the village was not frequently travelled, especially at night, there was a risk of being caught out in her deception.

So far the only person she had frightened was her inebriated father, and that little more than half a dozen times. One good scare tended to keep him home at night for a long time. But when he was drunk enough, he forgot how scared he had been the last time.

Forgot that he could not speak of baby Laura, his adorable grandchild, to anyone else.

Olive hastily shrugged into the rest of the highwayman costume.

Eliza made quick work of draping the horse in ghostly gauze.

'Give us a dreadful snort, Star,' Eliza sniffed while Olive mounted the saddle.

Having been secretly trained to do so, the horse made a fierce noise while rolling her eyes until the whites showed.

'Good girl, Star! You are a smart one.' Eliza fed the horse an apple from the barrel.

'Be quick. I think I hear Father singing like a strangled cat.'

Eliza rushed for the doors. She pushed them open.

Lantern glow shone out ahead of Olive. The path went dark when her sister drew the doors closed again.

Urging Star to a trot, she wondered why it was that when Father saddled his horse for the ride to The Shepherd's Keep, the tavern, not the chapel which shared the name... but to the point, how was it that Father never noticed that

Star was missing? Perhaps because he was well along in his drinking by then and his attention was set on only one thing…drinking even more.

And chatting. Father would talk about anything that crossed his mind when he was drunk and in the company of neighbours.

It was before dawn when Joseph Billings mounted his horse and rode along a rural path toward his father's newest property acquisition in North Yorkshire.

Having spent the night in the village of Fallen Leaf at a quaint tavern with rooms to let, he was able to venture out before daylight. It was the time of day he enjoyed most, when night and morning were nearly balanced.

Joseph could not help but grin while he rode though a pretty valley dotted with cottages and small farms. He smelled smoke, but the light was still too dim to see it rising from chimneys.

While he was doing his father's bidding, seeing to the condition of the new property, he found it a pleasure and not a duty.

It was worth the travel north if only to escape London, where people of rank tended to sleep past sunrise and miss dawn's splendour.

More than that, though, he was glad to be rid of Lady Hortencia Clark's attention. In London, there was not a time he did not feel her avaricious eye cutting him between the shoulder blades.

The woman had an unhealthy obsession with him. Or not him so much as the Claymore fortune. She was determined to have him and all that came with him.

Joseph snorted, resentful that the grasping woman even occupied his mind for a moment.

He would not let her ruin this special hour of the day.

Out here in the country, he could breathe. Life in the city and the social obligations that went along with being Viscount Claymore's only child were not what he was made for. Damned if it didn't feel like a polished boot heel pressing on his soul.

He may have been born into society, but he had never particularly felt like a part of it. Just because he had been raised to respect the rules of proper etiquette did not mean he was going to dance to them…insofar as was possible.

Nothing in London could compare to sitting atop his horse, Dane, while watching the sky turn pink behind the hills. The manor house was said to be located on the hilltop where this road ended.

At first Dane's hoofbeats were the only sound he heard. Then birds began to chirp. One, then two, and within moments the trees growing along the path seemed fully alive.

From what he could tell so far, this might be his father's finest purchase. The land leading to the new property was the prettiest he had ever seen. Even while it was half-hidden in the shadows of near dawn, he sensed the estate would be exquisite.

He had not felt such peace in a place since he was a boy and had spent his summers in Scotland with his father's cousin, as his own father had done as a child.

The estate in Scotland was not a grand one, but humble and comfortable. More of a farm, really, he thought, where he and his cousins were free to run and leap. Father's cousins' home was a place where the most common sound was laughter… games were played and books read around the hearth at night.

Each year when it was time to return to London, he'd felt the loss of family and freedom keenly.

It was not as if he did not love and miss his parents during those summers, but their lives were focused on social commitments, and the travel which was required of their positions. Even when they were at home, it often felt as if they were not. Back then he had imagined society to be a thief, robbing him of his family…always taking them here and there, away from him.

When the day came for him to take the title, he would not travel far and wide. If he had a family, he would put them before any social obligation.

'It isn't that I am not appreciative of what I was born to,' he said to the horse. Only, it felt good to say things to an animal which you could not say to anyone else. When one spoke to a horse, there was no chance of being misunderstood. 'It's a bit like how you would be grateful for having a good stone stable to be in during a storm, plenty of oats and hay to eat rather than not. You'd be grateful, aye?'

He patted Dane's neck. 'But what if the cost of the comfort was being away from the other outdoor horses? You'd be safe but lonely. What if all you could think about was leaping the paddock fence and going to them?'

His parents had always loved him. He well knew it. It was only that with all they had to do for Claymore, they were simply too busy to spend much time with him.

He was grateful that his father had sent him to his cousin's estate where there were aunties, uncles, and cousins aplenty who loved him, too. They never looked at him differently because he was the only heir to a very wealthy title. They were close enough to one to not be impressed. To them he was simply Joseph.

In London he had no cousins, only a few friends. But did those friends even like him? He never really knew if it was him they admired or the Claymore wealth and influence.

'I shall tell you a story from my past.' The horse's ear twitched. 'As an example of my two lives. Once when I was in Scotland, I was sick as anything…fever, cough and the like. My parents were in Paris and could not come to my bedside. My aunties were there, though. I remember how there was always at least one of them sitting beside me, stroking my brow and singing to me.'

Joseph paused, remembering…smiling while he thought of his sweet aunts and how devoted they'd been to spooning broth into his mouth.

'Another time, and this was in London, I was sick again, much like before. This time my parents were in Spain and could not be with me. There was a doctor at my bedside and a nurse. Highly qualified, both of them. But they did not sing or call me their sweet handsome boy.'

Dane snorted and shook his mane.

'You understand then how cut up I was when Father decided it was time to end those childhood visits. Time, he said, to be trained to one day take his place as Viscount Claymore.'

Ach, he'd been crushed for a time, putting that part of his life away. Back in London he had worked hard, studied hard, and yet he still felt he did not fully belong amongst the glittering nobility.

The sense of having two lives never really went away.

'I will tell you another secret, Dane. There is more than a whisper of Scots left in me.'

Riding past several farms, rich and fertile-smelling, he felt the land begin to rise toward the hills. Trees here became thick, branches arched over the path, creating a leafy canopy.

While he rode, savouring the fresh, crisp scents of morning, the sky began to brighten.

He heard a goat bleating, looked that way and noticed a path which led from the narrow road to a cottage. A distance beyond the first cottage, he spotted another.

A woman was singing. He paused to listen. Someone must enjoy daybreak as much as he did. It seemed that the voice came from outside the first cottage, but he did not see anyone.

Seconds later, he heard the faint cry of a baby coming from the second cottage. It reminded him that morning was moving on and, just as the child's mother certainly had things to accomplish, so did he.

Father would be waiting for his report, a detailed narrative about the property's condition. The house, the land, the area surrounding it…his father would be anxious to read every detail.

A short distance past the cottages, there was a bridge. Dane carried him over a wide stream. The water looked cold and sounded as if it rushed rather than gurgled. He swore it sang a song as lovely as the woman's had been.

On the other side of the bridge, the path rose sharply, carrying him to the top of the hill where the manor house was reported to be. If it turned out as he imagined, the view of the property's acreage would be stunning.

Something stirred him about this place. From the moment he'd arrived in Fallen Leaf, he'd felt…well, something…but he knew not what.

The curious sensation had grown while he'd crossed the valley. Now, the further up the hill he rode, the stronger the feeling became. He could not say he'd ever experienced anything like it before, not since those summers in Scotland. There was an abiding sense of well-being here.

Perhaps, having been stuck in London for a year, it was only that he felt stirred by the natural beauty of the land, refreshed by the sounds and scents of nature.

It seemed more than that, though.

The road ended and became a driveway which wound left and slightly up. A grove of trees hid the house from view. All he could see of it were chimneys. Three of them poking over the treetops. The stones would be cold since no one had lived in the house for two years.

At last the full house came into view. It was three stories tall with morning light glinting off a dozen or more windows. A wide porch stood proudly at the front.

Again, a sense of well-being made his heart swell. Odd how a place he had never been to could cause such a reaction. A breeze kicked up, shuffling leaves against one another in a whisper.

He knew they were not whispering 'welcome home,' but it felt as if they were.

How could one feel he had been missing a place he had never been to?

It made no sense.

Sense or not, he was glad to be here.

Once again, Olive sat atop Star under the limbs of a great dripping tree at night.

Truly, she did not feel like a dastardly highwayman riding a ghoul horse.

What she did feel was wet and miserable.

She stared at the curve in the path, wondering how far

out her father was. Straining her ears over tapping rain, she listened for hoofbeats. At their first echo, she would draw her sword, gathering her terrifying persona about her.

It never failed to amaze her that her father, being frightened of the apparition lurking on the road at night, continued to go out. So far he had not made it all the way to the pub but raced for home as soon as he spotted her. A bit of a wail and the brandishing of her foil were enough to give Father the shakes.

As far as Olive was concerned, the deception she played on him was his fault as much as anyone's…if one did not count the drifting scoundrel who had landed them in this predicament in the first place.

Clearly this was completely that wicked man's fault.

What she and her sister needed to do was convince their father to allow Eliza to marry. Only then would they have a chance of putting all this behind them.

To Olive's way of thinking, a married woman had a certain respect in the eyes of the village. If said married lady then adopted a child, no one would remark upon it.

Thinking she heard hoofbeats, Olive rose in the stirrups and unsheathed her sword with great drama, even though Father had yet to come into view. It was important to draw on her character for a moment before letting him loose to do his villainy.

By nature, she was not a spooky marauder, but once she settled into the part, it became alarmingly natural. For a woman who was truth-loving to her core…mostly…the sensation was disturbing.

Whatever sound she thought she heard went away, so she settled back into the saddle to wait, sword resting across her thighs.

It was taking Father longer than usual to come around the bend. Hopefully he had not fallen from his horse. His heart might fail if a hellish brigand helped him back into the saddle.

She and Eliza both loved their father, for all his awful stubbornness and his dependence on the jug. There had been a time before Mama died when he had been a man who laughed and danced…who sang sweet love songs to them all. Mama's death had changed each of them, naturally, but Father most of all. After the grief settled and life began again, he became determined to be in control of everything. He could not control letting go of his beloved wife and so was now fixated on having everything else happen according to his will.

The trouble was, she and Eliza were what he wanted most to control. It was only a shame that he did not direct his stubbornness to turning away from drink.

Still, he was their father, and they loved him. So, with some worry, she strained her ears, listening for hoofbeats on wet earth.

There! *Clop suck clop…*but coming from the wrong direction. While it was not unheard of for travelers to take this path, it was rare. The only two cottages out this way were the Strickland cottage and their own, a situation which had made it easier to keep Laura's existence a secret. As luck would have it, or providence perhaps, Laura's and the Stricklands' babies were similar in appearance. So far, they had been able to make it seem that the two children were actually only one.

Certainly, the older they got, the more difficult it would be. Eliza simply must wed.

*Clip clop, clip clop…*the sound came closer. Who could

it be? There was a mansion on top of the hill where the road ended, but no one had lived there in the last two years.

She backed up into the deeper shadows of the tree. So far, Father was the only victim of her terrorizing, and she would like to keep it that way.

Of all the wicked timing, here came the sound of Father's horse picking her way along in the mud.

Since Olive could not allow her father to go to The Shepherd's Keep, she would have to expose herself to both travelers.

Wouldn't this end in a fine mess?

The riders stopped and spoke quietly to one another for a moment. Neither of the men noticed her lurking in the shadows.

Olive did not recognize the other fellow in the dark, bundled against the rain as he was. She probably knew him, though, since Father did.

Neighbour or not, she must do what she could to prevent her father from speaking of private family matters.

Very well…she took a deep breath then wailed. The sound echoed through the treetops…eerie, sinister. She would have frightened herself if she had not been the very ghoul howling a warning.

She emerged from under the tree, but only a few steps. It would not do to be recognized.

Star reared, snorted and rolled her eyes.

Father immediately turned his horse and dashed for home. The other rider screamed, nearly falling off his horse. The nervous animal raced back toward the village with his rider barely hanging on.

Olive waited a few moments, giving her father the time to get home. Eliza would be waiting in the stable to help him put the horse away. At this point, Father would be too frightened to turn back toward the village.

Please, oh, please let this be the last time she was forced to do this.

The whole matter grated on her. She hated deceiving her father, even if it was for the good of them all.

The worst of the night's affair was that another man had seen the apparition. This was no longer simply a family matter.

Word was bound to spread. News of a spectre terrorizing the road would be the only thing anyone spoke of.

'It was fierce as anything I ever saw. Not even human,' Father declared, sitting close to the hearth in an attempt to chase away a chill which no doubt went to the bone.

'The eyes of a phantom and no mistaking it. Flames is what they were…red and fearsome. Such heat! I must be burned. Do I look burned?' He stared at his arms, turned his hands this way and that. 'Ach, but you would not believe it.'

'You are correct, Father.' Olive handed him a cup of tea, and he curled his fingers around the prettily painted china. It was not likely that he would drink it, but she must encourage him to drink something calming which did not come from his jug. 'I would not believe it. You were drinking and had no business going to the village. When one is not in his right mind, one is bound to imagine all kinds of nonsense.'

'I was in my right mind, daughter. And I was not alone. Just you ask Homer Miles. He wasn't drunk. Only looking for a lost sheep. Got the buzzard scared out of him, he did.'

That was a complication, to be sure.

'Heavens, Father, I am certain as can be there is no phantom highwayman. Shadows are all you saw,' Eliza declared, then sat down in the chair across from him.

'No, my girl. I saw a horse with eyes of fire and hooves that sparked when it reared up. The rider smelled of brimstone.'

'Surely not!' It was entirely inappropriate to feel like grinning...but brimstone? Apparently her performance had been a grand success. She pressed her smile to the rim of her teacup, then sat in the chair beside Eliza's. It was all sorts of wrong to feel proud of her deception and yet...it must be noted that she had put a great deal of effort into her evil persona, even if she only noted it to herself.

'Homer will say it's the truth. From now on, you girls will not go out after dark, not even to go to the stable.'

Olive shot Eliza a glance...a wordless message. Eliza answered with a blink and half a nod.

With any luck, Father was in a mood to be receptive to the idea they had been wishing to present to him.

'If only we had husbands to watch out for us,' Eliza said with a sigh.

'Oh, indeed.' Olive leaned forward in her chair, making sure she had her father's full attention. 'James Foster is a big, strapping lad. A woman would be safe with him as her husband.'

Father set his tea aside with a thump. He nodded, then cocked his head to one side in thought. 'I have long admired the young fellow. A man could do worse than having a baker as his son-in-law.'

A blush rose in Eliza's cheeks. Olive knew it had nothing to do with hot tea or the reflection from the hearth flames. Her sister was more than just a bit taken with James Foster. She was in love with him and had admitted as much to Olive.

Having seen Eliza and James together, how special looks passed between them whenever she and her sister visited the bakery, she believed James returned Eliza's affection.

If Father gave his approval of a marriage between them, it would be an answer to their prayers.

Eliza would have the man she loved.

And perhaps the child she loved as well. Of course, her sister could not marry James without revealing the truth of Laura's birth. It would not be fair to James.

It would take a great deal of courage on her sister's part to do so, because only the best of men would be willing to overlook her fall from grace.

James, she did believe, was such a man, so all might work out well in the end.

Prayerfully, Olive slipped to her knees...mentally, not on the floor. Please, oh please, let it be so. Only then would Olive would be free of the phantom highwayman. Nothing would please her more than being the honest woman she used to be.

'Perhaps, Father...' Olive said, her heart in her throat, her palms as slick as wet leaves. So much depended on what her father's decision would be. If he decided that Eliza should marry James...prayers answered, indeed. If he did not, no amount of pleading would convince him to change his mind. Father was more stubborn than ten men at their worst. 'You ought to speak to James. He would be an excellent addition to our family, and we would no longer have to make our own bread. I suspect other fathers are eager to have him as a son-in-law.'

'I have heard whispers about it,' Eliza added, making a show of shaking her head.

If Olive was this nervous, her sister must feel like a beehive twitched in her veins. Eliza's very future would be determined by what their father decided in the next moment.

'It is indeed time you wed, Olive. Time and past. Your mother was much younger than either of you when she did. So, I will speak to the young man. Make him aware of your interest and my approval if he wishes to court you.'

'Me?' Olive gasped, casting Eliza a horrified glance. 'I do not wish to wed. It is Eliza who wishes to marry James.'

'But you are the eldest and must wed first.'

'That makes no sense.'

'Sense is whatever I say it is, miss.' He stroked his beard between his thumb and finger.

Stunned, Olive leapt to her feet, staring down at her father. Oh, what a horror.

'I should not have to explain it to you, but I do know what is best for you, my daughters. Time is creeping on. You, Olive Rose, are in danger of becoming a spinster. Once you wed, then your sister will be free to do so as well.'

'But I do not love James Foster. Eliza does.'

'Love?' Father spat into hearth. 'We are speaking of marriage.'

'You loved Mama,' Eliza pointed out bravely, for all the good it would do her. Poor thing looked so pale, Olive thought her sister would faint if she tried to stand up.

'Greatly…but to my eventual sorrow.' A shadow passed over his expression. Even six years after their mother's death, Father was not yet over the grief. 'A logical union is what you girls shall have. It is logical for Olive to wed before she grows any older.'

'You make me sound ancient!' She sat back down on her chair…hard. 'I am twenty-four years old. Not even two years older than Eliza, may I point out?'

'My mind is set. You will wed the baker, Olive. Eliza will have the next man I find worthy. Oldest, then youngest. It is the way things will be.'

'But, Father.' Eliza swiped at her cheek. 'I love James. And I believe he loves me.'

'Ah, but this is not the first time you have thought such a thing.' Father's expression was not hard when he said so, but rather soft and concerned. Which did not mean he was going to change his mind about what he had decided. 'You are not at all wise when it comes to love, Eliza.'

With a screech of frustration which was not a bit uncalled for, Eliza leapt from her chair and rushed out of the parlor.

Olive leaned forward, her hands braced on the arms of her chair, her expression hard on her father.

'You are as stubborn as a stone. But so am I. I will not wed the man my sister has her heart set on.'

That said, she stood to follow Eliza out of the parlor.

'I will visit our young man next week and give him my blessing to court you.'

He was not stubborn as a stone, then. Rather, set as a boulder.

Chapter Two

'Come, Dane.'

Joseph led his horse under a large tree. Its limbs nearly swept the ground. What moonlight might reveal would be hidden by brush and branches. This was a good place to watch the road for a dead highwayman.

'Stand courageous while we wait for the ghoul and its fire-eyed horse. Pay no mind when sparks fly from its hooves. Stand your ground in our righteous cause against evil, my good steed.'

Perhaps it was not right to make a jest of the matter. The people of Fallen Leaf were uneasy. It was said the poor fellow who encountered the monster could hardly tell his story for fear. Even so, the tale had spread quickly.

Aye, the poor soul—Homer was his name—had been terrified by something while out looking for his sheep, and another man along with him.

But a creature from the underworld?

It was absurd.

Someone was scaring the people of the village, and Joseph meant to find out who…and why. While the people of Fallen Leaf were not his tenants, they were his neighbours, and he would not stand for them being menaced.

What reason could there be for it? No good one, he would wager.

This was the third night he'd waited under this tree. It was where the witness claimed the horror had happened, so it made sense to watch this part of the isolated road.

The villain might see this as only some sort of jest, but the tavern was suffering from people being too ill at ease to leave their homes.

Ach! The owner of the tavern feared he would soon have to shutter his doors.

'Tonight is our night.' He patted the horse's neck. 'Don't you feel it in your bones?'

What Dane probably felt is that he would rather be in his stall.

It was still early enough in the evening that if he managed to capture the culprit, he would have time to escort him to The Shepherd's Keep, where he would present him to any patrons stout-hearted enough to brave a ride to the tavern. Then he would force the man to explain his mischief.

It was not acceptable that the people in the village should shiver in their beds.

This nonsense would come to an end this very night… as long as the cowardly fiend made an appearance. Each passing moment that he sat here made him feel like he was wasting his time.

All of a sudden the wind kicked up. It howled along the woodland path, twisted branches and made them creak.

'It does certainly set the mood for mischief,' he told Dane.

If one was inclined to fear, this would be the stage to make one quake.

But what was that? His nerves prickled in anticipation.

He leaned down to whisper in Dane's ear. 'I think I hear something.'

Mostly it was wind rushing past his ears. The whistling kept him from hearing the sound which had first caught his attention.

Dane's ears twitched, so Joseph knew he had not imagined the clop of hooves deeper in the woods.

One would not ride through trees, avoiding a proper path, unless one wished to remain hidden, and perhaps was bent on a bit of mayhem.

'I reckon we've finally got him, Dane, but hold here.'

Let the villain be the one to thrash about and announce his presence.

Joseph did not move so much as maneuvered his weight in the saddle.

The terror of Fallen Leaf emerged from the darkened woods, revealed moonbeam by moonbeam. It did not come fully into the open but sat on its underworld mount, keeping to the dappled shadows of the tree on the other side of the path.

The figure sat still as stone, except for his head, which he cocked to the side as if listening for something…for his poor victim, probably.

Aye, but not tonight. Tonight he would be exposed.

As Joseph expected, the rider was mortal. Surely an apparition would sense when its victim was approaching without having to listen.

In a quite benign manner, the rider shifted, bending to pat his horse's neck.

Then he drew a sword from a sheath and rested it across his thighs.

The man was rather slight of build for a highwayman sprung from the underworld.

With the element of fear removed, the fellow did not seem altogether fierce.

One would expect such a dastardly figure to be singed with hellfire. Not look as fashionable as this villain did. To Joseph's way of thinking, whoever had created the costume had done so with great care. Shiny brass buttons winked in a shaft of moonlight. A long red feather fluttered from a hat brim.

Hoofbeats pattered on the path, approaching from the direction Joseph had just come.

All at once the highwayman lifted his sword and charged out from under the tree. The horse gave a fearsome snort and rolled its eyes until the whites showed. The animal did look impressive and quite fierce, rising up and pawing the air.

The approaching rider rounded the curve in the road.

Joseph burst out of hiding, giving a shout. The approaching rider pulled his mount about and dashed back the way he had come.

The highwayman's horse pranced nervously. The rider got him under control, then turned the animal and raced into the woods.

The sound of the second horse's retreat grew fainter while Joseph urged Dane through the trees in pursuit of the highwayman's mount.

'Halt!' he shouted at the fleeing highwayman.

The man did not slow down, but no matter. This night his mischief would cease.

It was evident that the 'apparition' was not accustomed to being chased. The man wobbled in the saddle, his rump bouncing with the horse's fast gait.

It would take only a moment to run the villain to ground and have the truth at last.

'Halt!' he shouted again. Racing madly like this through dense woods was not safe.

An unexpected tree could loom out at one…a low hanging branch could—

Dash it! As if he had conjured the peril himself, it happened.

The highwayman hit a branch, fell off the horse, then grazed his head on a rock.

His horse must have been a loyal animal, because it immediately stopped and spun about, sniffed the fallen man, then turned nervously in a circle. The filmy gauze draped across the horse snagged on the tree branch which had brought down the rider.

Wind caught the fabric, blowing and twisting it in a way which did look ghostly.

The horse finally trotted away.

Leaping off Dane's back, Joseph knelt beside the unconscious rider. With great care, he turned him over.

The red hat fell off, revealing the culprit's face.

What the blazes! A hank of hair fell across his wrist. The lock was the colour of strawberries swirled in honey, then drenched in moonlight. Odd that he should take particular notice of the shade of the lady brigand's hair in this moment, but he couldn't help it as it slid over his palm, the silky strands tickling his skin.

The terror of the night was beautiful with fine features saved from looking aristocratic by an adorable round nose. The mystery deepened.

'Miss!' He jiggled her ever so gently, but she did not stir. 'Wake up, miss.'

Not so much as a fluttered eyelash. A trickle of blood dripped from her temple, down her cheek. Luckily, it was not a great deal of blood, which gave him hope that the injury was not too awful.

It did need tending, though, and right away.

Who was she? He did not recall seeing her in the village.

'I would certainly remember if I did,' he murmured, slipping his arms under her shoulders and lifting her from the dirt.

'Kneel, boy,' he said to Dane.

Luckily, Dane was a well-trained animal, which meant getting a limp woman, as slight as she was, into the saddle was possible.

He steadied the lady, gripping her arm. Then he ordered Dane to stand. Without letting go of her, he lifted himself up behind, clutching her securely to his chest.

With a light touch, he checked the bleeding. So far the swelling was not too bad. He wondered where the nearest physician was. Not in Fallen Leaf. He did know that much.

Even if he knew where to find a doctor, he could not leave the lady alone to summon him.

Dressed as she was, he would not take her to the village to be tended, not until he knew why she was acting the part of a villain. His curiosity demanded it.

There was nothing for it but to take her to the manor house and hope she would rally soon.

What a dashed shame that his first guest to the manor was unconscious and bleeding. This was what he thought while carrying the lady highwayman up the manor steps, then through the entrance hall.

In part, he was to blame, but only to a degree. True, she

had fallen from her horse because he'd pursued her, yet her behaviour was what had caused the pursuit to begin with.

Not that blame mattered in the moment. Only one thing did. Her recovery.

Up another flight of stairs, and then a right turn down a long hallway brought him to his bedchamber. There was no choice but to put her in there since it was the only bedroom habitable, as yet.

It was far from proper to lay a woman upon his bed.

If this had happened in London, he would find himself wed to her as soon as a special licence could be had.

He would have a pretty bride, in that case. On the outside. He had no way of knowing if she was equally pretty on the inside.

She had been terrorizing her neighbours. Not a respectful thing to do any way one looked at it.

Ah, well…until he knew the reason for her behaviour, he would do his best to withhold judgement.

Striding to the water basin, he snatched a clean cloth, dampened it, then brought it to the bed, dragging a chair with him.

He sat down, then lightly dabbed a line from her temple to her chin, wiping away a red smear.

A smattering of dried blood stuck to her curls. He stroked it away.

Light from the bedside lamp reflected on her still form. Interesting how it seemed like she had sunshine in her hair. There was no telling what colour her eyes were. Her eyelashes were thick as a fringe and curled up at the tips.

Even after hitting her head on a rock, her complexion had the same pink hue as the rose he had put in a vase beside the bed this morning.

It must be a good sign that her face did not appear pasty.

And yet he worried. The longer she lay without waking, the worse her situation seemed to be.

There was nothing for it but to sit and listen to the clock tick in the hallway.

He wondered if he should remove some of her clothing so that she could breathe more easily.

With his arms folded across his chest and tipping back in the chair, he wondered if putting her in his bed was inappropriate, then…removing her clothes was completely unacceptable.

Except in dire circumstances.

He watched her chest rise and fall. Which was not proper behaviour either, not by a measured mile, but how else was he to determine if her condition was a dire circumstance?

Her complexion remained rosy. That was encouraging.

Still, it was her breathing that concerned him.

'Damn it.' The curse rolled easily off his lips, but he doubted that she was aware enough to hear it. 'I need to know if your stays ought to be loosened. Even a highwayman ghoul needs to breathe.'

Breath huffed on Olive's face. Masculine breath!

Certainly a woman would not carry the unique sweaty, woodsy scent of a man who had recently been exerting himself.

Heat skimmed her nose, warmed it. She must be in a dream in which she was about to be kissed by someone wonderful. The sort of dream which always left her feeling bereft once she awoke and realized she was not about to be kissed by someone wonderful.

Something cold touched her cheek. Cold and wet.

What on earth?

She tried to open her eyes, to see what was happening. Oddly, her eyelids felt sewn closed. Her head was heavy, and yet at the same time, light with dizziness.

What was the last thing she remembered? Oh dear… someone had spotted her and given chase. Yes! She had been running away, and then…

Then something happened which she did not recall. Whatever it was had resulted in her lying in a bed which was not hers.

But whose was it?

How had she got from racing through the woods to here? Wherever here was.

And why did she smell a rose? Perhaps she was not in a bed, but lying on the forest floor near a wild rosebush.

'Damn it. I need to know if your stays ought to be loosened. Even a highwayman ghoul needs to breathe.'

She had been breathing, but hearing that, she suddenly was not.

Wherever she was, she was clearly not alone. No indeed, there had been a man's breath near her face a moment ago.

A hand touched her middle, lightly pressing the fabric of her highwayman costume.

She tried to bat it away, but her fingers merely twitched at her side.

'No stays,' she murmured but was not certain the words emerged.

The hand lifted from her ribs at once.

'Oh…yes, I probably should have guessed a highwayman would not have them.'

Whoever spoke had a deep, comforting voice. Contrary to common sense, she was not afraid.

Helpless as a soggy butterfly, but not frightened. She ought to be terrified, for all the good it would do lying here as defenceless as said insect.

'Why…' She struggled to speak, to ask why he had chased her. He must be the one who had, after all. The better question was, 'Who…'

No matter how she struggled, she still could not open her eyes.

'Imagine my surprise to find the terrible phantom haunting Fallen Leaf to be a woman. A rather small woman at that.'

'Imagine…' At last she gained control of her tongue and managed to pry open one eye. 'Did you hit me?'

He shook his head, brows arched in astonishment. 'I would never hit a woman.'

Perhaps not, but how was she to know that for certain?

'You were hit, but by a branch. It knocked you off your horse. Then you smacked your head on a rock.'

She had a quick flash of memory…of a branch looming suddenly out at her. She had no recollection of a rock.

'Star!' she exclaimed and tried to sit up. Oh, but it just murdered her head.

'Hold up, there. Don't do yourself more harm.'

'How harmed am I?'

'You are awake and speaking, so I expect you will fully recover.'

She managed to open the other eye. A handsome face came into focus.

'Star is your horse?'

She reminded herself not to nod. 'She is. Did you bring her here? And where is here?'

'She took off into the woods.'

He shrugged, smiled at her. His lips were handsome

with compelling brackets nudging the corners. Her stomach reacted with the oddest shiver. But of course it was due to her woozy head and not a stranger's smile.

'I suppose she went home, then,' Olive said. 'She knows the way.'

'Where do you live? Who should I contact?'

Not Father.

She winced. Truly, she was far too dizzy to have a conversation. What she really ought to do is get up and go home.

Since she could not even sit up, that would be impossible.

With a resigned sigh, she closed her eyes again.

'I'm not certain you should sleep, miss. Not with the way you hit your head.'

'Can't help…it.' She really could not. Everything felt so heavy…so distant all of a sudden.

'Go ahead then. I'll sit right here to make sure you keep breathing.'

At least, that's what she thought she heard.

She believed she said something in reply but may have only thought the words. Hopefully, they reflected gratitude.

Whatever the case, she would believe that's what she would have said.

Although she did not know where she was, or who her guardian was, he had claimed he would watch over her, to make sure she continued breathing.

She was fuzzily grateful for his presence.

Fuzzily grateful?

Had she truly thought that earlier on? Lying in a stranger's bed, in a place she did not recognize?

How much time had passed? She had no way of knowing.

This would not do, not for another instant.

She turned her head to see the handsome stranger sitting in a chair next to the bed, his gaze shifting between a sheet of paper he gripped in his hand, and her chest.

Seeing her awake, he crumpled the paper in his fist and shoved it in his shirt pocket.

'You did not stop breathing.' He gave her a weary-looking smile which crinkled his eyes at the corners.

'You really watched me?'

'For three hours.'

'No one has ever done anything like that for me… Perhaps my mother did when I was a baby. But it is what mothers do. Not what strangers do.'

'Somehow, after spending the night in the same room, it hardly seems as though we are strangers.'

'It might seem so to you, but I slept through it. If we became acquainted, I do not recall the moment. We do not know one another's names. Nor where each other lives, who our families are, or…'

Oh, no! For all she knew, she was sleeping in a married man's bed!

'Or,' he said, bending forward, peering deeply into her eyes…into her very thoughts, 'why you are terrorizing your neighbours.'

Yes, or that.

'I shall begin, then.' He sat back, crossed his arms over his chest, and gave a great yawn. 'My name is Joseph Billings. This is Falcon's Steep. I live here.'

'The manor on the hill?' She lifted to her elbows but a searing pain shot though her skull. 'Ouch.'

Despite the misery, she held the pose.

'You are the viscount?' She tried to sit taller, but light flashes pierced her brain.

'No, I am the viscount's heir.' Joseph Billings made as if he would touch her shoulder to prevent her from rising further but then jerked his hand back. 'Wait a while. There is no rush.'

'There is a great rush. My sister will be worried. How long have I been here?'

'Six hours or so.'

'I must go home.'

He shook his head. A lock of golden-brown hair shifted across his forehead. His gaze on her was intense, penetrating. And when had she ever seen eyes so blue? Although she was not herself in the moment, she could not help but notice their resemblance to the sky.

Good then. She must not be in too wicked a condition if she could appreciate vividly blue eyes.

'You will need to gather your strength first. I shall bring you a bowl of broth. If you can manage to keep it down, we will think about getting you home.'

'Oh, well, I suppose so.' It was the sensible thing to do. She eased back onto the pillow. 'Please thank your cook for getting up in the night to prepare it.'

'Aye, well, about that. I am afraid I have not yet hired any servants.'

'Do you mean to say we are here alone?' She had feared as much. The manor had been awfully quiet.

He nodded, then strode toward the chamber door.

'I am here in your bed, and no one is…there is no one to…'

He turned in the doorway, gave her a half smile. 'I promise your virtue is safe.'

'It was my reputation I was thinking of.' She struggled

to get up. She absolutely must get home. One ruined sister in the family was quite enough.

Oh, dear. She made it to her feet, but the room spun. Blackness tugged the corners of her mind. Her legs went limp. The floor rose to meet her.

Strong arms came under her, lifting her against a firm chest. When she landed it was on the soft mattress, not the floor.

'Do not try that again. It is far too soon for you to get up. I promise to take you home, miss. But not until it is safe.'

'It must be safe to do so before dawn, then. If my father wakes and finds me gone…well, I can tell you that neither of us would wish for that to happen.'

'We shall see how strong you are after the broth.'

'And my sister!' Her voice quavered for an instant. Normally she was not one to dissolve in a fit of weeping, but poor Eliza. 'She will be frantic by now. I imagine she is contemplating searching the woods for me.'

'Very well. After I see that you are able to keep down your meal, I will take you home, even if I must carry you.'

That would not do. To be carried in the strong arms of a stranger…the handsome son of a viscount…no, it would never do.

And yet, she would have been carried by him already. She had not floated from the forest floor to his chamber, had she?

'I am sure it will not be necessary. I will be right as a rainbow once I finish.'

'We shall see.'

'Thank you, my lord…for not leaving me on the ground as you probably think I deserve.'

'We shall discuss what you deserve after you eat.' She

would have been alarmed by what he said except she caught a glimmer of a smile in his expression. 'Please call me Joseph...or Mr Billings, if you must.'

'I am Olive Augustmore. I live in the first cottage we will come to. The one at the bottom of the hill.'

'I know of it. Do you sing in the morning? On the way here my first morning, I heard someone singing...and a baby crying.'

'It was probably me you heard. Singing is how I greet my goats each morning. The crying baby would have been my neighbour's child.'

Perhaps it was the neighbour's child. Or it might have been her niece, although she would hardly admit that to a stranger. She would not admit it to anyone.

Guarding the secret was what had led to her being stranded in Joseph Billings's bed in the first place.

Her stomach fluttered. This time she did not mistake the reason. The viscount's son had a smile that a woman could simply not help but react to.

'I'll fetch your broth.' He gave her a wink...and more flutters. 'Get a few moments' rest, Miss Augustmore. I will not be gone long.'

The very last thing she needed was to feel her heart reacting to a gentleman so above her own class...flapping about like a moth in a beam of moonlight.

Joseph sat on a stool near the stove, waiting for the broth to heat.

'Curse it, then,' he mumbled while drawing the letter from his shirt pocket.

It was from his mother and had been delivered earlier in the day, but he hadn't had time to read it when it first came.

Needing a distraction from watching his highwayman breathe, he had done it then.

Apparently, his parents were coming for a visit. Father was anxious to explore his new property. Thinking about it now, Joseph wished he had not presented such a glowing report of it.

It was not as if he did not wish to see his parents. He did, of course. Only, his mother had written that they were bringing 'Dear Hortencia' with them.

'Dear Hortencia?' Even saying her name made his tongue sting.

The woman was a viper. A pretty one, to be sure. It was why most people, his mother among them, never saw past her smile to the icy soul beneath until it was too late.

Cold as a stone in a stream, it was. Joseph did not wish to share a conversation with her, much less his life.

For years the woman had been after him, and with his mother's full approval.

Appearances meant a great deal to his mother, and Hortencia appeared to be perfect. A lady of good breeding, her father being a marquis…a woman of grace and beauty. Mama believed Hortencia would be a credit to the family's standing in society.

Added to that, his mother and Hortencia's late mother had been friends many years ago. A situation which Hortencia was using to her greatest advantage, he thought. The closer she was to Mama, the easier it would be to get to him.

He had never understood why Hortencia wanted him and only him when she could wed higher. The Claymore wealth, he supposed…and Mama's encouragement.

If only his mother could see what he saw.

He likened Hortencia to a cat who stared up at a bird in a tree while ignoring the mouse who crossed her paws.

He shifted on the stool, feeling tense.

This visit was a trap. He felt it to his bones. Hortencia meant to entangle him in something he could not get out of. Out here, away from society, it might be more easily accomplished.

He stood, looked at the broth and decided it was warm enough.

After placing it on a tray with a slice of bread, he carried it upstairs.

Going up, he strove for a pleasant demeanour. There was no way his pretty guest should have to suffer the dour mood that thinking of Hortencia brought on.

It was evident the lady had troubles enough of her own.

With his hand on the doorknob, he made sure to smile.

He did have another month before his parents came. He meant to appreciate the time. The last thing he wished was to taint the good feeling he had right now for his new home with fear of the future…and of what Hortencia might try to do to it.

Chapter Three

Joseph entered his chamber to find Olive Augustmore sitting at the edge of the bed, her fingers pressing circles on her temples.

It would seem that she'd refused his logical admonition to rest.

Even though, clearly, sitting up was causing her a great deal of pain.

He set the tray he carried on the bedside table.

'Broth and bread,' he announced, then pointed at the pillow.

'Are you always this overbearing?' she asked.

'I am rarely called out on it, but yes, I suppose I am in certain circumstances.'

Although she had ignored his advice to rest, she did seem somewhat improved.

He sat beside the bed, picking up the bowl of fragrant broth. After dipping in the spoon, he brought it to her lips. Swirls of steam curled in front of her nose, drawing attention to its sweetly rounded shape. It gave her face a soft, amenable appearance.

Except that she then pressed her lips thin, casting him an arched brow.

Oh, aye? She was not the only one skilled in the gesture. He sent it back to her, slick and easy.

All at once, her frown vanished, and her lips quirked at the corners. Amusement made her eyes twinkly green.

'Is something funny, Miss Augustmore?'

She pushed the spoon away, her lips now parted in a smile. 'You and I are at an impasse over whether or not I will open my mouth. Aren't we a pair of petulant children? You must admit, it is absurd to be scowling at one another over a spoonful of broth.'

Ah, it was good to know the lady was able to look at adversity with a sense of humour. He liked that about her.

Hopefully her lightened mood indicated that her condition was improving.

'Shall we call a truce?' He grinned because her expression was fetching, engaging in a way one could not help but respond to. 'But you must eat and drink if you wish to have the strength to make it home before dawn.'

'I do not believe a bowl of broth will do that. However, you did go to some trouble for me, so…'

She took the spoon from him, dipped it into the bowl herself, then lifted it to her mouth.

Her fingers trembled. Broth dripped onto the waistcoat of her costume.

With a despondent sigh, she handed him the spoon, then brushed the spill off her clothing.

'It seems that what I wish to do and what I am able to do are at odds.'

He filled the spoon and extended it to her. She touched his hand, helping him to guide the broth to her mouth.

'There is no shame in it. You took a nasty fall, but you will be back to yourself in no time.'

She pressed her fingertips on his knuckles while he scooped the next spoonful, offering it to her.

Ah, good, no more trembling.

Within moments she'd finished the broth and indicated she would like to try the bread.

She managed that on her own. He was not really disappointed that she was no longer required to touch his hand with soft, warm fingertips.

The bread was delicious. Olive recognized it as a loaf that James Foster sold every Monday and Thursday. It had always been one of her favourites.

Between bites she asked, 'What did you intend by chasing me, sir?'

How could she not ask? Although it was no surprise that he had pursued her, she did wish to discuss his motive for doing so.

For all she knew, the man meant to have her charged with a crime, although in her opinion, she had not committed one. Until recently, her mischief had been a family matter. One that involved no one but Olive, Father, and Eliza.

Who was Joseph Billings, really? Just because, for reasons she could not begin to understand, she felt safe with him, did not mean she ought to feel that way.

He might be a liar who had no intention of seeing her safely home...carried in his arms.

The image blossoming in her mind made a sticky lump of the bread going down her throat. Oh glory fire. The fact that he was a mysterious stranger made the image all the more interesting. Bordering on downright fascinating, is what it was.

Enough of that, though.

He would escort her home, and there was nothing gallant to it. He was simply stuck with her unless he did.

Besides, she was the one who had insisted on being home before daylight. He was only doing what she'd demanded of him.

To read anything more into it was not level-headed.

The quirk in his smile was a little too compelling. A prudent lady would not be fooled by it. For all she knew, he was as deceptive as she was. 'What I intended to do was to take you to the tavern, where you would explain why you were scaring people.'

Thank goodness she had been knocked senseless by a rock, then. How would she have explained it to everyone?

'Perhaps you have a good reason for causing fear among your neighbours. If you admit to me what it is, I might keep silent about all this.'

'You must keep silent about it, regardless of my reason. If anyone discovers I spent the night here unchaperoned, our reputations will be ruined.'

'I am aware of it. You need not worry. No one will learn of this. But I am curious. Why are you causing mischief?'

'You may rest assured that I have an excellent reason. I do not haunt the roads for my own amusement, I promise you.'

'Please, enlighten me. Once I understand your reason, perhaps I will no longer pursue you. You do know that the tavern is now suffering a loss of business because of you. I do not wish for the owners to fail.'

'No one does, naturally. The truth is, I never meant for anyone to see me but my father.' Causing fear to her neighbours was the last thing she'd intended.

Small furrows cut his brow while he silently waited for her to elaborate.

'Very well.' She leaned back on the pillow, gingerly so as not to jar her head. 'I will tell you.'

Some of it, but certainly not all.

Even though her only lie would be one of omission, and she told that for the sake of her sister, it did grate on her truth-loving soul to do so.

Choking down the last bite of bread, she began to tell him what she could.

'It all has to do with my father. He drinks, you see, far too much. I dress like this to scare him away from going to the tavern. My sister and I fear he will fall off his horse on his way home and be injured.'

This much was the truth. She did worry about his safety.

'Your method seems extreme. You have all of Fallen Leaf afraid to go out after dark. Perhaps giving your father a stern warning would do. Remind him of the danger.'

'Your bedpost would be more attentive to what I say than my father is. He is as stubborn as anything you ever saw. You cannot imagine what my sister and I must deal with because of it.'

Joseph Billings was an easy man to talk to, even though he had it in his power to reveal her charade to the village.

How odd. She really ought to be less forthcoming about everything. Then again, he was demanding that she be.

He seemed a decent man, and yet he was the one who held all the power here. He knew her secret…well, some of it.

'But surely he would not wish for you to scare everyone half out of their wits?'

'I am sorry for that, truly. I never meant for poor Homer to see me, only my father. It is rare for anyone to be on that path at night. I suppose it is a wonder I did not get caught before now.'

'I am surprised that your father did not tell anyone about what he saw.'

Indeed, it is something that she and Eliza worried about.

'Who would believe him? I suppose he did not wish to be thought a fool.'

With the broth and bread finished, she stood up, grasping the bedpost for balance.

'I am ready to go now.'

He tilted his head, arched both brows. 'Not yet, Miss Augustmore. You still need more time.'

'Ready or not, I must go home.'

But then, perhaps he was right. She was woozy-headed. Without his help, she would not even make it to the doorway.

She lowered herself back to the mattress and sat.

'I am curious about something.' He took the tray which she had set aside and placed it on the bedside table next to the vase. The pink rose looked far too cheerful. Her head hurt too wickedly for it to be of help.

'I am curious about something, too.' It was not quite about the rose, although she did wonder what made an important man like he was put a flower next to his bed.

'Shall we each take a turn slaking our curiosity?'

'I will slake mine first,' she said, since the answer was of the utmost importance.

'Very well, ask me what you wish.'

The smile he gave made her feel...probably not dizzy since she already was that, but as before, fluttery. How curious that the sensation came from her middle and not her head.

'Do you still intend to haul me before my neighbours to admit my crime…which is really no true crime at all but only what a dutiful daughter would do to protect her father?' She did not think he meant to expose her, but she needed to hear him say so.

'I understand why you felt you needed to act the way you did. Your secret is safe with me.'

'Thank you. I am grateful.'

'Now it is time for you to slake my curiosity.'

She could not imagine what more there was to be curious about but… 'You may ask, of course.'

The answer would be as honest as she could make it.

'You mentioned that your father's stubbornness made things difficult for you…and your sister, too.'

'I suppose there is no harm in telling you about it. My father has decided it is past time for me and my sister to wed. He has decreed that I, being the oldest and in great danger of spinsterhood, will wed first. He had also decreed that I will wed the baker, the very one who makes the bread you just served me.'

'And you do not wish to marry him? He seemed a decent fellow to me.'

'He is, of course…but he is in love with my sister, and she with him.'

'That does present rather a problem.' He gave her a long considering glance. 'One thing, Miss Augustmore. As I see it, you are in no danger of becoming a spinster.'

My word, the man was appealing, the way he scrubbed his hand over his grin, as if he wanted her to see it and not see it at the same time.

'Of course I am. Since I will not wed the banker, I will not wed at all. Therefore, I am doomed to spinsterhood.'

What? Why had he burst into a grin which he made no effort to hide? 'I cannot imagine why you think it is funny.'

'It is both funny and not funny, Miss Augustmore.' He leaned forward in his chair, looking as if he had a great secret to share. 'We are birds of a feather, you and I. You see, my mother also wishes to force me into a marriage. However, the lady in question is not at all likeable. I will fight the necessity as hard as you will.'

Joseph stood up. Walked halfway across the room and then held out his arms to her.

'Shall we test how ready you are to make the trip home now?' He flexed long, bold fingers in invitation. 'Come to me.'

'I must be ready, mustn't I? It would not do to add being caught alone together to our troubles.' She snatched up her hat from the end of the bed and tugged it back on her head. 'If Father gets wind of this, it will not go well for either of us.'

She took a step toward him, then another, before her strength gave out.

Joseph was beside her at once, scooping her up in his arms.

'Fathers are funny that way.' He smiled, looking handsome and mischievous all at once. By the looks of it, he was laughing inside.

'This is not a bit funny, you know, Joseph! Viscount or not, you will find yourself wed to me within a week if we are discovered.'

'Son of one. But then, if you and I were married, at least I would not need to worry about the woman my mother has chosen for me.'

'It hardly matters. Wed is wed.'

Going out of the chamber, he paused in the doorway and gave her the oddest look. She could not begin to guess what it meant.

'Is something wrong, Joseph? Is my weight hurting your back?' She doubted that was it since his back was broad and his arms were strong.

'No.' He plucked the feather from her hat, tucking it into the buttonhole of her waistcoat. 'The feather was tickling my nose.'

It was not until they reached the bottom of the stairway that she realized she had called him by his given name, twice. What had come over her to use it so easily and after such a short acquaintance?

'I will walk now,' she said, tugging on the shoulder of his coat. 'You cannot possibly carry me all the way home.'

'It's downhill.'

That said, he did not speak again until they arrived at the arbor where the path met the lane leading to the cottages.

'You must put me down now, sir. Don't you see my sister standing there?' Olive wagged her hand at the shadowed figure wringing her apron halfway between the cottage and the path. 'We should not be seen like this.'

Especially by Eliza, who would think the worst. 'I knew she would not sleep until I was home.'

Spotting them, her sister raced forward.

'Now she will see that she had no reason to worry,' he said. 'Finding you hale and whole.'

And in the arms of a handsome stranger.

'She will see no such thing. She will—'

Breathless, Eliza slapped Joseph's arm, yanking on his sleeve.

'Unhand my sister, you lout!'

'She'll fall if I do.'

'Fall? What have you done to her?'

Joseph loosened his grip, allowing her to slide to her feet, but did not let go of her.

'I am steady enough now, I think. Eliza can help me the rest of the way.'

Her sister slipped an arm about her waist.

'You, sir, are a villain.' Eliza gave Joseph a hard glare. 'You shall answer for what you have done.'

'Good night, Joseph...umm... Mr Billings, I mean.'

This was the worst time for her to make a slip of the tongue. He was not Joseph to her, but a viscount's heir.

'Do not judge him so harshly, Eliza. All the man did was come to my aid when I fell off Star and hit my head,' she explained, making her way toward the cottage one cautious step at a time.

'Heavens, how did that happen? I know you are a better rider than that.'

'Ordinarily. But he was chasing me. It wasn't me, though, was it?'

'Your injury is worse than you are letting on. You are not making a bit of sense.'

'I'm making perfect sense. He was chasing the phantom highwayman.'

'Chasing you.'

'Yes, but the point is, he did not know that.'

When they reached the cottage door, she glanced back over her shoulder.

Joseph was still there, standing under the arbor, watching her go. Her heart went soft. It was not so awful having a future viscount watching to see that she made it safely up the lane.

She lifted her hand and waved.

He waved back.

In the dim, predawn light, she doubted he saw her smile.

'Why are you smiling at that man, Olive?'

'I might like him.'

'Like him how?' Eliza took her by the shoulders, staring hard into her eyes. 'You spent the night with him, and I only pray you did not make my mistake.'

Once inside the cottage, Eliza and Olive went to the kitchen, beginning their day as they normally did with toast and eggs.

Father would not rise for another hour, so she and her sister had a few moments to talk before she would need to dress and then begin the daily chores.

'I did not make your mistake. My time with Joseph Billings was nothing like that.'

'Billings? You cannot mean the viscount?'

'Joseph is his son.'

'It is all the same. He is not one of us.'

'It is the oddest thing, Eliza. I get the impression that he does not wish to be seen as lofty. And he behaved like a complete gentleman.'

'He had his hands on you.'

'Because he feared I could not walk safely on my own, that's all. Like I told you, I fell off my horse when he was chasing me, and I hit my head on a rock. He made me broth and gave me bread.'

'Which he would not have needed to do had he not been pursuing you in the first place!'

'He would not have been pursuing me if I was not terrorizing the village. Someone was bound to come after me at some point.'

Eliza had been about to say something else but seemed to catch her words.

'It is my fault, of course. All you have done is try and protect me. I am sorry, Olive.' Eliza folded her arms on the table, placing her head on her forearms. 'I suppose the truth will all come out now. I cannot imagine he did not drag an admission from you.'

'Naturally, he did. Discovering the truth is the reason he chased me. I told him that I wished to keep Father from going to the tavern and drinking to excess. And also that Father is determined to get me wed to James when you are the one who is in love with him.'

Eliza turned her head. One green eye peeked up at her. 'That is all you told him?'

'It is. But I wonder…no, I think… I have a feeling he would keep our secret even if he knew all of it.'

'It is not wise to have a "feeling" about a man you do not know well.' Eliza lifted her head from her arms and shook it. 'Be very wary of him.'

'Of course. But really, Eliza, Joseph is more of a gentleman than you are giving him credit for being. I would not have made it home without his aid.'

'Oh? He might have brought you home on a horse, not in his arms!'

'I shudder to think how a horse's gait would have jarred my head. The pain would have been awful.'

As it turned out, being carried along in his arms had been gentle. At one point she had even rested her head on his broad shoulder, closed her eyes and breathed in the scent of his coat…of his neck.

It would be a lie to say she did not regret it when he set her on her feet at the lane. She'd felt a silly little lump in her throat when his steadying arms were replaced by Eliza's tense ones.

Her life was so full of lies, she would at least be truthful to herself in this one thing. Despite the situation she had landed herself in, she had been comfortable with Joseph.

It made little sense, but there it was.

'Since he went to such trouble to bring me home, I will take him some of our cheese as a thank-you. Please say you will come along as chaperone.'

'Who was your chaperone last night?'

Olive did not answer because clearly this was an accusation, not a question.

'I promise that nothing untoward happened.'

'You are the one who will pay the cost if it did.'

'You are not the only one who learned that lesson, sister. But come, Eliza. It is time to wake the goats.'

Rising, Olive went out the kitchen door, then walked toward the stable singing, as was her custom.

Once inside the stable, Olive took her gown from its hiding place in the trunk. She put it on while Eliza stowed the costume away, then slid the trunk into its spot under the cupboard.

She ought to be exhausted but actually felt quite recovered. In spite of the risk to her reputation last night had posed, her time with their new neighbour had been interesting.

What a handsome, charming man.

And, by glory fire, she was completely safe from developing an infatuation for him.

A cottage lass and an heir apparent?

It was too far-fetched to give a moment's thought to.

Which did not mean he should not be thanked for taking care of her. She would bring him her small gift of cheese.

It was the neighbourly thing to do. Proper any way one looked at it.

Walking in the woods behind the stable where the stream gurgled cheerfully to the right of him, Joseph went over last night in his mind. It had probably been the most interesting night of his life.

Rising yesterday morning, he would never had guessed how it would turn out. How in apprehending the terror of the village, he had become acquainted with an intriguing woman.

A lovely woman whom he thought he had got to know rather well, for all that they had not spent a great deal of time together. Only hours, but it seemed as if somehow in that time they had become friendly. It was interesting how easy conversation could be when one did not have to weigh each word and decide if society would deem it proper.

Talking to Olive had been natural…an echo of the past, he thought. It took him back to when he was young, when life with his cousins had been unaffected.

Aye, last night, once he knew the lady would recover with no great harm done, had that same quality to it.

A small bird hopped onto a branch to peer at him, first with one eye and then the other. The bird did not care if he was a viscount's heir or a commoner. He had to wonder if Olive Augustmore cared.

Not that it mattered really. It was only that he would prefer it if, when she looked at him, she saw a man and not a future viscount.

They were neighbours, after all.

He would like to fit in at Fallen Leaf. Somehow meld the two parts of who he was. It was not something he could do in London. The social demands of the city would only ever allow the noble side of him to flourish.

But here, yes, he thought it could be done. In time he might make acquaintances of the people who lived here. Hopefully they would come to see him as a man and not simply his father's title.

One good thing about his parents' visit was that he would be able to present his petition to Father to make this estate his home.

Coming out of the woods, he stood at the paddock fence, watching Dane prance in the sunshine.

Aye, this was home and where he meant to make his future. Mama would not be pleased for him to live here and not in London, but she was not the biggest obstacle he faced.

Lady Hortencia Clark was.

Joseph had good reason to dread her visit. He had barely escaped being trapped in a compromising situation with her a few times already.

Here at Falcon's Steep, she might succeed. He could hardly spend every moment of the day with his parents or with the servants his mother was already busy hiring.

Unless he was constantly in company, there was a risk of Hortencia springing out from behind a tree or sneaking into his bedchamber.

Last summer he'd caught her attempting to bribe a footman into claiming he'd witnessed Joseph in the act of compromising her. When the man had refused to do it, she'd berated him. Called him names that Joseph himself had never used.

With his ear to the door, he had then heard Hortencia threaten to spread a lie which would have the footman's employment terminated.

Naturally, when Joseph had stepped into the room to put a stop to her abuse, Hortencia had swiftly put on her mask of sweetness and smiles.

The footman did not dare accuse her of anything, so there was nothing he could do to set the matter to rights.

Nothing but remember, and be wary.

It had done him no good to warn Mama of Hortencia's flawed character. She'd dismissed his concerns as the simple aversion to marriage some bachelors had.

There were a few people, he believed, who saw Hortencia for who she was, but like the footman, they did not dare to speak against a lady of high rank who, with a word, had the power to sink a reputation.

Joseph groaned aloud, slammed his fist on the paddock post. He only gained a splinter for his effort.

'Dash it,' he muttered, then pulled it out with his teeth, spitting it onto the dirt.

Yet it was not really the splinter he cursed. It was that he refused to be bound for life to such a conniving shrew.

Not that he was entirely certain he could avoid it.

Unless…

He'd had an idea last night. An outrageous one. As ideas went, it was one of his worst. There was no way in which it could be successful.

His thoughts were interrupted by the high, happy lilt of women laughing.

Their voices came from the front of the manor. Coming closer, it sounded as if the ladies were taking the path which led to the rear of the house.

Surely there had not been enough time for the maids his mother was hiring to get here.

Looking away from the paddock, he squinted toward the direction of the sound.

Ah, there was a sight to brighten a man's mood. Miss Augustmore and her sister rounded the corner and were approaching the arbor which framed the kitchen steps.

Seeing Olive under a bower of blooming pink roses, watching her smile and chat with her sister, was a cheerful sight.

Cheerful was precisely the balm he needed in that moment.

Olive spotted him first. She and her sister came towards him across the grassy meadow that divided the manor house from the stable and paddock.

Olive carried a basket in the crook of her elbow. It bumped her hip when she walked.

Joseph did not consider himself a fanciful man. That didn't keep him from thinking she looked like walking sunshine, though.

It did not matter that he had spent only a short time with her, and much of that while she was asleep; he found he liked her.

There were certain people he had met in his life who he felt an affinity with straight away. Cousins mostly, and a few friends from school.

The odd thing was, he had never felt that connection to a woman before, unless she was a relative.

Interesting that he felt it now, and for a lady not of his class.

Interesting but not surprising, since given a choice, he

would spend as little time as possible among the class he was born into.

He crossed the meadow in long strides and met the ladies halfway, waving them around a patch of buttercups abuzz with bees.

'It is good to see you again, Miss Augustmore.' He nodded at Olive.

'And you, too, Miss Augustmore.' He nodded at her sister. Eliza, he recalled her name being.

Eliza did not look overly pleased to see him, but at least she was not scowling at him as she had done in the wee hours this morning.

Hard to blame her for it, though. He must have come across as a rake having kept her sister out all night and then bringing her home in his arms.

'Olive explained to me what happened, and I regret that I assumed the worst and glowered at you, sir.'

'Think nothing of it, Miss Augustmore. It was easy to misunderstand the situation.'

'Indeed… Well, I will say this one thing and then not speak of it again. You should not have been chasing my sister. Now I am done with it.'

'Eliza!' Olive shot her sister a reprimanding glance. 'Have you forgotten what we discussed? Did we not agree that it was a fortunate bit of luck Mr Billings caught me out and not someone else? That we can thank our lucky stars he has chosen to keep our secret?'

'I do recall it, of course. And we have brought you cheese from our very own goats to express our gratitude to you, sir.'

Eliza took the basket from Olive and pushed it at him.

'And a mince pie,' Olive added.

In the sunshine, Olive's eyes were a near match to meadow clover. He was so caught up in how pretty they were that he lost track of what the sisters were saying. But it wasn't only her eyes catching him up. It was her lips, too.

With a mental jerk, he reminded himself that it was inappropriate to be thinking of her this way, especially in front of Eliza, who did not trust him anyway.

'Thank you for the cheese and pie,' he said.

What he did not say but felt, was, *Thank you for bringing sweetness to a day which worry over Hortencia turned sour.*

Once again he wondered if he should present the idea to Olive that was niggling his mind. It was preposterous, though, so after another second's thought, he dismissed it. He did not wish for Olive to think him insane.

Too bad, because she did seem to have a gift for acting.

'May I just say…' Hopefully she did not take his compliment in the wrong way, but it was fair to give the lady her due. 'You did make a brilliant highwayman ghoul. I applaud both you and your horse. As a pair, you were truly frightful.'

'Thank you, I suppose. But the truth is, I am relieved it is over. I do not care for being dishonest.'

Eliza crushed a dirt clod under her boot toe, biting her bottom lip.

What a lucky thing he had not told Olive Augustmore what was on his mind, then. Honesty did not play into it.

'How will you keep your father home now?' he asked, because he sensed they were about to leave, and he wished for their company a bit longer.

'Hide the horses, I imagine,' Olive answered. 'It seems more respectful than drugging his tea.'

'Tea?' Eliza exclaimed. 'As if we could get a sip down his throat.'

'We should be on our way.' Olive nodded at her sister. 'We have schemes to invent.'

What would her clever mind come up with next, he wondered? If it was half as inventive as haunting the road, he would be impressed.

'May I help in some way?'

Aye, he would not mind being a part of whatever interesting mischief the ladies devised.

'You could tie him to his chair, but that would be less than subtle,' Olive declared with a quick laugh.

Somehow, and he was not sure how it happened, he found himself staring at her mouth again. This time for far too long. Riveted is what he was, caught by the appeal of humour expressed in her pretty, quirking lips.

She tipped her head, returning his stare in kind. It made his mouth tingle.

Something was happening here, but he was damned if he knew quite what.

It was not something to know, he imagined, but only to feel.

Then she blinked and broke whatever spell had momentarily held them.

Eliza tugged on her sister's sleeve, glancing back and forth between him and Olive with a less than pleased expression. 'We would not wish to involve you in it, sir. We will think of some other way to deal with Father. Come, sister, we will be on our way.'

'Good day, sir,' Olive said, nodding and smiling.

Watching the sisters walk back the way they had come, he clutched the basket of cheese to his middle.

Something was off with him. Hunger, perhaps, since all he'd eaten for breakfast was a slice of bread?

Surely he was mistaken about that long glance between them being a spell.

Olive Augustmore was a friendly neighbour. Nothing more and nothing less.

The good of it was that a social call required an answering one. The Augustmore sisters had paid him a visit, and now he would reciprocate.

Tomorrow he would pay his respects to Mr Augustmore.

If he managed to spend a bit of time with Olive during the visit…aye, well, he would not mind that at all.

Chapter Four

Sitting in front of the hearth that night, Olive had her knitting needles paused, her mind wandering here and there, but mostly up the hill.

What, she wondered, was Joseph Billings doing? Whatever it was, he would be doing it alone. Did he mind being alone? She did not know him well enough to know.

Eliza swept into the room, her knitting bag tucked under her arm.

'Father is in bed for the night.' Her sister plopped down into the chair beside her, heaving a sigh. She drew the knitting needles from her bag and clacked the pointed ends against one another. 'I visited the bakery this afternoon. Father gave James permission to court you.'

'Oh? I imagine poor James was properly stunned. Did he pummel Father with a baguette?'

'A fine waste of bread it would be, for all the good it would do.'

'Will James court you against Father's wishes?'

Eliza drew a skein of yarn from the bag. 'No. He says it would not be the honourable thing to do. I will admit his sense of honour can be trying. Although he did at least say he would not court you either.'

'It seems we are doomed to be old maids, then.'

It was more than that, though. Olive read the thought that crossed her sister's expression. Unless Eliza wed, she would never be able to adopt her child. 'I miss Mama. None of this would be happening if she were still here.'

'I miss her, too.' Every day.

'Wouldn't you think that since Mama wed for love, Father would allow me to do it?'

Yes, she would think so. 'Father was not as wrong-headed when she was alive.'

Their mother had wed beneath her station. Her father had been a vicar and gentry. The story was, their grandfather had been so angry that he had immediately cut her off from the rest of her family.

Olive and Eliza had never met the man. Not that they were terribly sorry for it. Their own family had been happy, and Grandfather's harsh attitude towards the marriage would only have cast a shadow.

If Mama had grieved the loss of her family, it did not show. She'd raised her girls with joy and laughter. She'd been devoted to Father.

Because of their mother's own upbringing, Olive and her sister had always stood out from the other women in the village. Mama had taught them the manners of polite society, and to read and write and talk. Since they spoke with the diction she'd considered proper, Olive and Eliza did not completely fit in with the other villagers. The men tended to pass them over for women who sounded and behaved more like they did. It was nothing so bad as being outcasts, only they were not quite like everyone else, either.

Luckily, James also had some education, so he and Eliza fit well together. If only their father would allow it.

'While I knit this scarf and you knit Father a pair of socks, we must find a way to keep him home,' Olive said.

'I say we feed his shoes to Gilroy.'

Sadly, that was the best idea they managed.

After wasting away the better hours of the night and much of the morning, Olive had not devised a scheme to keep Father at home.

Depriving him of his shoes would not be kind, and so the only other thing she came up with was to warn him of a plague in the village. Travel was forbidden.

Not a viable solution to the problem, but for now her brain was weary with chewing it over.

What she needed was a few moments of carefree fun, and she knew just how to get them.

She hurried down the back steps of the cottage toward the fenced meadow. Even from here, she heard young goats bleating in the warm afternoon sunshine.

Once inside the gate, she ran toward them, singing and laughing at the same time.

The herd was a perfect size. Large enough to earn money off milk, cheese, and soap, and yet small enough to be managed by Olive and her sister.

There were many wonderful creatures in God's beautiful creation. Of all of them, goats were her favourite.

Perhaps because they seemed to view life with humour. At least, that's how she interpreted them. Always leaping, climbing, and nibbling on anything that came close to their muzzles.

Gilroy was the first to spot her. He bleated and came trotting towards her. Four babies followed, not in an orderly line but bounding every which way.

'Hello, Gilroy.' She patted his head. 'Hello, babies.'

She scooped up a kid and twirled about with it. She nuzzled its head with her nose, then set it back on the grass.

The white-and-brown kid dashed away, followed by its mates. One of them got distracted by a bee and gave chase. Another went to its mother for a snack. The one she had twirled around stopped to nibble a flower.

It all looked like great fun. Which was the very reason Olive had come to the meadow.

She dashed after them, lifting her skirt high so she could leap like they did.

Finally winded, she lay down on the grass, arms stretched wide, while she caught her breath and watched a cloud changing shapes in the sky.

Something nibbled her sleeve. Absently she patted a soft little head. A cold nose pressed her cheek. Then brown eyes blinked at her, the pupils humourous-looking rectangles.

Some people thought a goat's eyes were eerie, but to Olive, they were sweet and funny.

'You are the dearest creature alive,' she said in the very second a different face filled her vision.

This one did not have goat's eyes.

No indeed, these eyes stared down at her with lines creasing the corners. This face had a mouth that turned upward in an effort not to laugh.

'Thank you for saying so, Miss Augustmore. But perhaps I have come at an inconvenient time?'

Truly, there could not have been a more inconvenient one. To greet a future viscount while sprawled in the grass with a small but persistent goat clambering over one's bosom would never be a lady's first choice.

'It is perfect timing if you care to frolic with my young friends.'

'Another time perhaps. I came to return your basket.'

His lips twitched. In another second, he was bound to

bend over in a fit of mirth. She knew because it is what she would do in his situation.

Sitting up, she carefully lifted the goat off her. Then she stood, swiping grass from her skirt.

'I assume you've met my father?'

'He seems a pleasant, reasonable chap.'

'Yes, well, it is still early,' she muttered, then regretted the slip. 'I trust you had a pleasant visit?'

'We spoke of your upcoming marriage.' How much longer could Joseph withhold his laughter? Not much, she guessed. 'He informed me that if I had a mind to court you, I would be refused. He did offer up Eliza, though.'

With that, he finally let go of the laugh. The sound gave her insides a pleasant shiver. Or maybe it was the attractive laugh lines bracketing his mouth causing the sensation. Both working together was her guess.

'I told him that, regretfully, I had only come to return your basket.' Joseph grinned at her, his eyes snapping blue with humour. 'Will you walk with me?'

How, she would like to know, was a lady to walk when her knees had suddenly gone soft?

What was wrong with her? She was not developing an infatuation for her neighbour. It would be all sorts of improper.

In her defence, his face would cause any woman's heart to stumble over itself, no matter her social status. It was not her fault that he was so appealing.

'There is a stream close by. Shall we walk beside it?' she asked.

'Yes, I know the one. It runs downhill from my property.'

Glancing back at the cottage, Olive spotted Eliza standing on the back porch, watching them.

Chaperone enough, she decided, in case the propriety even needed to be observed in her own meadow. London rules might require a hovering third presence, but fortunately this was Fallen Leaf, and life was more relaxed.

'I enjoyed the cheese. I assume it was compliments of one of your friends here in the meadow.'

'They do produce the best cheese. The mince pie was from me.'

'I enjoyed it even more.'

Handsome and with a sense of humour...society debutantes must fall at his feet on a regular basis.

'Your father does seem as determined as you said he was. Will you be able to go against his wishes? Refuse to wed the baker?'

'I shall stand firm in my refusal, I assure you.'

As always, the scent of rushing water was refreshing. Given her present company, she felt as if she could walk alongside it for hours.

'As I will stand firm in my refusal to wed the woman my mother has chosen for me.'

Joseph stooped, plucking a blue flower. Coming back up, he offered it to her with a smile. Oh yes indeed, the ladies of London would never be able to resist him.

'Will you allow me the familiarity of calling you by your first name?' he asked.

She thought about it for a full second, not certain it was appropriate. But she had already called him Joseph, and it had felt nearly appropriate.

'We are neighbours, after all,' she decided. 'And allies in the cause of not marrying as our parents decree. So yes, you may call me Olive as long as I may call you Joseph.'

Hopefully she had not overstepped since he was nobility.

She had some idea of who called who what in social situations, but still it was a little confusing. Too late to take it back now, though. And if he was going to call her Olive, then—

'It is agreed, then…we are Olive and Joseph.'

'May I ask you a question, Joseph?'

'Certainly, Olive.'

How pleasant this was, neighbours taking a friendly walk beside the stream, speaking of this and that, and—

'It is just that you know why my father is insisting I wed a man I do not desire. Why does your mother insist on it?'

The question was rather personal, but she really did want to know.

'Mama has been duped. Many people have. From the outside, Lady Hortencia seems a perfect choice. She is a lady of quality who will bring distinction to our title. She has an angelic look about her, speaks and behaves graciously when people are watching. It is not who she truly is. I will not wed her.'

'Surely no one can force you, a viscount's heir?'

Joseph stopped walking, ran his wide hand through his hair while shaking his head. He pointed to a fallen log beside the stream.

'Do you mind if we sit?'

Birdsong, leaves rustling in a breeze overhead…and sitting beside a handsome man…what was there to mind?

And yet Joseph seemed stressed. A companionable sit by the water might be just the thing.

Silently, they watched the stream gliding past. Dapples of sunshine glinted off the surface in a way which was mesmerizing. One could nearly get lost in the moment.

'It isn't true that I cannot be forced,' he said at last. 'A compromising situation would see me wed in a hurry. Men of my position must be wary of it at all times, you see.'

Hmm…would this be one of those situations? They were alone, after all. And not for the first time.

'I have reason to believe you would not compromise a woman, Joseph.'

'Aye, you do,' he answered with a lift of his brows. 'I wouldn't need to do the wicked deed. It would only need to look as if I had.'

He shook his head, and a ray of sunshine caught his hair, making strands of gold sparkle in the brown. Distracted, she nearly got lost in this moment instead. She really did need to keep her attention from foolishly wandering.

Olive clasped her fingers together, focusing her attention on his dilemma. She would be the worst sort of neighbour to act in a way that would add to his worries. Touching his hair would certainly do that.

'So, you fear this woman will catch you in a false but compromising situation and then demand you marry her, is that it?'

'She has tried before.'

'Presently, it does not seem to me that you are in great danger. You are the only one living in the manor.'

He stood up, pacing toward the water's edge and then back again. 'Not for long. I've received a letter informing me that my parents are coming to visit, and they are bringing Hortencia with them.'

He squatted in front of her, apparently to better get her attention. Truly, she could not recall anyone ever having it so completely.

'I wonder if…' he began. 'No, never mind.'

He looked hard at her, seeming to have lost his voice.

One of them needed to say something, so she did. 'You are wondering if luck will smile upon you, and she will not come? Is that it?'

He shook his head, still silent. There was something he wanted to say, though. She could nearly see the thoughts swirling behind his eyes. Not the exact words, naturally. She was not a mind reader, but she recognized the concern pressing upon him.

But who would not be worried, fearing he would be trapped in a marriage he did not wish to be in?

She stood up. Joseph did, too. Continuing to stroll beside the stream might ease his anxiety.

'Oh, she'll come. I am certain trapping me is the reason for the visit.'

'Perhaps if you write to your mother and explain.'

'She would no more listen to me than your father would to you.'

He nodded, almost said something else, but apparently changed his mind again.

'But possibly I will get lucky and she will not come.'

He said the words, but she knew he did not truly believe them.

Olive disliked seeing him so troubled. While the two of them were worlds apart socially, they did share a common problem.

A problem which neither of them had the power to help the other with.

'What if there was a way?' Joseph heard the words come out of his mouth but could not believe he'd gathered the courage to utter them.

'I am not certain I know what you mean.'

'No? Well, I am not certain I do either,' he admitted.

'What are we discussing then?'

'You...'

Curse it. Getting Olive involved in his troubles was wrong. Nor did he wish for her to think him insane.

'You have a gift for playing a part,' he said, deciding he actually was insane.

'You cannot possibly mean it?' Her eyes sharpened on him, and her jaw sagged a bit.

'I have not yet told you what I mean.'

'It is clear that you wish me to reprise my role as terror of the night and scare Lady Hortencia away from Falcon's Steep.'

Olive curled her fingers into fists, which she jammed on her hips. She shook her head forcefully and dislodged a strand of hair from her tidy bun. The curl hugging her neck went a great way towards softening her starchiness.

'I will not do it. I have only just regained my status as an honest woman. I am quite finished telling lies.'

This could not end in his favour. Honesty was the last thing he wanted.

'I was not going to ask you to become a ghoul.'

'No? That is a great relief.'

It was so wrong of him to ask her. She had told him more than once how highly she valued honesty.

Wrong or not...he must.

'Then what is it you were going to ask of me?'

'I was going to ask you to be my wife.'

'Glory fire, Joseph.' She placed her hands on her waist, tilted her shoulders back and gave him a wink. 'Wouldn't I make a fine lady?'

She turned in a circle, making her skirt swirl.

'As elegant as fine lace,' she went on. 'Refined, too. I suppose I will not be able to lift my hand for the size of the ring you will place on my finger.'

That said, she wagged her hand at him, shooting him a playful smile.

'You my friend, are a great jester. I will admit, laughter does go a way to ease the situations we find ourselves in.'

'I've made a mess of it all,' he groaned.

'Not at all. My spirit is quite lifted.'

'Indeed? I was not making a joke.'

'Of course you were. I am a cottager and you…you live in the manor on the hill. I do not believe for a moment that you seriously meant to propose marriage to me.'

She was correct. He had not meant that in the strictest sense.

'What I should have asked is, will you pretend to marry me?'

'What?'

She backed away from him, her expression suddenly blank. But only blank for the space it took to gather a thought, to gasp.

'You, sir, are a…something I shall not say. I retract what I said about you being a gentleman. Only a true cad would make fun of a humble neighbour in this way.'

'I wasn't doing that.'

'Ha! I only just admitted to you that I was happy to no longer be living a lie…how I valued honesty.' Red-faced, she marched back to him, pointed her finger and jabbed it at the centre button of his waistcoat. 'You, Lord of the Hill, may go back to it.'

Seeing her stunned expression and the offence she had

taken to his proposal, he wished he could take it back, present the idea in a more convincing way.

In for a penny, and all that, he might as well press for the pound. She could not think any worse of him than she did in this moment.

Spinning about, she bustled off, her skirt jerking with her angry stride.

He had to run to catch up. 'Wait, Olive.'

'I also retract my permission for you to call me that.'

'Let's discuss this.'

'I would as soon pretend to wed Gilroy as speak one more word to a man who would tempt me to return to being dishonest.'

'Are you tempted?' Perhaps this was a chip in her resolve. 'You did say you would not wed the baker, that you would be a spinster first…and your sister with you.'

'James is the baker. Gilroy is that goat over there. The one pointing his horns at you.'

He saw the animal, but it was, in that moment, settling onto a patch of clover for a nap.

'Olive—'

'Miss Augustmore to you.' She continued on her way without giving him a backwards glance.

He couldn't blame her. Seeing it from her side, it would seem absurd. All he needed was a moment more to convince her of the benefits to them both.

'Will you consider it before you completely dismiss the idea?'

'I have already dismissed it.'

'Don't you see how my proposal is the solution for both of our problems?'

'Oh what a tangled web we weave when first we practice to deceive,' she recited. 'It is my motto.'

'The damned web is exactly what I am trying to avoid.'

'Cursing will not win me to your cause, sir. I would think such language was forbidden to a man of your high rank.'

'I apologize for the outburst. Not the rest of it.' All he needed was the chance to show her the merit of his plan. 'In the name of neighbourliness, will you allow me to explain the benefits?'

'*Neighbourly* is an odd word to use to describe someone you have just belittled as of no importance.'

'It was not my intent. I vow it was not.'

All at once she stopped walking.

'It is clear what you thought. That poor humble Olive—Miss Augustmore, that is—would be oh so grateful to pretend to act the lady for however long you choose to continue with the deception. You should know that I have no desire to be a lady.'

'One week only…and that is not what I meant.'

He might as well turn around and walk back upstream toward home. This had gone all wrong, and there was nothing more he could say. Remaining in her company would only distress them both.

'I wish you good day, Miss Augustmore.'

He was several yards along his way when he felt a tug on the back of his coat.

'Why do think this makes any sense? How would such a deception benefit us both?'

'It is simple enough. If Hortencia believes I am already wed, she will not continue to pursue me. If your father thinks you are already wed, he will allow your sister to marry the baker.'

He nearly lost his train of thought for an instant, distracted by her eyes. The prettiest he had ever seen, even snapping with indignation as they were. No disguising how sweet her lips were, either, despite being pressed into a thin, tight line.

'Very well. While I understand your point, it is a great lie, one which will never work, and I will not be a part of it.'

Giving a sharp nod, she turned and walked downstream.

'Will you at least think about it?' he called.

'No!'

There was nothing to do but make his way upstream toward home.

To the devil with it. He was going to be on his own when it came to avoiding Hortencia Clark. He did not like his odds.

It was dark outside with no moon, only a fierce, stiff wind. Going to the stable, Olive had to lean into the gusts to keep her balance.

She would rather not be saddling Star for a ride to Falcon's Steep, but in spite of the fact that she had told her noble neighbour she would give no thought to his idea, it was all she had done.

One thing was for certain. She was no longer at risk of succumbing to an infatuation for Joseph Billings. Handsome could only take a fellow so far.

A decent sense of morality counted for quite a bit more. Clearly the man lacked that attribute.

To her utter consternation, the idea he'd presented might actually work to both their benefits.

And yet due to its many flaws, it could surely only end in disaster.

She wanted nothing to do with it.

And would not have done if only the possibility of Eliza happily living in the home of the man she loved—while holding the child she adored—had not taken root in her mind.

Taken root and blossomed!

'Glory fire,' she mumbled while riding Star out of the stable. 'I might be as wrong-minded as our neighbour on the hill. Nearly so, anyway.'

It did not take long for Star to trot the distance to the manor.

Hardly a surprise that there were no lamps flickering in the windows, as it was quite late.

No matter. He had left her sleepless, so she did not feel bad about banging on his front door and waking him from whatever sweet slumber he'd managed to indulge in.

It was only a moment before the latch scraped on the other side of the door. Just long enough for Olive's hair to fly about her head, making it impossible to see the man when he opened the door.

'What the bloody blazes! Olive?'

'Who else would it be? Unless you presented some other woman with your pretend proposal and left her sleepless, too.'

She scraped her hands across her face, brushing her hair aside to the right and left so that she could see.

Oh dear, that was a mistake. It would be better to be blinded than to be looking at Joseph Billings's muscular bare chest.

Any true gentleman would have buttoned his shirt to answer a knock on his front door.

He might even have tidied his hair. Who greeted a guest with unkempt locks poking from his head in such a wild-man manner? She would allow for his bare feet since he would not have taken the time to find his shoes while leaving a visitor standing in the dark and teetering in the wind.

The open shirt, though. It did present a problem for her.

If he wished for the dreaded Hortencia not to seduce him, he would have to do better than this.

'Come in before you blow away.' He caught her arm against a gust and tugged her inside.

This visit would be more successful if she was not struggling to ignore how delightfully rumpled he looked.

From a room off the hallway, she spotted a fire blazing. Well, then, it was satisfying to know that he had not been sleeping either.

'It is nearly midnight. What were you thinking, coming out in this weather?'

'That I have questions, and I will not sleep until they are answered.'

'Very well. Go and sit by the fire. I will tend to your horse and be back shortly.'

'Do not bother. I will not remain long.'

He arched a brow at her as if to hint she was mistreating the animal, and then he led her toward the room with the fire and its welcome glow. Her boots tapped the tile. His bare feet padded.

Being a highly bred society horse, perhaps Dane would be troubled by a bit of wind. Joseph was greatly mistaken about Star. She was a hardy farm animal and would not be distressed at all.

Olive nearly wished she had not come. It was probably too bold a thing to do. And yet with his proposal now lodged in her mind, how was she to move forward with her sweet, quiet life until she had the matter settled?

It would be easier to keep a clear head on matters if she was less focused on how the fire reflected in his hair, and how his very capable hand, with its large knuckles and long fingers, brushed it away from his face.

He indicated that she should sit in a chair near the hearth. It was a delicate-looking chair and one of only two pieces of furniture in the parlor. Lord Future Claymore would shatter it if he tried to sit on it.

The other piece of furniture was a couch.

'I do not need to sit. It is late, and I should not be here. I will ask my questions and be on my way.'

'Sit or stand. Either way, you have already ignored propriety by showing up at my door in the middle of the night.'

That was a valid point. She decided to sit.

He took his place on the couch.

'I would not be here were it not for your inappropriate and false proposal of marriage. Make no mistake, sir, although I have questions, I still believe the proposal to be ill-conceived.'

'Desperate, you mean.' He leaned forward, his hands pressing on the knees of his trousers. 'What would you like to ask?'

'Firstly, why do you think anyone will believe you married a woman from the neighbouring cottage? Peers wed equally well born ladies, not commoners.'

'Ordinarily, they would not. You make a valid point. But you made everyone believe you were a highwayman ghoul. I imagine you could act the part of a society lady rather well.'

She *had* learned proper manners from her mother, so maybe...

'You overestimate my ability, sir.' Truly, it was one thing to wail while hiding in the shadows, and quite another to act a part face-to-face with genuine ladies. In addition, one of those ladies was his mother.

'Olive, you have a skill for this sort of thing…acting, I mean. I will teach you what else you need to know. My parents will believe you to be a lady. With luck, Hortencia will, too.'

'You see? You thinking I can do this only proves that you are not thinking logically.'

'Aye, maybe so. But it is my freedom at stake. I might seem unhinged to have thought of it, but given proper consideration, it makes sense.'

In truth, she did not believe him to be unhinged, only possessed of a clever, manipulative mind.

To her shame, it was rather like her own.

'If you agree to live here with me for a short time, I will pay you handsomely.'

Pay? Surely she had not heard him correctly.

'I will leave now.'

She stood, confused at why his offer of payment offended her so badly.

It must be because accepting his money would put her on the same level as one of his staff. Until earlier today, she'd thought there was something special growing between them.

Something that money would diminish. Truly, if she wished for paid employment, it would not be as a false wife.

If only he had not asked her to live a lie, their budding friendship might still be possible.

She half regretted turning to leave. The more thought

she gave to his plan, the more merit it had. There was very little she would not do to ensure Eliza's happiness.

But really! Lie and get paid for it? To her way of thinking, it only compounded the sin.

She had not gone three steps before he strode after her. He reached for her arm as if he would prevent her leaving but then drew his hand back, clenched his fingers.

'Is it the offer of payment which is making you angry?'

'I am not angry, merely incensed.'

'I do not understand.'

She continued toward the door, trying not to let him see how hurt she had been.

He stepped ahead of her and blocked half of the doorway.

Mercy but he was large and impressive, for all that she hated to take note of it in the moment.

Even his fingers pressing the door frame gave her heart a little flip. His toes did the same thing to her. All ten of them peeked out from under the hem of his rumpled trousers.

'Tell me what I have done wrong, Miss Augustmore.'

How was she to explain that this division between them troubled her? Especially when much of it was her own doing. She had been the one to insist he call her Miss Augustmore again.

At the time, it had felt the righteous thing to say…but now? She could not recall ever being so confused.

'When you offered to pay me, it was a reminder of the distance between our stations. And I thought there might be an understanding of friendship between us, I was reminded of who we must be to one another.'

'It is not at all what I intended, Olive. Surely it is only

fair to pay you for your service? Any actress would expect it.'

'But I am not an actress.'

She squeezed past him, caught the scent of his skin. He really should have buttoned up. It was not her fault that she felt a sweet shiver while going past him.

Let it be a warning to you, she told herself. *Acting the part of this man's wife would leave any woman wanting more.*

She had her hand on the front door knob when his voice came softly to her.

'Olive, think for a minute. This would be a way to give you and your sister the freedom to choose who you will spend your life with. It might be worth the risk.'

Softly spoken, his words had the impact of being shouted…because he was correct.

'Even if it were true, and I agreed, I would not accept a penny of your money.'

'Will you do it then, if I withdraw my offer of money… and apologize for offering it? It would mean a great deal to me to be restored to your good graces.'

'You are restored, Joseph…only I cannot say about the other.'

'Will you think about it at least?'

That was the problem. The more pondered, the more inclined she was to think…just maybe.

'I do believe you have not given this enough thought,' she said. 'Caution was called for. What is your plan to get out of the marriage when the acting is over? How do we stop being wed?'

It was a valid point. They could hardly proceed until it was addressed. 'We can hardly be married one day and then the next, not.'

'I do not have an answer for that bit yet.'

'Which only shows that you have not thought this out properly. On the surface the scheme might have a small speck of merit. But the truth is, it cannot believably be accomplished.'

'You may leave that to me.'

'Even if you could, which you cannot, I will fail at playing the part.'

'You were a convincing highwayman.'

'Which I no longer am. No matter how well I might play my part, it will end. I cannot simply exist as your wife one day and then be vanished the next.'

'A problem, yes. One that I believe can be solved.'

'How? I cannot think of a way. I do not see that there is one.'

'It is illusive, that's all.'

'You have until I open this door and mount Star's saddle.'

Dastardly wind! It blew her about, dizzy as a willow. Her insides were dizzy enough as it was.

'May I try something before you leave?'

His grin would do her in one of these days.

'What do you wish to try?'

Not kiss her. And why had she thought that? Just because his hair blew all wild about his face and his feet were bare… Just because… When was the man going to button his shirt?

Even if he tried to kiss her, she would not allow it.

'To rehearse, as much as try. I will act the part of a gentleman, and you will act the part of a lady. Just to discover if you feel you have a knack for the part before you completely reject it.'

Not a kiss, then. Good.

'Very well. But you must instruct me first on my part.'

She knew a lot more than most cottage girls because of her mother, and from what she read in novels, but surely not so much that she could accomplish what Joseph was asking of her.

Rather than playacting, she ought to be halfway home right now.

'We will act a greeting,' he explained. 'Try not to blow away during it.'

Since she was here, she might as well give it a go, just to see what she could do.

'Is this our first meeting, or are we already acquainted?'

'We have met one time already.'

'Do we like each other?'

'Quite well. In fact, we were taken with one another at first sight.' Seen in the dark, eyes should not look so blue. It must be her imagination making them that way…blue and sparkling with mischief. He gave her a slight bow at the waist. 'Lady Olive, what a great pleasure to meet you again.'

He reached for her hand, picked it up, then lifted it to his lips as if he would kiss it.

Although he did not, he might as well have, given the sweet shiver that raced across her fingertips.

'How lovely to see you again, my Lord. I pray you are well.'

She dipped a small, polite curtsy. She had never engaged in this type of greeting before. Such formality was uncommon in Fallen Leaf. She would need to call on what she had read and imagined.

She blinked at him, slowly, flirtatiously, because it

seemed a society thing to do. And also he had said they were attracted to one another at first sight.

'How could I be otherwise in your delightful presence?' He must have had a great deal of practice with saying that.

'Oh, my lord.' She offered a great deep sigh which lifted her bosom. A society lady might do that. 'If we hurry, we can be out of this wind and tucked up as warm as hatchlings in our respective beds. Now, that would be bliss, would it not?'

'Olive…you do have a gift. A debutante making her debut would not appear so accomplished.'

'I do not know exactly what I accomplished, Joseph.'

Glory fire, it was good to say his name again.

'We just proved that you have the ability to act the part of an exquisite lady of society. If you are comfortable with the part, perhaps we can continue with the lessons. It might help you decide if you can do this for us or not.'

'And if I decide not to? Will it change our…' She waved her hand between them, not certain what words were appropriate. 'Budding acquaintance?'

'You must decide as you will, Olive. Whatever your choice, it will not change my admiration of you.'

If it was within her power to unite Eliza and her daughter, Olive must give this false marriage serious thought.

Setting her foot in the stirrup, she felt his hand at her waist, assisting her up. Although she did not need the help, and had been mounting a horse unassisted since she was ten years old, the attention made her feel appreciated. Feminine in a way no man had made her feel before.

For Joseph, treating a lady like this was simply good manners, and she should not take the attention to heart.

He was a nobleman, and she was a cottager. They were acting a part. There was no more to it than that.

And yet, here in the dark with the wind gusting around and between them, with it wailing in the treetops, the world around them seemed to seemed to fade.

When he grinned up at her, the divide between their stations did not seem as wide.

'If the weather improves,' she said, 'meet me tomorrow at the stream where our properties join. I am curious about what other ladylike things you can teach me.'

'I will meet you regardless of the weather.'

She nodded, then turned Star toward the road.

His eyes were still upon her. She knew it as surely as if she had turned around and looked for the proof.

Which did not mean she did not wish for proof.

Drawing Star to a halt, she glanced back over her shoulder.

'Come at noon. I will bring lunch,' she told him.

'I will bring a bottle of wine and a blanket.'

She waved goodbye to him, wondering what it would be like to blow him a kiss…to practice what a loving wife would do.

Something was wrong with her. She had never blown a man a kiss for any reason.

She nudged Star on towards home.

'I think perhaps it might be done.' She patted the horse's neck. 'The thing is, I do not know how it might be undone again afterwards.'

And she was not speaking only of ending the sham marriage. Her heart was far too tender when it came to the future viscount.

She would do well to remember that his station in life and hers were worlds apart.

Still, what harm could there be in indulging in the delightful, tickling warmth she got when thinking of him?

Unlike true love, which endured forever, an infatuation burned bright and in secret for a moment and then was gone.

There could be no harm in pretending.

Chapter Five

Joseph watched a bee crawling on a yellow flower, productively gathering pollen near the blanket he sat on. Sunshine warmed his back.

He rolled his shoulders in pure pleasure while listening to water gurgling in the stream, and to the pleasant tone of Olive's voice as she practiced words.

Not words that were new to her, but she was learning to pronounce them in an even more refined way. Proper diction was crucial if she was to fool his visitors. She did not need much work in this area since, as she had told him, her mother had been gently born.

All at once she stopped speaking, took a sip of wine, then set the goblet aside in the grass.

'This is delicious, Joseph,' she said, giving her lips an appreciative smack. After a sigh of satisfaction, a mask descended over her natural expression. 'But pray, my lord, how long would I be required to engage in this farce? As delightful as it may be.'

If she actually found this exercise delightful, he'd eat that bee. Her true feelings did not show behind her smile, which was a testament to her skill. A born and bred lady would appear to find everything delightful even when she did not. Putting her guests at ease was a lady of privilege's first order of duty.

'One week, that's all.'

'Sir, may I take you at your word? This is an agreement which you vow to honour?'

'Indeed. On my honour, I vow it.'

'Then, yes. I will do it.' She tipped her wineglass at him in salute. 'To our success.'

He tipped his glass back at her, but it took all he had not to leap and shout in triumph. If he were free to express himself, he would pick her up, swing her about.

'To winning our freedom,' he said instead. 'And to our friendship.'

'To our friendship.'

He could not look away from the blush in her cheeks when she sipped the wine. It might be due to the weather, or the drink…but hopefully it was because she was excited about the venture they were undertaking.

Her lips twitched.

'I will hate to see our alliance end, of course.' She cast him a charming smile.

'You really are good at this,' he admitted. 'If we had just met, I would not question that you were not born a lady.'

'I do not think you would believe it,' the genuine Olive said. 'As you see, I am dressed as a commoner. And I smell a little like goats.'

He shook his head. 'More like fresh air…grass and flowers. Natural. Not like some women I know who drench themselves in so much perfume it makes everyone's head ache.'

She laughed. For as much as he appreciated her portrayal as a fine lady, the real Olive was far more interesting to him.

'Tell me your secret, Olive. How do you play a part so well?'

'I've a good bit of it from my mother, as I said. That much is not acting.'

'However you come by it, you are a natural actor.'

'The acting comes from books.'

'You studied acting?'

'I would not call it studied so much as living the adventure. How do you imagine I learned my talent for highway terror? In print, fine ladies are in distress even more often than ghouls haunt the woods. Upon occasion the poor lady is in distress because of a ghoul. I, though, do not expect to be in distress. Rest assured, Joseph, I intend to cause distress.'

Heaven help him if he was not beginning to adore this woman. She was perfection. Lady or lass, he had never enjoyed a woman's company more.

'Oh, I believe that. I nearly pity poor Hortencia.' He did not, but was beginning to wonder if Olive was a match for her.

Not that the women were at all the same. Olive would be acting in an unselfish cause. Hortencia was all about attaining a selfish goal. Matters of right or wrong did not matter to the woman who intended to trap him.

'I need you to tell me more about her, Joseph. As your wife, I should know how to deal with my nemesis.'

It took half an hour to explain all of Hortencia. How selfishness was her guiding light. How she did not care who got hurt in her quest to have what she wanted…his title, the extensive family fortune and lands.

The way Hortencia ferreted out a person's secrets and used them to her advantage.

At that news, Olive frowned.

'I am sorry,' he said, 'but the woman is part hound. Do not worry, though, we are cleverer than she is. She will not discover that our marriage is false. Only…be wary, Olive, she will come across mild and sweet like a newly hatched chick, but you must not trust her.'

'Glory fire,' she muttered when he finished. 'Now tell me about your parents.'

'They are honourable, but still, they will present a challenge. Especially my mother.'

'I have always got along well with mothers.'

Olive looked sad, somewhat melancholy when she said so. Probably because she missed her own mother.

Not wishing to make her feel that he was looking into her thoughts, he gazed at the treetops. Leaves shivered in a breeze which felt soft on his face.

'Tell me more about your mother,' Olive said.

'She is a force in society, and charitable to go with it. But position is important to her. To Mama, family security is gained by allying ourselves with another family of the highest rank we can marry into. Which is why she is set on having me wed Hortencia. In my mother's eyes, she will be a credit to us all.'

'But surely what you wish for your life also matters to her?'

'No more than it matters to your father.'

She reached across the blanket and squeezed his hand. 'We will strive hard for our futures, Joseph.'

He would kiss her in thanks, but he did not wish to scare her off. Aye, and likely scare himself off along with it. Something warned him a kiss of thanks was not all there would be to it.

'My father will be easier. His way of promoting the health of the estate is to add to it. Property is what he has his eye on. My job in the family is to visit his purchases and report on them. In the past, I never minded the travel. It was a relief to get out of London for a time.'

'In the past, you say? Am I to understand that now, you do mind?'

'There is something about Falcon's Steep…' He glanced north as if somehow he could spot the tall chimneys through acres of woods between here and there. 'Of all the properties I have visited, none of them ever felt like home to me. This place does. It grabbed me from the first moment.'

'London does not feel that way for you either?'

'Never did. I think I was born all wrong. I would rather have grown up with your goats than in the city.'

'Do you intend to remain here, then? Once this is all finished?'

'I'll try. I am not sure if it will be possible.' He did his best not to scowl, but damn it! His future was not his own and never had been. 'I was born to obligation, you understand.'

'It seems a tiresome burden. But perhaps once you have discouraged Hortencia, you will find a bride who appeals to you more. Then your future will be bright wherever you live.'

A long shadow crept across the blanket. Joseph jolted in surprise. He was rarely taken off guard.

'May I join the picnic?'

'Oh, do, Eliza. The reason for this meeting concerns you, after all.'

Olive's sister cast a glance between him and Olive.

'I will leave you to discuss this with your sister.' Rising, Joseph nodded politely at them both.

Olive stood up as well, handing him what he had brought.

'Return at the same time tomorrow, Joseph. I still have so much to learn before your family arrives.'

Once again he had the urge to kiss her. Too bad even a brief salute on the cheek would be inappropriate despite the friendship growing between them.

'Good day, ladies.' He bowed, then strode beside the stream toward home.

It had taken Olive all afternoon to explain the situation to her sister, and then until bedtime to convince her to go along with the plan.

Oh, what a night. If convincing Eliza of the wisdom of what she was doing had not been enough of a challenge, Father took it in his mind to go to the tavern.

What a shame it was about the plague, though. However, he would believe the story only until he paid a visit to the village and discovered there was not some wicked illness striking people down.

But that was a problem for later.

Now she was for bed. Having agreed to act as Joseph's wife, she would need her wits rested and alert in order to succeed in the course she had turned her hand to.

Climbing the stairs to her chamber, she had doubts… new doubts.

Although she had spent so much time convincing her sister all would be well, she herself was not as certain as she had been earlier today.

Weariness wore at one's confidence. She had passed the

weary mark while bedding the goats down in the stable, and that had been hours ago.

Entering her bedroom, she fell face first on the mattress.

She and Joseph had settled many things having to do with her being his false wife…how they had met and had fallen instantly and irrevocably in love, which had led to their sudden vows. They did not wish to live in sin, after all. They had even made up a family of rank for her. What a shame it was that they lived all the way down in Cornwall and had never visited London.

Also agreed upon was that she would need to live in the manor house with Joseph. If she did not, Father would not believe she was married.

Was she about to live in sin, or was it pretend sin, she wondered?

She felt bad about leaving all the work of running their small goat farm to her sister. Worse about giving her the full burden of their father's care.

Even though she was doing all this for Eliza, Olive was the one who had chosen this path for the both of them.

She rolled over onto her back, yawned and spread her arms.

Yes, indeed. This was all for Eliza. It had nothing to do with being able to see Joseph Billings every day. To enjoy his smile, to inwardly sigh over the sound of his voice.

She might, in the moment, be indulging in fantasies, but that was not the reason for pretending to be his wife.

Again, this was all for Eliza, who was now quite on the spot. Once it became known that Olive was married, her sister would be free to tell James they could wed.

Which then put her in the position of having to tell him the truth about Laura.

Between them, Olive would rather be in her own challenging shoes than her sister's.

If James rejected Eliza for her indiscretion, this would all be for naught.

No, that was not right. It would be for Joseph.

Joseph, who looked into a woman's eyes so deep and true that she believed she was the dearest person in his world and he wanted her desperately.

She knew this was not the case. It is only how her weary mind wished to see it.

As she drifted off to sleep, her thoughts became jumbled. A bit of this and a bit of that which made no sense. Then an image of Joseph's smile hovering over her lips came to mind. She would take that one to her dreams.

Tomorrow she would worry about what fancy knife and fork were used for what food, about what was the most appropriate word to speak in any given situation.

How to make someone feel welcome in her home when, in truth, they were not.

In the morning she would consider ways to keep Joseph out of the clutches of the evil Hortencia.

Tomorrow.

Now, seconds before sleep dragged her under, she was going to spend time with her pretend husband's lips.

Two days after their second picnic, Joseph invited Olive to the manor. She would need to be familiar with the place if she was to live here for a time and to be believed as its mistress.

'I am lost with all these rooms,' she told him, wandering from one to the next. 'And servants, you say? I will not know the first thing about being in charge of them. I have only ever been in charge of goats and my father.'

'We have a little time before they begin to arrive. But really, Olive, for all that you are not used to servants, I believe you will find them helpful.'

'I suppose I will not mind having someone to do the cooking for me, but you may tell the woman who is to dress me to find something else to do.'

'If I must be dressed by my valet, you must be dressed by your lady's maid.' He could not help but grin at the resistance shooting from her eyes. Green was a good colour for the emotion. 'She depends upon you for her livelihood. It is the way things are done in society.'

'No wonder you want nothing to do with it,' she commented while staring up at hallway's high ceilings. 'How is a person to clean, to dust the cobwebs all the way up there?'

'That is not your chore either, in this house. But come, Olive. Would you like to see your chamber?'

She did not answer but looked up the stairway.

'Is something wrong?' he asked.

'It is only that I have never slept anywhere other than the cottage. I imagine this will be very different.'

'It will not be for long. Only until my parents leave.'

'Not long enough to become spoiled by all the luxury, I suppose.'

'Do not expect luxury in your chamber yet. The furniture I ordered will be here in a few days, along with what is needed for the rest of the house. But there is already a wardrobe with plenty of room for your gowns.'

'I do not own a single gown…work dresses only, and a better one for church. I never even considered the need for fancy clothes. I am sorry, Joseph, no one will believe

I am your wife. Everything I wear smells like cheese and animals.'

'Olive, I never expected you to be responsible for that expense. A seamstress and her team are due this morning to fit you. Before the servants arrive, you will have appropriate clothing to suit our needs.'

'I can only imagine what the help will think of me having a chamber along with a wardrobe full of gowns.' She tapped her fingers at her waist and the toes of her shoes on the floor. 'Yes, I can imagine. They will assume I am a strumpet, a kept woman who sells her virtue for a bit of silk and lace.'

Laughing was not what he ought to be doing just now, but it escaped him nonetheless.

'Your reputation will do just fine,' she said. Her glare might be the prettiest thing he had seen in a long time. 'You are a man.'

'I beg your pardon, my dove. I will present you as my wife when they arrive.'

'Your dove?'

'If I use an endearment, our love will be more believable.'

'It sounds absurd. Dove? I think not.'

'Pet? My dear one? Or perhaps, my sweet.' She shook her head at them all. 'Would you care to pick your own endearment?'

'I ought to. Let me think on it a moment.'

He watched her eyes, wondering what was going on behind them. She might be reviewing the many endearments she had read in her books.

'My treasure…that would be lovely. My kitten…no! My vixen.' She smiled, then winked. 'My vixen. I like that one.'

'Shall we settle on "my love"?'

'I like that one as well, Joseph. And I will call you "my dear".'

All at once her expression dimmed, and she bit her bottom lip.

'What is it, my love?'

'It is only, my dear, that I have no ring on my finger. No vow of any sort. It will be difficult to feel a sense of being wed.'

'Come with me.'

Scooping up her hand, he led her to his study. There was a battered-looking desk which had been left behind by the previous owner. He was using it until the new furniture arrived.

He opened a drawer, drew out a velvet bag and emptied it onto his open palm.

'This ring belonged to my father's mother.'

'Now, that is convenient. But do you bring it wherever you go?'

'I do. I loved my grannie deeply. She gave me the ring during my last summer in Scotland. Keeping it with me makes me feel closer to her.'

'I do not feel right wearing it falsely. I am sure she never intended it to be used for this kind of mischief.'

As always, thinking of his grandmother made him grin. Her smile, her bright laughter, were as fresh in his mind today as they had been years ago.

'Ah, no. Grannie had a fine sense of mischief herself. If you ever hear laughter whispering out of nowhere, it will be her.'

'You have heard such a thing before?'

'I've heard something. I choose to give Grannie the honour.'

'Then she might not mind having a former highwayman ghoul wear her ring for a time?'

'Keep your ear open for a distant giggle and that will be your answer.'

'It is a beautiful ring. I will protect it so that when the time is right, you may give it to your bride—your real one, I mean.'

'I thought you might keep it.'

'Oh no, I would not dare. It is far too precious to be given away. I will give it back to you once we win this game.'

'As you wish, then,' he said.

He circled the ring around her fingertip, thinking he would not mind her having it as a remembrance of him. 'I believe that words of some sort are called for.'

'What sort of words? This is a unique situation.'

He could scarcely imagine one more unique.

'Vows,' he said. 'Suitable to our endeavour.'

With a smile which teased and insinuated that he was addled, she said, 'Very well. You go first.'

He cleared his throat, squared his shoulders. 'I, Joseph Billings, heir apparent to Claymore, do swear by all that is prankish to pretend to be your husband. I will protect you from the wiles of Lady Hortencia Clark to the best of my ability, and be a true and faithful friend to you always.'

He nodded, indicating it was her turn to say something.

'I, Olive Augustmore, loyal sister and friend to goats, do swear by all that is preposterous, to play the part of your loving wife. I will protect you from the wiles of Lady Hortencia Clark to the best of my ability and be a faithful friend to you always.'

He slid the ring on her finger. 'Should we kiss to seal the vows? It would seem appropriate.'

'Nothing about what we are doing is appropriate, Joseph.'

'So then, my love, a small kiss will not hurt.'

'One to practice on, my dear...that might not be amiss.'

If he gave her the kiss he'd been thinking about, it would absolutely be amiss. Friends did not smother one another in a passionate embrace.

Instead, he bent, intending to kiss her cheek.

Ah, but then Olive went up on her toes, touched his chin with one finger, and breathed a kiss on his mouth. He barely felt it, and yet it left him off balance for a second.

'This sort of thing will be expected if we are so madly in love that we eloped,' she said. 'We might as well get used to it.'

Used to what? To kisses that were not genuine...to passion pretended for the sake of their scheme?

Only an idiot would believe it was possible.

While Olive had not considered that she would have nothing fitting to wear...dash it, he had also failed to consider something. What her breath would feel like skimming so close to his mouth, how the briefest graze of her lips would make him imagine so much more.

He may have landed himself in a fine predicament.

There was some connection bubbling between them even if he could not say exactly what. But it sizzled down the back of his neck. Made his fingertips itch so that he had to curl them up into fists.

Just in time, he caught up with his self-control, clung desperately to it.

'To us,' he muttered, lifting her hand, as if he were offering a toast to their success but without flutes of champagne.

'To the success of our endeavour.' She squeezed his fingers.

The ring caught a glimmer of sunshine streaking through an open window. It sparkled.

He was close to certain that was not a ripple of laugher in the curtain when a gust of wind twisted it in the open window.

Five days later, Olive walked toward Falcon's Steep with Eliza.

'It all begins today,' Olive said, seeing three tall chimneys come into view over the treetops.

She carried nothing with her. Whatever she would have brought would have been too humble for a lady of quality to own.

Even the gown she was wearing would not stay here but would be taken home by her sister. She had seen the gown she would change into, and it nearly rivaled the cottage in value.

'We are in this for good or ill now,' Eliza said bravely. 'You cannot come home until it is finished, or Father will know you did not elope.'

'I will be stunned if he believes it in the first place. I am hardly the type to be swept away in a fit of passion.'

'I will weep on his shoulder because you treated us so heartlessly by running away. He might believe it then. But the one thing you must not do is let him see you. You can hardly have eloped and be here at the same time.'

'He is bound to notice all the activity up the hill.'

'We discussed this, Olive. Of course there is activity when the manor is preparing to receive a new mistress. I will tell him before anyone arrives so that when they do, he will not question it.'

'I cannot imagine how you will keep him from getting curious and coming here.'

Truly, this was never going to work. If Father came knocking at the manor door asking for his daughter, no one would believe she was a lady of society. The lie would be instantly exposed.

'I will do it somehow. Perhaps I will be able to convince him that since you are on a grand honeymoon tour, there is no point visiting until you return. But don't worry, Olive. You act your part, and I will act mine.'

'Thank goodness this will only be for a short time.' Otherwise this would fall apart, lie by lie.

Even if Father never set foot outside of the cottage, it might be impossible to accomplish a phony marriage.

Arm in arm, she and her sister mounted the stairs of Falcon's Steep as if they were marching to battle. Which was rather how she felt.

She was not ready to meet any of the people soon to be arriving. However, she had made a vow and would keep it no matter what.

'Of them all, I most fear meeting Hortencia.'

'She will quake before you, Olive. I have no doubt about it.'

The front door opened before she and her sister made the top step.

Joseph smiled at them both. Olive gave her sister a sidelong glance. Eliza did not seem to have gone all breathless over his smile. But then, her sister was in love with James, so that would explain it.

Olive felt breathless, and it bothered her. It was one

thing to feel that way in the moments before falling asleep, quite another now that she was here to assume her role as his infatuated bride.

This, she reminded herself, was all a great act, and squishy feelings had no place here.

'Are you ladies ready?' Joseph asked, glancing between her and Eliza.

'Nearly,' Olive answered. 'When will the servants begin to arrive?'

That was when her role would start. Making them believe she was their mistress was nearly as important as making Joseph's parents and Hortencia believe she was his wife.

'Later in the afternoon.'

'Come to my chamber, Eliza,' Olive said. 'It will take until then to put on all the layers of clothing I will be required to wear. Wait until you see it all. You will never believe the extravagance.'

'I will see you soon, then.' Joseph turned and, whistling, walked down a hallway which she knew led to the garden.

It was a nice sound, his whistling. She could stand here for an hour just listening to it.

'Hurry, Olive. I cannot wait to see your new gowns.'

'Give it a moment and you will be happy it is not you who must wear them every day. It is a great responsibility caring for such fine fabrics.'

'But you will have a laundress to take care of them.'

Eliza rushed up the stairs ahead of her.

'That is beside the point!' She called up after her. 'Each one of them costs more money than a year of selling goat's cheese would earn…no, two years!'

Eliza did not seem to care about that. She continued up, laughing and clapping her hands.

Chapter Six

Days later, Olive stood on the front porch of Falcon's Steep, curling her fingers into her expensive skirt. In an attempt to divert her attention from the arrival of Joseph's family…more, from the dreaded Hortencia…she watched a butterfly flit from one overflowing flower urn to another. There were several urns, a pair of them flanking each step leading to the front door.

The new staff had done an amazing job of preparing the manor for the visit.

Joseph had been pleased with their work and had praised their efforts many times. When the day came to take his place as the next Viscount Claymore, she felt he would be excellent in the role whether he wished for the title or not.

Now he stood next to her, watching the drive. Joseph had not wished to be taken unaware of his family's arrival, so he had assigned the new gardener to trim the hedges where the drive met the road.

A few moments ago, shears in hand, Mr Kathol waved his arm, signaling that he spotted carriages approaching.

And so here they stood, the great deception ready to be played out.

Wind gusted about, billowing Olive's skirt. A chill

whirled up her legs. Dark clouds to the south began to pile upon one another in an ominous way.

Hopefully Eliza would get the goats inside before the thunder began. The animals became agitated by storms.

Joseph took one of her hands and carefully held it in his. 'Do not worry, Olive. You will shine. The servants believe you are my wife, and they are not an easy group to fool.'

'Perhaps they believe I am your wife, but I cannot think they believe I am of the upper class.'

'Perhaps not, but they accept that as my wife, you are entitled to the respect they would give to a highborn lady.'

'What if they say something about it?'

'They will not. It is not their place to do so. Besides, from what I can see, they are particularly taken with you.'

'I wish you had informed your parents of our marriage beforehand. It will come as a great shock to them.'

'It is best this way. Trust me on it. It is better that Hortencia does not have time to plan anything devious in advance.'

'I trust you.'

Too soon, she heard the clop of hooves. Any second she would see carriages rounding the curve of the drive.

Inhaling deep and long, she closed her eyes. She went to a place in her head where Olive Billings lived. She stepped within her fictional self, drew in another breath, and left cottage lass Olive behind…at least, hopefully she did. The strategy had always worked when she was a highwayman.

Blinking her eyes open, she smiled up at her husband.

'Well, my dear,' she said. 'Here we go, for better or for worse.'

'For better. We will prevail. Wait and see.'

He squeezed her hand, then bent to kiss her cheek. From

the corner of her eye, she caught a movement, the carriage curtain being drawn aside and a face peering out.

A streak of lightning cut the clouds, but the thunder was still too far off to hear.

The driver of his parents' carriage stepped down from his perch, lowered the steps, then opened the door. Hortencia would be in that one as well. The second carriage would carry his mother's and Hortencia's personal maids along with his father's valet.

Six more people whom Olive would need to convince that she was his wife. He marveled that her hand was not trembling.

Both their futures depended upon a convincing portrayal.

Glancing at Olive, he saw her smiling. She leaned her head briefly against his shoulder in a gesture of affection and excitement.

Mama was first to step out of the carriage. Her surprise at seeing Olive standing beside him was revealed by a flash of alarm widening her eyes, there and gone in an instant.

His mother also knew how to play a part. Viscountess Claymore was gracious in every situation. Although she could not know the situation she was walking into, she did so with a smile.

Olive went down the stairs before he did, confidence marking each step. He came down behind her, returning his mother's smile.

Seconds later, his father stepped from the carriage. Spotting Olive, he seemed curious, but after an instant, his attention was diverted by the newly manicured grounds.

'Outstanding,' he announced.

Father was easy. It was Hortencia's reaction he dreaded.

The toe of her fashionable travelling boot hit the first rung of the carriage. He set his shoulders. Let the battle begin, then.

As if issuing a warning, a roll of thunder boomed toward the manor.

He clasped Olive's hand, not for show but for mutual encouragement.

'Joseph! We have missed you, dear boy.' His mother rushed to hug him, breaking his hold on Olive's hand.

He understood what was first on everyone's mind. Who was this lady offering them a welcoming smile? And why was it her place to be welcoming them?

Perhaps he was a coward not to inform them immediately of who Olive was. He needed a second more to gather the perfect words before making the formal introduction.

Conveniently, Father filled the second.

'This property is as fine as you told me it was, son!' He clapped Joseph on the shoulder, half his attention on Olive while he added, 'I cannot wait to take a tour of the house and the grounds.'

Next, Hortencia made a move to embrace him. 'Joseph! Oh, how I have missed you.'

'My dear.' Olive subtly changed position, blocking Hortencia's attempts. 'This must be the family friend you mentioned. She is as lovely as you told me she was.'

Hortencia stepped backward, jerking as if the compliment had been a slap in her face.

Well done, Olive, he cheered inside. Clever of her to place herself as his intimate and Hortencia as just a visitor, first thing.

Mama's well-honed smile slipped.

Father's brows rose over a grin. From the beginning, Father had never been Hortencia's biggest admirer.

Hortencia's expression went blank. He didn't want to know what was going on in her head.

'Mama, Father,' he said, intentionally leaving the family friend out of the announcement. Hortencia must be made to understand that she was not, nor would she ever be, a part of his family. 'It is my great pleasure to introduce you to my wife, Olive Billings.'

Father, bless him, found his voice at once.

'My dear girl! Welcome to the family.' He opened his arms. 'May I offer my congratulations?'

Olive stepped into his embrace and returned it.

'I have been so anxious to meet you all.' Olive shifted her attention to the viscountess. 'I would say I have been anxious for a very long time, but your son and I wed too quickly for me to be anxious for long.'

'I…well, what a surprise.' His mother made a valiant effort to gather her social wits but appeared to be stumbling.

Hortencia always had her wits about her.

'My word, Joseph,' she said smoothly. 'What a wonderful surprise.'

Next Hortencia turned a luminous smile on Olive. 'Welcome to the family. I am so pleased to meet you.'

Curse it. The woman was not pleased, nor was she in a position to be welcoming anyone into the family.

Giving every indication of friendliness, Hortencia slipped her arm though Olive's. 'I am certain we shall become great friends. Oh, but you cannot imagine the tears that will be shed in London over the news. Of course, I understand perfectly. In time the ladies of society will as well.'

'There will not be all that many tears,' Joseph pointed out curtly. He was hardly society's bad boy.

'I did not mean to say so, Joseph. But love does result in a hasty marriage…upon occasion.' Hortencia made quite a point of smoothing her skirt where the pleats lay neatly over her middle. 'For some ladies.'

'Hortencia!' Mama exclaimed, her face blanching at the ill-disguised intent of the comment and the gesture.

Olive, though…she pressed her fingers to her slim waist, and laughed in good humour.

His bride turned toward his mother, clasped her hands, then gave them a squeeze.

'Hortencia was merely indulging in a jest, a bit of humour among new friends, isn't that right?' Olive arched a brow at her nemesis.

'Oh, please, do not think I meant any offence, Lady Claymore. Your new daughter-in-law is correct; only a little teasing among us women.'

The explanation might have been passed off as genuine, except that he and Father were among the company, so it was not simply teasing among women.

'Rest assured, Lady Claymore, preventing such a catastrophe is the reason your son and I wed so quickly. I am not with child…not yet.'

Olive said that last with a pointed glance at Hortencia, which his mother would not have seen.

'I fear we have got off to an uncomfortable start, and it is all my fault.' Hortencia wrung her hands, giving every appearance of being distressed.

Very likely she was, only not for any insult she had caused.

Her distress would come from finding him happily married and now beyond her reach.

He could only pray she would accept the situation. He would still need to be wary in case she decided to test his faithfulness to his bride.

No, not in case she did. Rather, *when* she did.

'Come,' Joseph said, waving for everyone to come up the steps and into the house. 'The storm is moving closer.'

He slipped his arm around Olive's shoulders and began the procession inside. In a backward glance at the clouds rushing in, he noticed that Hortencia had slipped her arm about Mama's waist.

The reason for it was clear. She was claiming a spot as the favourite, no matter that she had been displaced as his bride by another.

'Joseph,' Olive whispered, casting him a subtle glance. 'That storm…it isn't coming. It's upon us already and walking into your house.'

Noise in the house increased more than six extra people in residence would account for.

There was really no mystery to it, Olive decided. It had to do with two of them being annoyingly demanding.

Her mother-in-law because she was making sure the staff was living up to the standards she required of them.

And the other, her foe, constantly nagged at the servants, demanding this or that extra service.

She imagined they must be frustrated by the constant attention ladies of quality required. Not that they were likely to let on about it since they did not wish to risk their employment.

Perhaps now that everyone was seated for dinner, things

would settle. Surely the guests were weary from travelling, and with a spoonful of luck, would retire early.

Olive needed a few hours alone to slip out of character and breathe. Being constantly on guard against the war of words Hortencia waged was exhausting.

That woman was a sly one, coming across as sweet and companionable. Syrup was also sweet, yet it made a sticky trap for unwary flies or ants.

Luckily Joseph had warned her to be on her guard. Otherwise she might have been drawn in, stuck as miserably as an insect.

Why, oh, why had the cunning woman made a point of sitting beside her for the meal?

The conversation went on innocently enough until—

'I must apologize for my words earlier. Truly, Olive, I did not mean them as they came across. I would never suggest you were a fallen woman and so forced to wed. I know Joseph well enough to understand he is not easily fooled. Only a clever harlot would be able to trap him that way.'

'You are correct. My husband is ever discerning when it comes to a person's character.' Olive speared a piece of cheese with her fork but did not lift it to her mouth. 'But tell me, do you believe it is only harlots who get caught up in what nature intends to happen when a man and woman… come together, shall we say?'

Lady Claymore must have heard the exchange because her spoon, brimming with turtle soup, hung halfway between her mouth and her bowl.

Glory fire, Olive was too far into the conversation to let it go now.

'A lady would never allow herself to be in a position for

such a thing to happen. A true lady would not even know about "coming together".'

'I see. As a true lady, then, there are matters you do not understand?'

'Naturally not!'

'I must warn you then, in all friendship, that there are men who might take advantage of your ignorance. You might find yourself in trouble without you even seeing it coming. If you do not mind me saying so, your mother did you no favours by keeping you ignorant in the ways of men and women.'

Hortencia blinked. Her mouth opened and closed like that of a fish tossed on a streambank to flop about. It might not be charitable to feel satisfaction at the woman's consternation, but she did nonetheless.

'I know this is a distressing topic for ladies of our station, Hortencia, but it does no one any good to be unaware of certain ways of…well, of biology, shall we say? Do not worry, though. I will explain it all to you, if you wish.'

'You make it sound as if a woman with a dirty secret is a victim. Not the lowest and most immoral of us all.'

Soup dripped from Lady Claymore's spoon…plop, plop, plop, into the bowl.

Olive had done it now. This was not at all appropriate dinner conversation. Not appropriate conversation for a lady to engage in at any time.

Joseph would probably send her home after dinner ended.

What could not be seen but was true nonetheless, was that Olive had steam coming out of her ears. What an outrage it was for someone to call Eliza immoral…pronounce Olive's sweet niece a dirty secret.

Laura might be a secret, but dirty?

Glory fire! She called on what authority she thought the wife of a future viscount might have and pressed on to make her point.

'I understand what you are saying, of course.' And it made Olive want to spit. 'But you speak out of naivety. There are ladies who find themselves in delicate situations and by no choice of their own. Men are stronger than women are, if you understand what I mean. And often women are simply too innocent to know what is befalling them until it is too late. You, my dear, are in danger of that last example. But if you wish for me to advise you on what to watch out for, for the warning signs if you will, I will be happy to do so.'

'This is the most inappropriate conversation I have ever been engaged in.' Hortencia pushed away from the table and stood up. 'I am overwrought by it. I shall retire to my chamber.'

'I meant no offence, truly.' Oh, but yes, she did intend it. It was beyond gratifying to see her foe rise from the table and flee the battlefield. 'Forewarned is forearmed, you must agree.'

Hortencia snapped her fingers at the footman who stood at attention near the wall. 'Have a meal sent up.'

Joseph gave Olive a considering look from under lowered lashes. He would no doubt have heard the conversation. They all would have.

He'd probably decided she was a miserable failure at being his false bride, and who would blame him?

Who would ever consider her an appropriate future viscountess after this? She was certain that Lady Claymore had never engaged in such a conversation.

Joseph could only be thinking he would be better off with no wife at all.

'I suppose Hortencia is weary from travel,' her father-in-law declared lightly. 'We shall miss her.'

One thing Olive was certain of. No one would regret seeing the last of her.

Indeed, what noble family would appreciate having such a bluntly spoken daughter-in-law at their dinner table?

Only half a day into her role as wife and she was an utter failure. She was as far from genteel as a woman could be.

There was but one thing to do. She must leave this fancy home and its refined people before she brought shame on Joseph. More shame, that is.

A rather tricky obstacle stood in her way. What would she wear home? Her own gown was at the cottage, and she could not wear one of the ornate garments hanging in the wardrobe. It would feel like thievery.

She felt the same about the undergarments she wore, but she could hardly abandon them.

Heavens, what a predicament.

She shrugged and twisted out of the elegant dinner gown she had on. It was not an easy task to perform without the aid of the maid who had helped her into it.

When the gown hit the floor, she scooped it up and spread it across the bed.

Shed of the dress, she faced the next obstacle to her escape.

How was she to get out of the house wearing only undergarments? Even if the family was settled for the night, which she did not believe they were, there was the issue of servants travelling the hallways, performing their night-time tasks.

She could not hope to evade them.

And yet, there might be a way… Hmm, with a bit of luck, she might escape the house.

Going to the corner of the room, she yanked three times on the cord which would summon her maid.

Within moments, the woman bustled into the room, saw the gown on the bed and looked surprised.

'My lady?'

Was she supposed to apologize for undressing herself when it was this woman's job to do it? Here was one more failure at acting a lady.

'I shall put the gown away and brush your hair for bed.'

'I would ask a different service of you tonight, Collins. All of sudden I am feeling rather faint.' Fine ladies did feel that way upon occasion, or so she had read. In Olive's opinion, it was a bit of fiction contrived in order to draw attention to oneself. 'I would like a bit of fresh air.'

'Sit down at once, my lady. I will open your window.'

'Garden air, I mean. I need to sit amongst the shrubbery for a time. I have a small problem, though. I do not wish to dress again, but at the same time, I cannot be seen in my shift. Perhaps you know of a private way out of the house?'

Mary nodded, but not without a frown. Going to the wardrobe, the maid took out a lacy robe, then put it on Olive. Next she found a blanket in another trunk, and folded it over her arm.

'The rain only just stopped, my lady. Everything will be will be wet. But if you truly wish it, I will take you down.'

And so, by way of a back staircase which led from the bedchambers to behind the kitchen, Olive was able to get out of the manor unseen.

Convincing Mary to leave her alone in the garden

proved to be more difficult. In the end, given Olive's 'superior' position, the maid had no choice but to go back inside the house.

Once Collins was out of sight, Olive set the blanket on a bench. She shrugged out of the robe, which was far too elegant to take with her, folded it, and placed it on top of the blanket.

Oh, brrr…it might not be raining, but it was chilly. Still, she did not wish to take anything that did not belong to her even if it meant a bone-chilling walk home.

'I'm sorry, Joseph,' she muttered even though he could not possibly hear her from the house. 'I am not qualified to be your wife, even in jest.'

What she was, was a coward. It was not right to leave him struggling to explain to his parents where she had gone.

Worse, she was abandoning him to the wiles of Lady Hortencia.

Worse again, where was she to hide until her sister wed her baker? In the stable, she supposed. There was really no other place.

Rubbing a chill from her bare arms, she glanced back at her chamber window. It had been lovely and comfortable. She would never forget her time there.

'Please forgive my awful behaviour during dinner.' It did not matter that Joseph would never know she apologized. She simply felt the need to do it.

No matter how she tried to act the part, she was not a lady. She was a far better goatherd than a false future viscountess.

'I do not,' said the tall bush she stood beside.

Leaves rustled, and branches spread apart. Joseph peered narrow-eyed at her through the opening.

'Then you will agree that I must be on my way.' It was a relief to know they were of a same mind on the matter… at least, she thought that was what he meant.

The branches snapped back into place. Joseph stepped around the bush, facing her square on the path.

'How can I forgive you for something when there is nothing to forgive?'

Poor man thought she was only asking his pardon over her dinner behaviour. He would feel quite differently when he knew she was backing out on their agreement.

The sooner she made it clear, the better. She would rather not be standing in the cold discussing matters wearing this thin shift which did not even belong to her.

There was not much to the garment. If she was beginning to feel warm, and she was, it had to do with the way Joseph was looking at her.

Had she not just given Hortencia a lecture on the risk to a woman? How a situation might come upon her quite by surprise?

Very well, she would not leave the robe behind after all. It seemed prudent in the moment to put it back on. To tie the ribbons securely at her neck where it might choke her with good sense.

'Of course there is something to forgive. Even at a cottage dinner table, my conversation would have been unacceptable.'

'Which is what made it so entertaining. Olive, it was all I could do to remain in my seat.' He picked up the blanket, tugged it across her shoulders, then bunched it under her chin. 'I came much too close to laughing out loud when Hortencia got up from the table.'

'I nearly made your mother choke on her soup. She must think me the worst daughter-in-law ever.'

'You won over my father, though. He's never been fond of Hortencia. Come, Olive. Let's go back inside. It is too cold to be out here…especially undressed.'

'There is a reason I am out here undressed.'

'To entertain your husband amongst the shrubbery?' He gave her a teasing grin…one that that smacked of shenanigans.

She was struck dumb for an instant by the mental image of the two of them frolicking about the garden.

'When you have a wife, a real one, you may give her that grin. You may not give it to me. I insist you take it back.'

'Tell me, Olive, why are you leaving me, as clearly you are doing? Have I done something to offend you?'

Other than frolicking about the garden with her in his mind, he had not.

'I only assumed after the way I embarrassed your guest you would not wish for me to remain.'

A gust of wind came up, snatched raindrops from the leaves, then deposited them on her face and hair. It blew the clouds away, revealing a bright, fat moon.

Joseph brushed a damp trail from her temple to her chin, giving her a thoughtful look. It was hard not to notice how raindrops also dotted the hair of his forearms.

In all honesty, and honesty being her guiding light, she was not sorry he had, at some point, rolled back his sleeves and left his arms bare to her view. He had nice, muscular arms. She could not be faulted for noticing.

In that instant, she was noticing far too many things about him. Which would not be so awful if it remained merely observation. But no, there was more to it than that. There was reaction.

All around them, moonlight glistened on water drops, sparkling as if brushed in enchantment. And there was the whisper of his slow, deep breathing and her own quick heartbeat in her ears.

She knew quite well she was not warm because of the blanket he bunched under her chin.

Caution was called for here, because she was looking at Joseph in the way Eliza had probably looked at the travelling poet-singer. In the way that Hortencia claimed to know nothing of.

In the way she had no experience with either, but felt by instinct what was happening.

Instinct suggested she open the blanket and draw Joseph close to her bosom, to share heartbeats and…

Experience—Eliza's, not her own—warned her to run from this folly and go home the way she had planned to.

Which is what this conversation was about. It was only her imagination taking it in another direction.

'I must go, Joseph. This all seemed a brilliant scheme in the beginning, but now that I have met your parents and Hortencia, I can only think I will make a muck of it all. You will end up worse off than you would have been without me.'

'I do not think you truly believe that,' he murmured, looking terribly vulnerable all at once.

For as much as she'd thought it best to go home, to avoid the trouble this marriage ruse was bound to cause, at the same time, she felt wicked for letting Joseph down. He was counting upon her. Eliza was counting upon her.

'You were magnificent at dinner, Olive. I have never

seen anyone get the best of Hortencia, and yet you did it quite handily.' Then his lips twitched, and his eyes sparkled…not figuratively, either. She actually saw a glint. 'Admit it, my friend, you enjoyed every second of it.'

'Glory fire, but I did.' Her lips twitched, too. She could only wonder if her eyes were sparkling like his were. It felt as if they were.

'Please stay, Olive. You are only having a bit of stage fright.'

'But you thought I was magnificent?'

Magnificently inappropriate is what Olive thought.

'Oh, aye. Even better than when you were the terror of the road.'

'I suppose you are right about the stage fright. Please forgive me, Joseph. I will not run off again.'

He let go of the blanket he had been holding in place at her throat, then slipped one arm companionably about her shoulder.

'I am grateful, more than you can know.'

'So am I.'

Because of Joseph, Eliza would have her family.

'If you are worried again, please come to me. We will figure things out.' He led her toward the house. 'Now, we should get back before you catch a chill.'

A chill? That would be the last thing she felt with his body heat wrapping her up in delicious waves.

He kissed her hair in a sweet, friendly gesture. He urged her closer to his side. A woman could rely on a husband with shoulders so strong and broad. One day, some lucky woman would.

However, that woman would *not* be Lady Hortencia Clark.

Chapter Seven

The next night, Joseph sat in the parlor after dinner with his father, legs stretched before him, watching the inch of brandy he swirled in his snifter go round and round.

His father smiled and lifted his own glass.

'To a job well done, son. This is the finest property we have purchased so far.'

'I agree. It felt like home here the first time I rode up the drive.'

'Because you were bringing your bride with you, I would think.'

He nodded, grinned, striving to play his role as husband as brilliantly as Olive played his wife.

'I remember when your mother and I were in love.'

'You say that as if you no longer are.' Perhaps he should not have pointed that out, but Joseph had never considered his parents to be in love.

'That is not what I mean, not quite. I am very fond of your mother, naturally. It is only that life happened, and our young passion for one another grew up. Over the years, it became more practical in nature, I suppose one would say. It is an adequate arrangement.'

He was not surprised to hear his father admit this. His

parents seemed much like many other society couples…bound to one another by duty rather than love.

'You are fulfilled with adequate?' Was this even an appropriate conversation for a father and a son to be having? It might be, now that he was married, or at least perceived to be.

'I have my lands. Your mother has society to keep her entertained. Although I suppose her adventures will be curbed somewhat now that you have married. Your mother was certain she would have you wed to Hortencia, and all of society would be gasping with pleasure over it.' Father took the last sip of his drink, long and slow. 'Well done escaping that fate, my boy.'

'This might be an uncomfortable visit for everyone. I suppose I ought to have told you of my marriage before Mama invited Hortencia.'

'If you want to know what I think, Hortencia would have come regardless. The fact that you have taken wedding vows will mean nothing to her.'

Joseph fought back a grin. He and Olive had taken vows, only not the sort his father imagined.

'I fear you are right.'

'Well, I would not over worry it. It does seem that Olive is Hortencia's match. It is good to see you so in love with your wife. I admit, it does bring back sweet memories.'

Olive must be doing a brilliant job indeed if his father saw him as being so much in love.

When the day came for Joseph to wed, it would be for love. He had seen marriages where a spark ignited between a man and wife had lasted over the years.

Father might be content with being fond of his wife, but Joseph would have more…or he would have nothing.

'I have a matter that I would like to discuss with you, Father.' Joseph finished his drink, long and slow, the same way his father had, as a way of giving brief pause to a conversation. 'I would like to make Falcon's Steep my home. I will still explore your new properties, but I wish to settle here.'

'I cannot imagine a better place for you to bring up your children. You never did appreciate London anyway.' Father stood up from his chair, clasped Joseph on the shoulder, and squeezed. 'Please accept the estate as our wedding gift to you and Olive.'

This was both wonderful…and horrible. Feeling a great deal of guilt, he stood to embrace his father. To accept a wedding gift when there had been no wedding made him feel like the worst of sons. And Father had no other.

However, saddling him with Hortencia as a daughter-in-law was unthinkable. She would make all of their lives utterly miserable.

The scowl he felt settling on his face, sinking into his soul, vanished when the women came into the parlor and Olive's smile rested on him.

He and the viscount stood. Olive hurried across the room, hugged his arm, then went up on her toes and kissed his cheek.

This woman sparkled. Her smile looked sincere, he could nearly believe she was truly his bride and so in love with him that she glowed.

'I missed you,' he said. Once the words left his mouth, he had to confess they were true.

What he ought to do was return Olive's kiss, but all of a sudden, he was not certain his motive was only to fool Hortencia.

'We have all missed your company, Joseph,' Hortencia declared, rushing forward to claim his other arm and, therefore, preventing the possibility of a kiss.

For the best, then. Some things were better left undone.

It left him wondering, though. What if he was not only lying to everyone else about who Olive was to him, but to himself, as well?

His pretend bride intrigued him in every way a woman could intrigue a man.

He was far from indifferent to her. Thinking about it now, how much more could he feel for a woman he one day courted than he felt for Olive, here and now?

It did not matter how much. He knew he could never court Olive properly. No more than Olive could accept his courtship.

A viscount's heir and a cottage lass would not be accepted. Not in London and not in Fallen Leaf either.

He shook out of Hortencia's grip on his sleeve, then led Olive to a couch which was barely wide enough for the two of them, even if they squeezed close together.

His intention when he'd ordered the piece was to fit a woman's generous skirt. Now, feeling Olive's thigh pressing against his, the warmth where her elbow rubbed his arm…he was glad it was no bigger.

This piece of furniture was perfect for cuddling, even if it was not genuine cuddling.

Conversation hummed pleasantly along without much challenge from Hortencia.

After about an hour, the viscount said, 'Amelia, let us retire to our chambers. I believe the newlyweds have better ways of occupying their time than speaking to us old folks. Begging your pardon, Hortencia. I did not mean to suggest you are old. Only that Joseph and his bride would appreciate a bit of privacy.'

'Think nothing of it, my dear Lord Claymore.' Flushed, Hortencia stood.

Damn it but the woman was presumptuous. It grated on him that she used the endearment on his father. She was not family.

'As it is,' she went on, 'I am weary from a day in the wilds. My dear Olive, I wonder how you can take living out here with nothing for company but woods and birds...and squirrels, the dirty, chattering little creatures! It must be so dull with no proper company to keep you entertained.'

'It is not so difficult,' Olive answered, giving his hand a squeeze. 'I have Joseph. He is never dull.'

'Yes, I do recall that about him. Good night, my dears.'

Hortencia sent him a smile that was far too intimate to offer a married man, or a single one, for that matter.

With a dramatic swirl of satin and lace, Hortencia swished out of the parlor.

Moments later, Mama hid a yawn behind her hand. She stood and crossed to where he and Olive sat pressed together. She patted his cheek.

'Good night, son.'

She nodded at Olive. Then, linking her arm with Father's, she led him out of the room.

Out of sight but not of hearing, his father said, 'Hortencia is not a good sport, if you ask me, Amelia.'

'No one did, Marshall.'

'I suppose I should not be offended that your mother likes Hortencia better than she does your wife, Joseph.' Olive said.

What could it possibly matter? Olive was not his true wife, nor a true daughter-in-law either.

She was offended for Joseph's sake, that was all.

Oh, very well…it was only fair to admit that was not all there was to her opinion on the matter.

Still, out of loyalty to her son, Joseph's mother should show a preference for his wife.

Especially since Hortencia was so disrespectful of the wife…of her.

There was constant competition between herself and Hortencia. It had begun that first moment on the steps when Olive threw down the gauntlet, so to speak.

Not that the gauntlet would not have been thrown by one of them eventually, and Olive was only glad she had been the one to do it first. For some reason, being first gave her a sense of advantage. A perception was all it was, because in truth, she didn't have the advantage, not in anything.

'I can only hope that seeing me happily wed will open my mother's eyes to who Hortencia is at heart.' With an arm companionably around her shoulders, Joseph led her from the parlor toward the grand staircase which led up to their chambers. He bent his head close to her ear to whisper, 'Now that she has no hope of making a match between me and that woman, perhaps Mama will look at things differently.'

The warmth of his breath made her wish, if only for an instant, that things were different. That this was not just for show.

But no. A performance was all this cottage girl would ever have of a noble gentleman. It would be futile to wish for anything more than what she had in this moment.

Besides, she was happy with what she had. It was true

in life that the present was all one ever had. No living in the past. No living in the future. Only what was offered right then.

They arrived at her chamber door first. His was one door further down the hallway.

She leaned back against the door, looking up into a face that would leave every woman in London sighing, high- or low-born.

'Well, good night,' she said, half sorry the day was over. She had enjoyed most of it.

Joseph braced his hand on the door frame, leaning toward her, his expression intent as if trying to decide whether to kiss her or not.

She got lost in his eyes. Her heart beat every which way of mad.

This, she reminded herself, was not the first time she had anticipated his kiss, and yet it had not happened.

But this time…oh, this time she felt it pulsing between them. There was a dance of sorts going on…a waltz between what was forbidden and what was desired.

Then, just like that, the music ended. 'Sleep sweet, Olive.'

Joseph lifted away from the door frame, nodded and then walked the short distance to his chamber.

At his door, he paused and gave her a considering look. Whatever he meant by it, she could not guess.

Was any of what just happened real? Had he only been acting as if he would kiss her in case someone was looking?

This game she had agreed to play held more risk than she had first thought.

Although the cottage was a distance away, Olive swore she could nearly hear Eliza warning her to be careful.

* * *

It was not wise to meet her sister in the meadow so near the manor. It could hardly be helped, though. Olive could not venture any closer to the cottage and risk meeting Father. Nor could she be away long enough for anyone to question where she had been.

'Everything is going well,' Olive reported, shading her eyes from the sun, which was warm. Also quite bright after the cloudiness of the past couple of days.

'I need more than that, sister. I require details.' Eliza pointed to a large tree which offered an inviting patch of shade. She tugged Gilroy on his lead toward it. 'This poor boy misses you. All the goats do.'

The trees would provide some privacy, but not enough. This would need to be a quick meeting.

Sitting down in the shade, Olive hugged the goat around his shaggy neck. He responded with a special bleat which meant he was happy to see her.

'I am sorry, Gilroy. It will only be for a few more days. How is Father, Eliza? I hope you have not had a difficult time with him.'

'He is doing well and has given James permission to court me. So thank you for that, Olive.' Eliza squeezed her hand. 'It is such a small word, isn't it? But it is all I have… so, thank you.'

'Has Father tried to go to the tavern?'

'You'd hardly believe it, but no. He sends me to the village every day to see if there is a letter from you.'

'I suppose I should have written one and left it for him. That was a bit of a slip-up. But just tell him I will not be gone long enough to write.'

Gilroy lowered to the grass and settled beside her.

This was lovely. She pitied the people of Joseph's circle who were not able to enjoy nature this way. Imagine a genteel lady sitting under a tree with a goat in Hyde Park. Eyebrows would arch so high they would float right off those proper faces.

She smiled at the mental image because, really, it was very funny.

'I want to know about the woman. Is she as awful as your husband claims she is?'

'You know very well Joseph is not really my husband. And yes, she is every bit of it. Pretty, though. She looks like a fair-skinned porcelain doll. And her eyes! You would not believe how blue they are. She is every man's dream and every woman's envy.'

'I do not dream of fair skin. I envy the freckles on your nose. I hope Laura develops them.'

Eliza sat down, looping her arm across Gilroy's back.

'Proper ladies do not have them.'

'Poor them. But tell me what it is like being married to that handsome man?'

'I will not lie. It is fun to play at.'

'My heart gets dizzy at the thought. But imagine, me the sister-in-law of a noble.'

'Imagining it is all you will do. Better you pay attention to your own coming marriage. I imagine James is happy about it.'

Eliza's gaze wandered to the treetops, and seemed to get lost in the shifting leaves.

'Eliza?'

'I have not spoken to him about it yet. Only Father has. I will, of course. It is only…well, I know he loves me as I love him, but I am so frightened to tell him about Laura.'

'You know you must.'

'Of course I do. But it scares me. Whenever I begin to admit the truth to him, I find I cannot.'

'You only have a few more days before I am no longer wed. You will lose your chance.'

'Pray for me then, sister. I have never been so scared to do anything in my life. What if he hates me afterwards? What if he tells someone about my sin?'

'If he does, he is not the man you want to marry, anyway.'

'But I will be ruined, and Laura along with me. No man will want us then.'

'A very good man will. One who loves you. I believe James is that man. You must trust him if you wish for any sort of happiness in your future.'

'This afternoon, then. I will gather my courage and do it.' All at once Eliza straightened. 'Who is that? It's her, isn't it? The porcelain doll.'

Good heavens! It was.

Hortencia had just come over the rise of the hill and was now making her way towards them.

'This is the first time she has been outside. She dislikes nature. So why is she out in it now? Probably up to no good.'

'She has followed you. Stand up, Olive. Pretend you have come to buy cheese.'

'Did you bring some with you?'

'No…you saw me and my goat passing and stopped me to order some…or something of that nature.'

'I am supposed to be new here. How do I know you sell cheese?'

'You saw the goat and hoped I did.' Eliza frowned at

the approaching image of female perfection. 'Perhaps she will not notice Gilroy cannot give milk.'

'She claims to be innocent of male parts and what they do, but even she cannot fail to notice he is a male. Well, we shall carry on as best we can, Mrs...Gilroy.'

The goat looked up at Olive and bleated. 'It is all I can think of in the moment.'

Then Hortencia was upon them, reaching down to pick leaves from her skirt and muttering unladylike oaths.

'Olive, I do not know how you can tolerate it here. Surely you miss London as much as I do.'

'I find the country far more pleasant. But take heart, my dear. Not much longer until you return.'

Eliza, dressed in her work gown, appeared as common as they came. Hortencia acted as if neither her sister nor her goat existed. She looked right through them.

Then her expression shifted from blank to speculating.

So, she did see them, after all. They were simply beneath her regard.

But what, she would be wondering, was the lady of the manor doing speaking with a commoner?

'Hortencia, may I present Mrs Gilroy.'

'Why would you? I am certain I have no interest in making this woman's acquaintance.' In spite of having no interest, Hortencia looked Eliza over with a sharp eye.

'Mrs Gilroy sells the best cheese in the area. I have made a habit of purchasing only from her.'

Hortencia's blue gaze slithered back to Olive. Olive's imagination supplied a hiss because there should have been one.

'It does surprise me, I must say. Why doesn't she come

to the kitchen door and deal with the cook, like any other vendor would do?'

Why indeed?

Olive stepped closer to Hortencia and whispered. Luckily her sister had excellent hearing and would not miss what she said in 'secret'.

'Mrs Gilroy, the poor soul, has had an accident, and she has trouble walking long distances. I promise you, Hortencia, once you taste the cheese she sells, you will not mind that she cannot make it to the back door.'

'Are you certain?' Hortencia did not bother to whisper. 'She does not look lame. This might be a lazy excuse to avoid walking so far.'

'Oh, no, my lady. I suffered a grievous injury when I was knocked flat by a nervous horse.'

'Really, Olive. I do not know why you believe the woman. She looks as hale as you do.'

'The story is true, Hortencia. I have heard it told among the villagers. It was all anyone spoke about for a while because the horse was fleeing a highwayman. The incident did cause a stir.'

'A highwayman?' Hortencia caught the bodice of her gown and twisted a hank of ivory lace. 'Here?'

'Some say it was a ghoul sprung from the underworld, but that does seem rather far-fetched to me,' Olive said.

'I detest this place. Ghouls and highwaymen. It is absurd. Superstitious delusion.'

'Beggin' your lady's indulgence, it is the very truth. Look, I shall show you the wound.' Eliza grabbed her skirt, drawing it up her leg inch by slow inch. 'It is still oozing a bit, though. As long as you do not mind a bit of pus, it is not so bad to look at.'

Hortencia spun about and stomped back up the hillside, not seeming to notice how her skirt snagged on the thistles.

Olive clasped her hand over her mouth, bent at the waist, suppressing hysterical laughter.

She spun away from Eliza and Gilroy, dashing after Hortencia.

Tears damped her eyes with the effort not to laugh because the urge pressed her chest without mercy.

Oh, but nighttime could not come soon enough. It had become custom for her and Joseph to spend a few moments alone before retiring in order to discuss the progress of their scheme. No one would admire Eliza's tale more than he would.

'A word, son.'

His mother's voice caught him as he was about to go to the garden, where the caretaker was at work trimming a rose hedge which had been neglected for two years.

Joseph had hopes of turning the grounds into a showplace one day. Not for hordes of admiring visitors but for himself. And for Olive, if she came to visit him once this was all over.

Only a couple more days. Thinking about that made him…not unhappy exactly, because it had been his and Olive's plan all along…but there was no denying he was going to miss her.

The two of them got along well, even though theirs was an uncommon friendship. Society, both his and hers, said it should not even exist.

'Of course, Mama. Would you like to walk in the rose garden? The weather is perfect this afternoon.'

'It seems private enough. Yes, then, let's go there.'

'Everywhere around here is private, and beautiful,' he pointed out.

'Your father tells me we are giving it to you as a wedding gift.'

'It is very generous of you. Olive and I are grateful.'

'It is so strange, Joseph…you and Olive. It was a shock to discover you had married her. The match is not at all what I had in mind for you.'

'My duty was to wed. You have never failed to point it out. When I met Olive, I knew there was no other woman for me, so I saw no point in waiting.'

'But Hortencia!' His mother shook her head, probably not even seeing the burst of yellow roses she passed by. Mama usually loved yellow roses. 'It was supposed to be Hortencia you married. I am certain you knew that was the plan. She was a perfect match for you.'

'That was your plan, not mine. She was not a perfect match for me, only a boon to the family name.'

'And for the title you will inherit one day. And therefore, for you.'

'One day far in the future, I hope.'

'Very far in the future, but it would have been wise for you to prepare for it now.'

'I am sorry you are disappointed with my choice, Mama. I never got on well with Hortencia. But Olive? I proposed to her the day after we met. She accepted it the day after that.'

This was somewhat true; it was only the nature of the proposal he was not forthcoming about.

'You are a young man in love. Be careful about that, son. Passion is fleeting. Now, duty…that is what is required of a man of your station.'

'Duty to whom? To myself and my wife or to my peers in London?'

'Who is this wife of yours, anyway? I am not familiar with her family.'

'They are not from London. Olive's father is a country baron. Neither he nor his wife has sought a life in society.'

'You must get along with them famously, then, being of like minds.'

Had they been authentic, he probably would have got along with them. A part of him did wish all this was real. What might have happened if Olive's family was titled?

She would not be who she was, that's what.

Which would be a shame. He would not change her for anything. To his mind she was engaging, clever and… perfect.

To chain such a woman to society's rules would be a crime. He could not imagine her being stuffy and stifled.

'The damage is done, I suppose, and we must live with it,' she said, her sigh resigned.

He stopped and stared hard at her, trying to remind himself that she was a product of her time and place. In her eyes, marrying less advantageously would be considered damage.

'I ask you to look at me, Mama.' He paused for a second to be sure he had her full attention. 'Do I look damaged?'

She let out a great huff. 'What you look is in love.'

He'd expected her to say he looked content…or something on that emotional level.

In love, though? He looked in love?

Very well, it was how he meant to look, so why did the statement shake him?

A man could appear to be in love without being in love.

But his father had said much the same thing…that it was good to see him in love with his wife.

At least Olive did not see what they did. She knew this was a sham, understood that the ruse would end in a couple of days.

'Well, my dear, being that things are what they are, we must celebrate your marriage. Share your joy, and ours.'

'Thank you.' He kissed his mother's cheek. He knew giving up Hortencia's family connections could not be easy for her. 'I hope you will become as fond of Olive as I am.'

'There is something about her…she is different than most ladies I associate with. But I can see why you are taken with her.'

All good…except that soon he would need to find a way to be untaken with her.

He had promised Olive he would think of a way out of this mess, but so far, no way had presented itself to him.

'I have spoken to your father, and we have decided to stay longer.'

They'd decided what? No…he must have misheard her.

'Surely you are anxious to get back to your friends in London.'

'Yes, quite. But I've already announced your wedding in the newspapers. We have invited a few friends to join us here. As I said, your marriage must be celebrated. Everyone must know how much we approve of it.'

'Do you approve of it?'

For some reason, he really wanted her to. And yet it might be easier to find a way out of this predicament if she did not.

'Just give me time, son. This has all come as a great surprise to me.' Then she smiled, giving his cheek a happy pinch. 'But as soon as the grandchildren come, no doubt I will be over the moon about it all.'

A wedding announcement…a party…grandchildren. Joseph did not know whether he was flushed or pale. Dash it all if he was not flashing from one to the next with each heartbeat.

'From the look on your face,' she said, 'I can only think the happy day will not be far off.'

How in the great bloody blazes was he to tell Olive of this turn?

To ask her to remain here longer than she'd agreed to and act as the hostess of a house party was too much to ask of her.

Once she heard the news, she would go home. The ruse would finally fail.

He would be vulnerable to Hortencia's attack. It played out before his eyes, making him cringe because he saw himself as a mole snagged in a falcon's claws. The more he struggled, the tighter the claws clutched him.

Chapter Eight

Given that Olive was required to be dressed by her maid in a new gown and her hair arranged just so, she was running a few moments late for tea.

Had she been allowed to dress herself in a comfortable gown, had she not been forced to sit impatiently while her hair was piled on top of her head in frivolous curls, she would have been early.

Rushing down the hallway to the drawing room, she thought fancy dressing was a waste of good time.

Why not spend those moments getting ready for tea, actually enjoying the company of Joseph's family instead?

She paused outside the door to catch her breath, and to listen for an appropriate time to enter. Although she had not learned any particular rule about entering a room, it only seemed right to wait for a pause in the conversation so that she did not interrupt one in progress.

'Apparently it is only you and I for tea today,' she heard Lady Claymore say.

'I do not mind,' Joseph's father answered. 'We spend so little time just the two of us. I miss that. Don't you recall when we were young…'

This was not a moment to walk in upon. From what Joseph had told her, his parents had been close once and then grown apart.

Besides, a frisson of alarm was creeping in her brain. It did not seem that Joseph was in the drawing room. As far as she could tell, Hortencia was not either.

Where, then, was he? Of a bigger concern…where was Hortencia?

For all that Olive was expected to sip tea and nibble on small sandwiches with Joseph's parents, she had made a vow to protect her un-husband from the claws of his enemy.

Tiptoeing back down the hallway, she wondered which way she should go.

She had no idea why Joseph had not attended tea and so could not imagine where to find him.

Since he would be most in danger from Hortencia in secluded places, she would search there first, then work her way towards the less obvious spots.

Coming out of the kitchen door at the back of the house, she wondered if the stable would be the battleground. She took several steps across the meadow between the house and the stable but stopped short when she saw the gardener and the stable boy come out.

Not in the stable then.

Olive closed her eyes, wondering if it was possible to feel another person's presence. She went utterly still while she conjured up Joseph's face in her mind, mentally reaching for him.

No, apparently that was not possible.

However, she did think of a place he might be.

If he'd needed a few moments of solitude, it made sense that he would walk through the woods and then stroll beside the stream.

At least, it is what she would do. Since she had no better idea of where to find him, she dashed the rest of the way across the meadow, then hurried around to the back of the stable, where the woods grew thicker.

It was tough going wearing yards of satin and lace. Oddly, tough going did not prevent a funny image from blossoming in her mind.

This was a time of urgency, not funny images. But still, she saw herself trudging through the woods, thistles snagging in the hem of her fancy gown while she carried a teapot in one hand and a delicate china cup pinched between the fingers of her other hand.

But then, perhaps it was not all that funny. Perhaps the vision symbolized her struggle with being one person and acting the part of another.

What was wrong with her? This was no time for deep introspection. Joseph might be in danger.

Might be. She did not know for certain that he was, only that neither he nor Hortencia was where she expected them to be.

Her hasty dash through the trees was making too much noise. She stopped, listening to the sounds of the woods, just as she did when she was hunting a stray goat.

Close by, she heard a man's voice over the rush of water. It was cursing.

Why would Joseph be cursing?

Peering hard through the trees, she was relieved to see him sitting on a log and very much alone.

Then she saw a flash of ruby-coloured fabric.

Ha! Hortencia should not be wearing red if she expected to successfully hide herself behind a shrub. And the woman considered herself to be cunning.

From where Joseph sat, he could not see his foe. She clearly saw him, though. The wicked woman stared at him with a calculating smile while unbuttoning the bodice of her gown.

'My dear!' Olive called.

She dashed through the high grass, launched herself at Joseph, and toppled both of them off the log.

They hit the ground hard, but she managed to whisper, 'Roll on top of me, Joseph.'

He rolled, giving her a puzzled look…well, not only puzzled, but rather pleased as well.

She curled her fingers in his hair, drawing his face down to her mouth, but turned her lips at the last second to say rather loudly in his ear, 'Ravage me, husband, here by the stream.'

Taking a cue from Hortencia, she slipped three buttons open on the neck of her gown.

'She's here?' His lips brushed her ear.

A swirly little shiver tickled her middle. Her body reacted as if it did not know this was all for show. Her heart did not recognize it either, because it pumped hard against her ribs.

'Peering at us over the log,' she whispered softly. His nod was as imperceptible as her whisper had been. She only knew he had done it because beard stubble scraped her earlobe.

He dipped his mouth to her neck, kissing it tenderly from the hollow of her throat to her jaw.

Glory fire…

'I am a lucky man, my love,' he said, his voice thick and husky. 'No man could ask for a better wife… A more beautiful or passionate lady does not exist.'

Hortencia would hate hearing that!

Completely immersed in her part, Olive did not mind hearing those words, feeling them whisper over her earlobe like curling steam. Nor did she shy from the warmth they gave her in places she supposed might lead an otherwise respectable woman astray.

In the novels, it was called delirious longing. Perhaps the books had the right of it, because here and now, the sensation nearly made her forget Hortencia was even watching… that this was all to convince the woman what a doomed effort it was, trying to seduce Joseph away from his bride.

To press the point, Olive lifted her leg and rubbed the toe of her shoe along Joseph's calf.

Had she read of this seductive movement in a book, or had it sprung from her heart? If it did come from her heart, then this moment was inappropriate. It would mean the line between acting a role and living it was becoming blurred.

She felt cool air when Joseph caught the hem of her skirt and began to lift it.

'Forgive me,' he whispered in her ear.

None of this is real, none of it, she chanted in her mind. *Only an act performed to discourage a villain.*

Olive heard her foe gasp in clear indignation. 'I have never seen anything so disgraceful!'

Joseph rolled off her, the two of them staring up at Hortencia's flushed face.

'Rolling in the grass like a pair of—'

'Newlyweds,' Joseph said, cutting off the rest of the insult she would have flung at them.

He sat up, reaching out his hand to help Olive upright. She could not be certain of the reason for it, but a shudder clamped his fingers tighter on hers.

Anger, she supposed…and shock that he had nearly been caught by Hortencia.

'Further,' he said while standing and drawing her up beside him, 'eavesdroppers have no right to be offended by anything they see or hear.'

'I did try to warn you about what goes on between a man and a woman, dear Hortencia…when they are deeply in love.'

Recalling the moment, that was not quite how Olive had presented the matter. It was more of the risk a woman took when she gave in to forbidden moments.

Until a few moments ago, her only experience had been what had happened to Eliza…and what she'd read in books. Now, though, she rather understood that under certain conditions, a woman's body could speak louder than logic.

If she was especially fond of the man…not in love perhaps, but maybe…oh, never mind. Runaway emotions made everything tricky, that was all.

Even if she did allow herself to fall in love with Joseph, the future viscount could never love her back.

Quick as a minnow, her motto flitted through her mind. This was a fine tangled web, indeed. She had not expected to become entangled in it quite this way.

The day after tomorrow, their charade would be over, she would go home, and hopefully her sister would have eloped to Gretna Green.

'I was merely walking and I came upon you quite by surprise, Joseph,' Hortencia said. 'I do beg your pardon for interrupting.'

At least the sneaky creature had buttoned up her gown.

Olive left her collar sagging open. The point must be

illustrated that between a married couple, certain behaviour was acceptable.

The same behaviour was forbidden to those who were not wed.

What she told the woman without using words was that she and Joseph were a couple in love.

Hortencia was the outsider.

There was nothing more to her gaping collar than a simple message to a nosy busybody.

Olive touched her throat, wondering if her skin looked flushed. It felt hot enough to have blistered. She also wondered if her pretend husband was flustered.

Not likely, him being a viscount who would be tempted by fine ladies as regularly as the seasons turned.

His temptations were none of her concern. Shame on her for wondering.

'Well,' Hortencia declared with a sudden fake smile, 'we are all late for tea.'

'You go ahead,' Joseph said. 'Please let my parents know we will see them at dinner.'

'As you wish, Joseph. I dare say we will miss you.'

If Hortencia had been shocked by what she saw going on between the bride and groom, she seemed suddenly recovered.

As soon as she was out of sight, Joseph fastened Olive's bodice buttons, slowly…one by one. His knuckles skimmed her neck. She wondered what was behind his thoughtful look. If he meant to cool off anything that had just happened in the grass behind the log, he was failing.

The show was over, but her heart had a difficult go of regaining a steady pace.

'Sit with me, Olive.' He drew her to the log. 'There is something we must discuss.'

She sat down beside him, perhaps closer than she ought to have. If he minded, he would move further away.

This conversation was going to be embarrassing since he could only wish to discuss her behaviour. How she might have rescued him from Hortencia in a less scandalous way.

Joseph kept a firm grip on Olive's hand. Once he told her of the guests who were soon to invade Falcon's Steep, she was bound to leap from this log and go home…leave him to his fate. He was not ready for that.

Not that holding on to her made a difference one way or another. He'd never had any intention of keeping his cottage lass forever.

Not that she was his, either. He did not know why he even thought that.

What he did know was that, in this moment, he liked the way her hand felt in his…small yet strong.

These were capable hands, he knew, as comfortable milking a goat as they were wielding a highwayman's sword. He also now knew how her fingers felt twining through a man's hair. Siren's fingers they were, which could draw an unwitting fellow in for a kiss.

Not that he would consider himself all that unwitting, only drawn in.

In the end it did not matter, not now that everything was changing.

'I beg your pardon, Joseph.' When she glanced up, her eyes shimmered, bright and green. 'I acted shamelessly and with Hortencia looking on, too. I am mortified.'

'You were brilliant. No need to feel mortified. It was lucky you happened along just then, or she would have caught me.'

'It was a near thing, wasn't it? I did not just happen along, though. I was looking for you. When you and Hortencia were both missing for tea, I became worried.' She wriggled her fingers out of his. 'I suppose we should join them now.'

'Not yet.' Curse his tongue for turning to a clumsy lump. His brain searched for words. How was he to inform her that Mama had invited guests?

He had vowed to her this visit would last only a week. To ask her to remain in the lie for who knew how long was not acceptable.

It was not what she'd agreed to. Not what she deserved.

'You look troubled,' she said. A sweet-looking frown cut her brow. 'Is there something else we need to discuss?'

'It is the last thing I wish, and yet, yes, there is.' He glanced over at dapples of sunshine riding the surface of the stream. This problem was not going to slide away on the ripples, so he looked back at her. 'Tonight, after everyone has gone to bed, I will take you home.'

'I know I was very forward with you a moment ago. Truly, Joseph, I promise, I have no intention of entrapping you.' She slid along the log, putting distance between them. 'You are safe with me.'

'I know that. And I must admit, a moment ago…it was not all about Hortencia.' He glanced over his shoulder. The grass was bent where they had lain. 'I think we both recognized what was happening…but it is not why we must cease our charade. Something has come up, and I am certain you will not wish to be a part of it.'

He was silent for a moment, working up the words. It seemed to be a failing of his…being at loss when it came to spitting out something important.

'Since you have not revealed what this "something" is, you cannot be certain I will have no part of it.'

'Mama has invited guests from London to celebrate our marriage.'

Olive stood up. Her eyes went wide. Then she blinked.

'That is indeed a complication,' she muttered.

'One for me to deal with. I do not expect you to remain here, too.'

There, said and done.

It might be best for her to go back to her cottage. The scent of crushed grass came to him, a reminder of just how desirable Olive had been a moment ago.

Awareness of her shape and her scent, of the little sound she'd made when he kissed her neck, all that seared him.

For an instant, there had been no Hortencia staring down at them like some voyeur.

There had been only him and his bride, except that she was not really his bride.

One thing was for certain—what had ignited between them was too intense to be indulged in again.

Despite the fact that Olive had lectured Hortencia on the dangers of unwed intimacy, she could not know all that much about it herself.

Teaching her would be the worst sort of repayment for all she had done for him.

'From what I just saw, Joseph…' She wagged her head at him, brows arched and lips pressed thin. No one else he knew of could wear that expression and still look pretty doing it. 'Taking me home to the cottage would be a great mistake. You will not last an hour without me.'

He would argue the point, but she was correct. He could feel his future turning to misery even while sitting here on a mossy log.

Hortencia would catch him and chain him to London, where all his joy in life would shrivel and die.

Olive stared at him, tapping her lips with her fingers. A thousand thoughts appeared to be going on in her mind.

One thing seemed certain—her thoughts could not be moving in his favour.

'What kind of friend do you think I am, Joseph Billings?' She took three strides toward him, bending at the waist to peer into his eyes. 'Not a loyal one, I'd wager. I am insulted.'

'I meant no insult to you, Olive. But this is not turning out as you imagined it would.'

'Ha! Do vows mean nothing to you? I took them, and so did you. Therefore, I am your ally for the duration of our scheme.'

'And I thank you for it. But it is one thing for you to play my wife in front of my parents and Hortencia. How will you manage with all the rest of them?'

'You will teach me what I need to know.'

Nearly nose to nose with her, it was not possible to look anywhere but into her eyes. The urge to kiss her became overwhelming.

'How many of them?' she asked.

'Six, as far as I know.'

'Formidable.' With that she straightened. 'Still, I will not let that woman have you, Joseph.'

'Why?' It was a foolish question. They had made a bargain which she meant to honour. He wondered if it was more than that, though. She was a friend…a loyal ally. Luckily for him, she was also as clever as a fox.

'Very well,' she said. 'I shall reveal something to you. You will be stunned to know it.' She sat beside him again but did not reach for his hand. 'May I trust you to never reveal a word of what I am going to say?'

'Of course.' What was this? Whatever her secret, he would take it to the grave. 'You may count on me, Olive.'

'Alright then. While it is true that the majority of the reason I am not letting you take me home tonight has to do with Hortencia and her wicked threat to you, there is more to it than that, quite a bit more.' She sighed, clearly hesitant to go on. After a deep sigh, she did. 'I am not confident that my sister has wed her James yet, and I cannot go home until she does.'

'Has she not? I would have thought she'd have got him away to Gretna Green as soon as she could.'

'I had hoped she would, but it is rather more complicated than that. You see, there is something she must tell him, and she is afraid to do it.'

'If they love one another, surely they can overcome it? Eliza must speak up.'

'Easy to say, but the fact of it is, it takes all I have to tell you. And all I am asking of you is your silence.'

'You have it. I promise.'

'Eliza bore a baby out of wedlock. She will have to ask James to raise her as his own. She will not marry him unless he agrees to adopt our sweet Laura, too. It is tearing my sister up, wanting her child so badly and not being able to have her.'

'Poor girl. She has every reason to be afraid.'

'You understand, then? If James rejects Eliza…if he speaks of it to anyone, my sister will be ruined.'

'Aye, she will. She will need a great deal of courage to carry through with what she must do.'

'Eliza has a great deal of courage.'

'Like you do.'

'Not like I do. My sister bears a great load. I only help her carry it. I admire her more than anyone I know.'

'Olive, after hearing this, I really must take you home tonight.'

There was danger here that she had not considered.

'But we are not yet finished,' she said. 'You and my sister both need for me to see this scheme to the end.'

'Do you recall when I told you Hortencia is like a bloodhound? How she seeks out other people's secrets and uses them to get what she wants?'

'And you fear she will discover this one? That she will use it to make me give you up so that she can have you?'

'It is precisely what she will do. I might as well surrender to her now.'

'You will not. Nor will I.'

Olive straightened, squared her shoulders. She gave him a smile so confident, so assured, that he felt her courage seep into him.

Perhaps they might pull this off in the end.

'Come, Joseph.' She reached for him. Her hand looked delicate but was as sturdy as the woman's spirit was. 'We are at war, and our next battle is tea.'

'On to victory, then,' he said resolutely, answering the charge.

He wondered if he might be falling a little bit in love with Olive Augustmore…

Chapter Nine

Guests! To celebrate her marriage? What a nightmare.

As he had done for the past three nights, Joseph knocked on her chamber door.

She could not possibly learn all she needed to in a week, but hopefully enough to make the visitors believe she was the lady of the manor.

He entered her chamber looking casual and too appealing with his collar unbuttoned and his shirtsleeves rolled up…and no shoes.

This was how he dressed each time he came. It was why she'd decided that if he could discard his shoes, so could she.

It was quite a freeing sensation.

'Good evening again, Joseph.' She closed the door behind him, thinking she smelled the flowers in the hallway.

'It is indeed good. I like coming here instead of sitting alone in my chamber.'

'Doesn't it seem a little scandalous, though?'

'Scandal is an odd bird. It only exists when someone else judges a situation to be so. Since no one would object to a man visiting his wife's bedroom, there can be no scandal.'

'What odd logic.' But it made sense if one looked at it

in the light if they wished to see it. 'I wonder what you will teach me tonight.'

Something to do with the bag tucked under his arm, she supposed.

He answered with a grimace, tossing the bag onto the bed.

'We covered dancing last night. Lord Helms and Lord Barlow will be taken with you if they have a mind to wind up the music box.'

'All well and good, but I think it is the ladies I must fool more than the gentlemen, and they will not be taken with me.'

'I do not think you need it, but would you like to practice a few dance steps before we begin our next lesson?'

He was correct. She did not need it, but still she lifted the sides of her gown and twirled toward him.

Catching her hand, he positioned them for a waltz. His palm open wide on her back felt warm, possessive.

She had never felt a touch like it. As lessons went, it was quite informative.

Not scandalous, of course, since there was no one present to judge it to be so.

Clearly music was not needed for dancing. Barefoot steps padding on wood, a man's and a woman's mingled breathing, was all the tune required while he glided her here and there...slowing ever so slightly when they passed the bed.

All at once he stopped, cocked his head.

'Is something wrong?' She missed the pressure of his hand when it fell away from her back.

'Probably not. I thought I heard footsteps pause outside your door.'

'Hortencia. I smelled perfume in the hallway when you came in just now.'

'Ah, good then, let her believe us to be so smitten we cannot keep our hands from one another.'

Yes, let her imagine that.

Joseph went to the hearth and squatted to stir the coals.

'What is in the bag? What new ladylike skill will I learn?'

Rising, he went to the bed and sat on it, then indicated she should join him.

Was it really true that scandal only existed if it was found out? It was what she believed about her sister's situation.

'It's a lesson easier taught if we are sitting next to each other.'

Very well. She sat down with the bag as a buffer between them. How odd it was that a moment ago, Joseph had his hands on her, and it did not feel wrong.

It was only…they were not dancing on the bed.

Heaven help her. For a distraction she opened the bag.

Peeking at what was inside, she laughed. 'Joseph? What on earth?'

He took the bag from her and dumped the contents onto the mattress between them. Four colours of embroidery thread lay on top of a rectangular piece of muslin. Three needles pinned into the fabric glinted in golden lamplight.

'Ladies spend a great deal of time sewing fancy stitches. I can't say whether they enjoy it or not, but it is what they do while they visit and talk.' He picked up a skein of green thread. 'But perhaps you already know how?'

'I know how to mend. And stitch sheets…plain work. I am good with knitting.' She should not be laughing at his frown, even if her mirth was on the inside, as much as she could keep it there. 'Do you intend to teach me to embroider?'

'You think I cannot?'

Oh, that grin was going to destroy her one day. Everything about it made her barmy inside, from the glint in his eyes to the turn of his lips.

'I do have my doubts.'

He held a needle up to the light, pushed the end of the thread toward it and missed the tiny hole.

'Aye, so do I. But I did watch this afternoon when Mama and Hortencia were busy at it.'

'Here, I will thread the needle,' she said. 'Mending and fancy needlework cannot be so different.'

'Does your sister know how? Perhaps she will help us.'

'Our mother knew how, but she never had time to do it or to teach us.'

'Here, then.' He took the threaded needle from her. 'I paid close attention when my mother was sewing a leaf.'

'She must have thought it odd, you watching her sew so intently?'

Joseph pushed the threaded needle into the fabric, down, then back up.

'I doubt she noticed. She and Hortencia were discussing our guests. One of them especially— Curse it!' Joseph tugged at a knot in the thread which would not pull through the fabric. 'Forgive my language, Olive. This is trickier than Mama made it appear.'

'Let me try.' She took the cloth from him. 'There are supposed to be hoops to hold it flat.'

'Hoops are tricky things to make off with.'

'We will manage as best we can.' It was a stubborn knot.

She had to bite it with her teeth in order to get the thread loose. 'You hold the muslin tight while I try a leaf.'

Her attempt failed, her foliage looking more like a thistle.

'Perhaps I will plead a sick headache,' she mumbled.

'Shall we practice that instead? I believe it is a social skill. That and fainting.'

'I refuse to feign a faint. If you see me go down, it will be genuine.'

The closest she had come to fainting was when Eliza had confided that she was with child. If she'd survived that without a swoon, she supposed nothing would fell her.

'Tell me about the guests. Why was one of them being gossiped about?'

'Ah, Vivienne Curtis. She has the misfortune of wishing to become a photographer and not a marchioness.'

He took the needle and thread from her fingers, apparently wishing to make another go at a leaf. Joseph Billings was unique among men. She could not a recall ever seeing a fellow attempt fancy-work…plain work either, for all that.

'Surely she can be both?'

'Her father is a noble, so no, she cannot.'

'I pity your class, Joseph. It seems that no one has a choice at all when it comes to their future. It is a shame, really, that you must one day wed for position, and that the unfortunate Miss Vivienne cannot have her camera as well as a husband.'

'Rebels have little hope of finding fulfilment in society. Worse if the rebel is a woman.'

'I always considered Eliza's plight to be desperate, but at least she has a chance at love.'

'Have you spoken to her? Has she revealed her secret to James?'

'Not unless she has done so since this afternoon, when I met her to pick up cheese.'

'It is rather urgent, I think. What if our ruse fails? She must be safely wed by then.'

'It is what I've told her time and again.' Olive well knew this was one of those easier-said-than-done situations. 'The odds against us being successful in our deception are not good, not now that we must keep at it longer. And I do not know how long Eliza will be able to trick our father into believing I am away on a honeymoon trip. Especially with the increased traffic on the path. He will be curious. It would ruin everything if he came here.'

'I wonder what he thinks of our marriage?' He shot her an owl-like wink and a teasing and oh-so-compelling grin. She would miss seeing it each day once this was over.

'I am sure he is more thrilled than he is confused. But don't you think the bigger question is, what will he think once we end it?'

'The one good thing about having guests is that it gives us more time to discover a way to become unwed,' he said.

'Us? As I recall, you told me you would think of a way.'

'A reckless promise, that. Now that we are mentioning it, I might need your help.'

'I have no idea whatsoever. We could be falsely wed forever, trying to come up with a way out of this mess.'

His laugh rumbled deep, giving her a curious tingle. 'It's not all a mess, Olive. But can't you see us? A pair old dodderers sewing leaves on handkerchiefs?'

'We will be rather good at it by then, I imagine. My question is, will I be a false viscountess, or will you be a false goat farmer? It seems some sort of choice will need to be made.'

Although they made jest of the situation, the problem was a real one.

Joseph bent his head to the task of demonstrating how to embroider a leaf. He poked his finger with the needle, then pressed his thumb to the wound.

'Wicked little weapon,' he muttered.

'It takes practice, I think.' She took the weapon and the wrinkled muslin from him. 'Does your mother knit? Some ladies do, our Queen among them.'

'I cannot recall. Until now, I never paid attention to what sort of stitchery she was creating. Is there such a thing as fancy knitting? It might do.'

'Most knitting is practical, but years ago, my mother taught Eliza and me to knit flowers to decorate our bonnets. They were as elegant as anything you ever saw.' It had been great fun for a while. 'But it has been years since either of us had time for it. Pretty stitches are very nice in their way, but they do not earn much money.'

'Knitting flowers will have to do, because I do not think we will learn this…' He took her needle, punched it into the muslin, then scowled at it. 'It would take a wizard and a magician working together to make a leaf out of thread.'

'I will ask Eliza to bring my needles and yarn when we meet tomorrow morning.'

'Be careful. It would not do for Hortencia to see the two of you together. We know she is watching.'

'We have the advantage, Joseph. She is not aware that we know it.'

'I nearly pity the woman, having to outwit you.'

'Not me, us.'

She took the moment to appreciate the turn of his mouth when he grinned, the laughter shining in his eyes made all the more intriguing because of where they were sitting.

The truth was that they would not be falsely wed forever, would not spend their doddering years stitching in their armchairs side by side while sharing stories about the exploits of their children and grandchildren.

Nor would she do it with anyone else if her sister did not admit her secret to James.

Once Father learned that Olive had not wed a viscount, he would push her at the baker again.

Not that he would succeed. No one could force her to marry Eliza's one true love.

'You are troubled.' Joseph reached for her hand. 'Tell me why.'

'It is what you just said about Hortencia watching Eliza. My sister needs to tell James the truth before it comes out on its own. I wish I could take her to James and stand beside her until she tells him the truth.'

'Shall we kidnap them and spirit them away to Gretna Green?'

'If only.' But the mental image of it did cheer her up.

'What will you teach me next about being a lady, Joseph?' she asked in an attempt to divert their minds away from the worry.

'I haven't decided,' he said softly, then touched her hair, drew a lock back over her ear. 'You are rather perfect as you are.'

The urge to lean across the heap of muslin between them and kiss him was too strong.

Nothing would come of it but heartache. More and more

often, she had to remind herself of who she was…and who he was.

They got on so well together that sometimes she forgot.

'Well, then, perhaps I will teach you something,' she declared, eager to redirect her thoughts to the display. 'How to make goat's cheese. That way, when our lie is revealed and you are disowned, you will have a skill to make a living at.'

'If you want to know the truth, given a choice between attending a season of balls in London and making cheese in Fallen Leaf, I would always choose cheese.'

She smiled at his playful jest, but not from the inside.

Joseph would never be free to make cheese any more than she would be free to dance at a ball.

He still had not let go of her hair, but twirled it around his thumb.

'You have pretty hair. I like it better when it is loose like this.'

She pulled the strand from his fingers, but slowly and with regret.

'I like it better this way, too,' she admitted.

She must not wish for something which was impossible. Once she did, she feared that she would never be able to un-wish it.

What kind of life would she have, longing for things which could never be? For a man who could never be hers?

A bitter life, that's what. In the past she had given little thought to love and its role in her future.

Now there was Joseph…and she did.

Two days later, Olive joined Lady Claymore and Hortencia in the solarium for an hour of stitchery.

Taking her place on a bench across from two ladies experienced in fancy needlework, she knitted her flower. It had taken three hours of practice in her chamber to remember how to make the complex stitches Mama had taught her.

She smiled looking down at it now. It was as pretty in its way as what Hortencia was stitching.

Not that she was not nervous. Although the Queen favoured knitting, it was slower to catch on in society.

Inhaling, she drew on her fictional self, who would be confident in everything she put her hand to.

When she exhaled, she was Lady Olive, her smile smooth and welcoming, as if these women were guests in her home and it was her place to make them feel at ease.

'Isn't this the best time of day?' she asked with the intention of beginning a pleasant conversation.

She removed a skein of yellow yarn from the satin bag, intending to show off her skill by changing colours. Last week the knitting bag had been made of an old shirt of Father's. Eliza had sacrificed a portion of her favourite petticoat and sewn her a new one.

'A lovely time of day, Olive, my dear. It is my favourite,' Lady Claymore commented.

The endearment made her feel wonderful. She also wondered if Joseph's mother meant it, or was she simply trying to mean it?

To find her son married to a woman she had never met, never even heard of, would be utterly shocking.

'It is getting cloudy.' Hortencia's sigh was heavy, dripping with drama. 'Solariums are meant for sunshine, and look how dreary it is becoming.'

Lady Claymore cast Hortencia a barely perceptible

frown. From what Olive was learning, ladies of rank did not frown, but smiled congenially in all situations.

'Olive, what a pretty flower. I envy your skill at knitting.' It gave Olive a glow inside, hearing Lady Claymore's praise even if it was only to be kind to her supposed daughter-in-law. 'I have never been able to hold the needles in the proper way to be skilled at knitting.'

'We are the same, Lady Amelia,' Hortencia put in. 'Knitting needles are far too cumbersome for my smaller fingers. I do not mind, though, since embroidery needles produce finer work. So much more delicate, don't you think?'

'I do not. In fact, I grow weary of doing the same thing over and over again. I have lost count of all the flowers I have embroidered over the years.' Lady Claymore secured her needle in the fabric and set it aside on the small round table beside her chair. 'Perhaps I should have another go at knitting. Would you be so kind as to teach me, my dear?' she asked Olive.

'I would be honoured, Lady Claymore.'

Amelia Billings rose from her spot, then joined Olive on the bench. 'Pah, I am not Lady Claymore to you, my dear. Please call me Mama. I know we have only recently met, but I would like it if you did.'

Resentment pulsed off Hortencia so hot it was a wonder it did not melt her delicate silver needle.

No surprise that she was provoked. To all appearances, Olive was taking the position Hortencia had fully expected to have.

Rather alarmingly, Hortencia had the skill to paste a smile over her anger. If Joseph had not warned Olive who this woman was at heart, she too might have been deceived by winsome blue eyes. By a smile sticky enough to trap the unwary.

'How wonderful,' Hortencia declared sweetly. 'We despaired of our Joseph ever making a marriage commitment. He must love you very much, Olive.'

'Some things cannot be hidden... I suppose it shows. But I love him just as much.'

'May I be honest, my dear?' Lady Claymore asked. 'I was taken aback when I first saw you standing on the steps with my son.'

'It is completely understandable, Mama.' Olive felt wicked and wonderful at the same time, calling her that.

'It is a marvel we did not faint, isn't it, Lady Amelia?'

Olive held her smile even though it was past annoying that Hortencia inserted herself into every turn of a conversation.

'Speak for yourself, Hortencia. I was quite steady.' Lady Claymore returned her attention to Olive. 'It is only that, had my son informed us beforehand, we would have been prepared for—'

'That was not well done of him, was it?' Hortencia disguised the insult with her sticky smile.

Olive wondered if Lady Claymore saw the woman for who she was. Perhaps not, or she wouldn't have been so set on a marriage between her and Joseph, no matter the social coup Hortencia's fine lineage would bring to the family.

'We all make mistakes, Hortencia, dear. Seeing how Joseph looks at you, Olive, it is quite forgivable. Not every couple is blessed with sudden love for one another.'

Hortencia set her sewing aside rather harder than she might have wished to. The action did cause the viscountess to raise her brows.

'I would adore learning to knit, if you will teach me as well,' Hortencia said.

'I would be delighted,' Olive said, but really, it was a pity that she could not answer with an honest no.

Hortencia squeezed in on the bench even though there was not proper room. Skirts and petticoats popped up at odd angles.

'Teaching others to knit must be something you enjoy, Olive.' Steely blue glinted in Hortencia's wide, blinking eyes. Seeing innocence and craftiness all in one glance was a bit unnerving.

The woman was laying some sort of trap for her, but Olive could not imagine how knitting could be a snare. Well, it could be if one was attacked by a large needle, but Hortencia was more subtle than that.

'It is not something I do all that often. But since you are my friend, I am delighted to instruct you,' she lied, because there was no way not to.

'I cannot tell you how thrilled I am to learn from you.'

She could not, because she was not. Still, Olive managed a smile while placing the needles in Hortencia's 'small' fingers in the proper position.

'I am confused about something, Olive. You say you do not teach knitting often? And do you only teach friends?'

'Yes,' Olive answered warily.

'Oh...but didn't I see you with that cottager who sells cheese? You had your knitting bag with you.' Hortencia snapped the needle tips together with a click. 'The two of you did seem particularly friendly. If I did not know better, I would have thought you to have been acquainted with her for a long time. But of course, it could not be, since you only just arrived at Falcon's Steep.'

The trap was sprung, and Olive was neatly snared.

'Hortencia, it sounds as if you are shooting some sort of jab at Olive. Although I cannot imagine for what purpose,' Lady Claymore said disapprovingly.

'There is no jab, I assure you. I only noticed the two of them while I was walking and thought they seemed friendly. But of course, I must have been mistaken, since our Olive would not have such a friend as that.'

'You were not mistaken.' Olive turned her attention to Lady Claymore because her approval was the object of this skirmish. 'I was teaching someone from the cottages to knit. The poor woman had suffered an injury. She is the one we purchase our cheese from, so I do see her upon occasion. I meet her in the meadow because she cannot walk the full distance to the manor to deliver her product, which is excellent, I have to say. Lately the poor woman's pain has grown worse. I was showing her how to make pretty knitted things to sell on market day. It seems easier than selling cheese.'

'It is commendable that you are able to have a friendly association with someone not of our own rank. I do not know if I could,' Hortencia declared.

'If you wish to make a first-class match, Hortencia, my dear, you must learn to do so.' Joseph's mother smiled when she spoke. Was it training which made that possible? Olive doubted she would ever learn that skill. 'A lady of breeding must know how to act congenially towards people of all classes.'

'Of course. I shall strive to be more like our Olive. I fear, though, that I will never learn the knack of making merry with my inferiors.'

'Making merry and being courteous are not quite the

same thing.' Lady Claymore's voice was crisper than Olive was accustomed to hearing.

Perhaps now that she had no hope of Hortencia wedding her son, she was beginning to look at her with more clarity.

Which was exactly what Joseph had hoped would happen.

'Olive, my dear,' Lady Claymore said, laying her hand companionably on Olive's arm. 'Shall we continue with the lesson? I cannot say how anxious I am to learn a new way to use needles.'

There was something in the older woman's gaze which looked different than it had mere days ago. In the beginning she had looked at Olive with reservation…suspicion, even. All for good reason.

Now the look appeared softened, as if she were welcoming Olive to the family. Perhaps even felt a bit of affection for her.

This was a complication Olive had not considered in the beginning but ought to have. At first, everything she had done was justified…necessary to protect Joseph and Eliza.

Nothing was too dear a price to pay for their well-being.

Only now did Olive fully understand that other people would pay the price as well.

She would leave wounded hearts behind when this charade came to its certain end.

Who among the ladies sitting here was the wicked one, she had to ask?

Before she entered the solarium, she would have known it to be Hortencia. But now she wondered.

If Hortencia was deceitful, what was Olive?

Birds of a feather, were they? Kindred spirits, perhaps?

There was one difference between them. Olive felt remorse for what she was doing. Hortencia probably did not.

Quite suddenly, Olive wanted to run from the solarium and weep.

To do a wrong and feel no remorse for it was far less wicked than feeling remorse and doing it anyway.

No wonder lying was a sin. It injured both the victim and the sinner.

'If you will excuse me,' she said, standing. 'Quite out of the blue, I need a breath of air.'

'Perhaps you are falling ill.' Hortencia gave Olive a considering look, one that said she suspected Olive did not need air, nor was she becoming ill.

'Do take care, my dear. We hope to see you at dinner.'

In that moment, Joseph entered the solarium, his smile so handsome it gave her an ache all the way to her soul.

She would fight Hortencia for this man with all she had…and in the end, she would lose him anyway.

However much guilt she felt for deceiving Lord and Lady Claymore, she would carry on.

Ending the ruse would only give Hortencia the victory.

Eliza would suffer. Joseph would suffer.

She would do this so that one day he could marry a woman who loved him.

Not Olive, because even if she did love him, it could not be her.

If she loved him?

Well, glory fire, she could not honestly say she did not feel anything akin to it for him.

Lady Amelia crossed the room and stood beside them.

'Are you well, my dear?' She pressed the backs of her fingers to Olive's cheek.

Tears cramped her throat. Having not had a mother's touch since her own beloved mama had died, she suddenly felt the loss and the longing quite intensely.

If she and Joseph were wed, she would have a mother again.

'Are you ill?' Joseph touched her cheek, frowning.

'I am not ill, I promise I am not. All I said was that I needed some fresh air.'

'We all need a walk in the garden,' Hortencia announced, reaching for Joseph's arm to claim him for the stroll.

'I believe my son came here seeking his wife. We shall give them some time. I will walk with you, Hortencia.'

Skirts brushing, Joseph's mother and Hortencia went out of the solarium doors, which opened to the back garden.

Joseph led Olive through the house, then out to the front gardens.

'You look as if you are about to weep.' His arm snugged tighter about her waist. Tears pressed harder against her eyes.

'I am not far from it.'

'Did Hortencia say something to you before I came in?'

'It was not Hortencia. It was your mother.'

'Mama? Was she pressing Hortencia on you? I hoped she would stop. Shall I have a word with her?'

Olive blinked, and even though she fought it, tears dampened her lashes.

'That is just it, Joseph. You have not chosen me. I am not the woman you love. This is all a great trick we are playing on the people who love you.'

And on her own father, too. He would be vastly disappointed to discover he was no longer the father-in-law of the wealthy neighbour.

Joseph had been looking intently into her eyes but then suddenly his gazed shifted to the rosebush to their right. The afternoon was dim with increasing cloudiness, which made the flowers look brighter against the foliage.

He picked a lavender-hued rosebud, twirled it in his fingertips.

'Maybe I...' His brows lowered in a frown. He tucked the rose into her hair behind her ear. 'Never mind...but in the end we will all survive it.'

'Yes, in the end we shall go back to being the neighbours we were always meant to be.'

Except they would not. For her part, she would always remember what it felt like, the fantasy of playing his wife. Every time she saw him pass by on the road, or spotted him in the village, she would wonder what could have been if he was not a viscount...if she was not a goatherd.

The thought had occupied too much of her mind lately.

She was far too taken with his smile, with his voice when he spoke softly to her...and how combined, they enamored her.

'The last thing I wish is for you to be sad, my dear.' He carefully swiped his thumb under each of her eyes, taking his time.

Had he noticed that he called her 'my dear' even when no one else was nearby to hear it?

Of course, it would be a slip born out of habit, nothing more.

'I am not sad, not really. It is only, your mother was so kind to worry about me. Her concern made me miss my own mother.' Sweet fragrance from the rose filled her senses, bolstered her. 'I hate deceiving her like this.'

His great, broad thumb touched her chin, lifted it while he looked deeply into her eyes.

What did he see?

That she wished for him to draw her in close to his heart?

Loving him was not a part of their agreement.

'This will all come out right,' he murmured, his fingers gentle while tracing the curve of her cheek.

Perhaps she was winning the battle against Hortencia, but she feared she was losing her heart in the process.

Chapter Ten

A scatter of lightning caught Joseph's attention as he strode past a window facing the front garden. He stopped to gaze out.

It had been two days since he'd walked in the garden with Olive, placed a rose in her hair and came so close to kissing her.

The moment left him unsettled, as if he stood on top of the black, roiling storm clouds, trying to keep his balance.

Thunder vibrated the glass, as much a warning as any he had ever received.

Kissing his pretend wife, except for the occasional peck on the cheek or the forehead, was not a scene in their show.

If he did kiss Olive, it would be because he wanted her in the way a man wanted a woman.

Damn it…a man who wanted a woman he could not have. Even if there was a way, he would not take it. To make Olive a lady of society would change her. He would never shackle her with those chains. Would that he could shed them himself.

A moment ago, he had left Olive in the kitchen, discussing the menu for tonight. It was an important meal since the guests arriving from London later today would be dining with them.

Mama had meant to instruct Cook, but Olive had stepped in first to perform her duty.

She was a wonder, his make-believe wife. He was amazed how anyone could look so natural playing a role she had no experience in.

When he'd left the kitchen, Cook was smiling and nodding her head. From all he had seen, she was not an easy woman to please.

Olive pleased everyone. Especially him.

No matter how he resisted wishing all this was not a farce but true life, he was failing.

Perhaps because his feelings for Olive were not what they had been in the beginning. He cared for her…deeply. More than friendship would account for.

He would never look at the lavender rosebush and not see the flower in her hair, not breathe in the enticing scent urging him to act on what he yearned for.

Turning away from the window, he continued down the hallway, lost in thoughts of lively green eyes and lips that were pretty no matter their expression.

The library door was open. He heard a fire crackling, his mother's voice in quiet conversation.

Perhaps Father was with her. A visit with his parents would be just the thing on this dreary day.

'There is something not right about them.'

Joseph came up short. Even if his father was in the library, so was Hortencia.

But what did she mean, something was not right? He stood very still, listening.

'It is just your imagination, my dear,' his mother said. 'Unless you have proof of wrongdoing, I think it is best to keep such nonsense to yourself. There is really no reason whatsoever for Joseph to pretend to be wed to someone he is not.'

'Perhaps he does not wish for you to know he has a mistress, Lady Amelia. If she acts the part of his wife, she can consort with him right under our noses.'

Of all things, his mother laughed.

Suddenly his clothes felt too tight, too hot. Hortencia had a scorpion's tongue…pure poison.

'You, of all people, know my son has never kept a mistress. You have had a close enough watch on him over the years to realize he would not. Do you want to know what I think?'

'Of course I do. We have known each other too long for anything but the truth between us.'

'Yes, well, you will not like it, Hortencia. What I believe is that you are seeing things which are not true because of your disappointment that our plans for you and my son have not worked out.'

'Surely you are also disappointed.'

'At first I was. But what mother can see her child so happily in love and not be glad for him?'

Was he in love? If so, he was not happy. Loving a lady who could not be his would only bring him misery.

In that moment, he did feel rather miserable, so what did that mean? He was in love?

'But you always said that having love in a marriage was not the most important thing. You believed that young love is gone too quickly to grasp. Did you not tell me that the family name is what matters, what lasts?'

'I did say that…but now, seeing my boy so happy, I begin to remember how it was early in my marriage. I wonder if I advised you wrongly.'

'You did not. I, for one, am not so quick to give up on our plans. I tell you, something about this feels off to me.'

'You must give up, Hortencia. We have no more plans. My son has made his choice.'

Joseph had had enough. He spun about.

'We shall see…' he heard Hortencia say.

Oh, aye, they would.

Olive felt snared in her elegant gown, trapped by the rain which forced everyone to remain indoors.

Not that she could go outdoors even if the afternoon was sunny.

The London visitors had arrived, and she was, right then, pouring tea. Hopefully, she remembered all the details of Joseph's instructions. This was a ceremony as much as just getting tea into cups.

What Olive needed to be doing was going to her sister, warning her that Hortencia might come snooping about. It was true what Joseph said about her. She was a bloodhound.

However, she was quite stuck here entertaining guests. Guests who already knew Hortencia from London. Friends who had socialized with her from forever ago and would probably believe every rumour she presented.

Joseph stood across the parlor, near the fireplace, speaking with two gentlemen he had known from university.

Peter was tall, Charles was short, but both of them displayed manners so polished they gleamed.

Joseph must have felt her attention on them, because he looked away from his friends and gave her an adoring smile, one so sweet everyone was sure to believe it sincere.

Nearly everyone. There was always Hortencia to threaten the show.

The taller of the gentlemen noticed the shift in Joseph's attention and nodded to her.

The reason for his friends' presence, Joseph had explained, was not only to celebrate with them. It was to balance the numbers. Two single ladies required the presence of two single gentlemen. His mother had insisted upon it.

Society was an odd bird, Olive thought, and not for the first time.

However, that being the case, the balance was off.

What gentleman was there for Hortencia?

The married one? Oh, but no… Joseph was not married. And yet her first reaction had been that he was.

It was not right for Olive to be possessive. Only Hortencia made her feel that way. When the right woman came along, the one who loved Joseph for the good man he was, Olive was sure she would not feel like that.

Not in the least.

For an instant, she forgot what she was doing. Hot tea from the china spout dripped on her fingers.

'Oh, let me help!' Viscount Helmond's daughter, the one who wished to take photos rather than wed, leapt up and dabbed Olive's hand with her napkin.

Olive blinked, came to herself and what she was doing.

'I know I shall never learn the knack for serving tea,' Vivienne Curtis declared.

'Olive has the knack,' replied Grace Curtis, the viscount's younger daughter. 'It was only when Joseph looked at her that she forgot herself. How perfectly wonderful it must be to be wed.'

'Nothing quite like romance to put one off-kilter,' Joseph's father announced. 'Isn't that right?'

The comment seemed to be made to everyone, but it was Lady Claymore who blushed.

Although she smiled, Hortencia's face flared.

The woman was hiding her animosity less with each day that went by.

It was time and past for Eliza to tell James the truth about Laura.

This marriage ruse would soon come to an end. Olive was determined that it would be on Joseph's terms, not Hortencia's.

Tonight, once everyone was retired for the evening, she would go to the cottage and make Eliza know how urgent it was.

'Please let me serve tea, Lady Olive.' Grace Curtis took the teapot from her, handling it with skill. Quite clearly she was presenting her accomplishments, showing what a beneficial wife she would make.

The young men flanking Joseph seemed to get the message, because they smiled at Grace, both of them clearly besotted.

Vivienne took the moment to slip her arm though Olive's and guide her to a couch. They sat down side by side.

'Please do tell me, Olive, what birds and wildlife inhabit the area. I am ever so anxious to capture them in a photograph.'

After a few polite words about nature, Vivienne said, 'I have always admired your husband. He is different from most society dandies. I cannot say how pleased I am that he married you. I feared that it would be that awful Hortencia, or no one.'

'Surely there were many ladies he could have chosen from, although I am glad he did not.'

'I am not certain if Joseph is aware of it, but Hortencia chased away his admirers with threats of ruin. Oh, she was subtle, but she could have done it with a word. No one dared cross her. But now look. Joseph is wed, and she is in danger of being left on the shelf.'

This fascinating conversation was cut short when Joseph crossed the room to stand behind her chair. In a touch that would appear loving, he caressed her shoulders with his thumbs.

How, she had to wonder, could he touch her this way and feel it a mere performance?

Her response to his touch was sincere. When she reached up to cup his hand, to caress his fingers…it was no act.

More and more often, when she touched him or smiled at him with tenderness, it was not a performance meant to fool others. If she denied how natural showing affection for Joseph had become, the only one she would be fooling was herself.

Head bent against the rain, Olive tugged her coat around her neck and hurried along the path toward the cottage.

The hem of her nightgown was getting caked with mud, but she refused to sacrifice an expensive gown to the downpour. It was not as if any of the dresses in the wardrobe truly belonged to her. Once this marriage ruse ended, she would sell them and donate the money to a charity.

She would not miss the gowns, not terribly. But she would miss the man who had purchased them, quite terribly.

That was a thought for another time. Right now, she

must warn Eliza about the urgency of being honest with James.

Rain and mud made it difficult going. Made it cold going, too.

If she had to drag her sister out of bed and take her to James, it was what she was going to do. Olive had every confidence in James to do the loving thing and take both Eliza and Laura to his heart.

Only a thunderbolt in her path would keep Olive from making her sister do what she must.

But what was that noise?

She stood suddenly still, rain dripping off her nose and sleeking down her hair while she listened.

Not thunder but horse hooves clopping in the mud. She knew the sound too well to be mistaken.

Knew the figure of the rider too well to be mistaken about him, either.

It took only a moment for Joseph to catch up.

She looked up at him, shielding her eyes from the rain with her hand.

'What are you doing here, Joseph?'

'Following you.' He bent low to peer down at her. 'What are you doing here?'

'I am going to tell my sister she must reveal the truth to James.'

For no apparent reason, he grinned.

'In that case, I am here to bring you back home.'

Bring her home? Did he think so?

Home was the cottage at the end of the lane. The manor was no more than Olive's stage.

'You go back. I must take my sister to James.'

'Come.' He reached his hand down for her, but instead

of clasping her fingers, he bent lower, caught her around her waist with his arm. He drew her up, then settled her in front of him.

'Put me down. I need to—'

'Trust me.'

'Do I have a choice?' It did not seem so since his arm held her snugly to him.

'No, you do not. I'll not have you becoming ill for no reason. Look at you, soaked to the skin.'

Judging by the arch of his brow and the glint in his eye, it was not all she looked. One would think a coat to be enough protection against that sort of gaze, but it was a short coat and bunched up about her thighs.

Joseph had not bothered with a coat. All of a sudden, the rain was no longer a nuisance but her friend. Water drenched his white shirt, making it nearly transparent.

Even though it was an indulgence she would pay for when the time came, she snuggled her shoulder against his chest, pressing her cheek to the wet shirt.

Heavens, how could a man feel steely and cosy at the same time? She was not going to waste precious moments wondering. She was simply going to appreciate the essence of Joseph Billings.

She was going to miss her pretend husband. Grieve his loss dearly. Although he lived close by, he might as well be an ocean away. Swimming the social distance between them would be impossible.

Joseph was silent on the ride back to Falcon's Steep, but they arrived at the stable in short time. He settled Dane himself rather than waking the stableman. Then he struck a fire in the stove.

'Sit here.' He pointed to small bench in front of the stove. 'I'll get you a blanket.'

He went into a tack room and came back out carrying a blanket of red and green plaid.

He heated it over the stove for a few moments before sitting beside her and placing it around both of their shoulders.

She was warm because of the blanket, but more because of the man next to her, who was as wet as she was.

He picked up the end of the blanket and dried her face with it.

'I was perfectly safe,' she said, fending off the scolding that was sure to come.

'I'm aware. I was behind you most of the time.'

'If you knew I was safe, why didn't you just let me continue on? Eliza's whole future is at risk.'

'Because she is not at the cottage.'

'If she is not there, where is she? And how do you know she is not in her bed?'

'Oh, well, I suppose she is in her bed…but in Gretna Green, with her new husband in it with her.'

Olive leapt to her feet. She stared at Joseph's grin for several seconds before she exclaimed, 'What! But how?'

'It was easy enough to arrange a few things and send them on their way.'

'Arrange a few things?'

'The trickiest part was getting them together in a private place so they could talk. Once that happened, it was simple enough to arrange the travel and the accommodations for them.'

'I cannot believe it!'

'All they needed was a bit of a shove. They were eager enough to go once they made up their minds.'

She sat down, and gave him a quick, wet hug. 'You, Joseph Billings are my hero.'

'Oh, aye?' He gave an impression of preening. 'A grand fellow, am I?'

'The best false husband a woman could want. Joseph, we are halfway there, then. All we need to do is get through a few more days until everyone goes home.'

And make up a believable story about why they were no longer wed. One that would keep Hortencia from coming back and beginning her pursuit of Joseph again.

He frowned. 'There's another reason I got them off to Gretna Green in a hurry.'

'Not for true love to find a way?'

'Because Hortencia suspects we are not wed and has told my parents that.'

'Oh no.' This was worrisome news. Not terribly unexpected, though. 'You may count on me to do my utmost to convince her that we are.'

Even though it would lead to her eventual broken heart, Joseph deserved everything she could give him, especially after saving Eliza and Laura.

Chapter Eleven

Except for the niggling worry of what Hortencia might do, the next few days passed pleasantly.

The thing for Joseph to keep in mind was that there was nothing Hortencia could do. The woman could not prove he and Olive were not married. They presented a convincing show of being in love. His parents believed it, and as far as he could tell, everyone else did, too.

In spite of it all, Joseph found he was enjoying himself. Entertaining friends at Falcon's Steep was not as stressful as he had expected it would be. It was different from in London, where one dashed from ball, to tea, to the theater, and all for the main purpose of being seen. Here in the country, he had time to leisurely enjoy the company of his friends.

But enjoying leisurely company was not all of it—not most of it, even. Joseph's greatest pleasure came from watching Olive playing mistress of the manor.

He had to remind himself that she was, indeed, only acting. She played her part so well that sometimes he forgot.

For Olive's sake, he was glad it was an act. It would be wrong of him to want her to be who she was not. To try and keep her with him, even though it was not what would make her happy, would make him selfish in the worst way.

Just now, he stood in the shade of the porch, watching while Olive walked near the edge of the woods with Vivienne, pointing out trees and birds.

Despite everything he had just considered, Olive looked like she belonged at Falcon's Steep. Or maybe it was simply what he wished to see, and so he did.

Judging by their gestures and smiles, the ladies were looking for the best spot for Vivienne to take her photographs.

He wished for a photograph of Olive as she was right in this moment, gripping the ribbons of her bonnet while her pale blue skirt ruffled in the breeze.

It was sad that all he would keep of her was a photo. Not even one he could hold, but only the one which existed in his mind.

When he was not with her, all he thought about was when he next would be. To say he ached for her company would not be an overstatement.

The only thing preventing him from telling her so was the circumstances of their births.

Star-crossed, were they?

No, that would imply that they were lovers, which they were not. And yet, he would be a fool not to recognize that whatever was between them was changing. What had begun as an alliance had quickly become friendship, and now…

Now he ached for her company.

Ach, well…it was foolish dwelling upon what could not be.

Olive would not be better off for bearing a title.

When he wed for real, it could not be to a commoner, no matter how uncommon she was.

He was supposed to wed a woman of noble birth in order to help secure the family's social status for generations to come. If he spurned that duty, it would harm the family name…the name his parents had spent their lives keeping above reproach.

While he could largely avoid London by living here, he could not avoid his duty to the title. One day he would be forced to fill his father's shoes.

'A damned curse is what it is,' he mumbled, not that he resented his life or his family…only the demands society placed on a first-born son.

He was startled by the rustle of skirts approaching from behind.

'My dear, unfortunate friend…a curse?' Hortencia gave a great sigh, then stood beside him. 'Have you come to regret your hasty marriage so soon?'

'I only regret that I am forced to share my wife's company with other people.'

'Surely you do not mean me.' Most men would be delighted to be the recipient of her engaging smile. He was not among them. 'I have been your dear friend for a long time. I do recognize when you are troubled. You may confide in me, you know.'

Oh, aye, he was troubled. It was because she was standing so close to him.

'Hortencia, there is something you need to understand. I am well aware that my mother held hopes that we would wed. She has finally put those hopes aside. I need for you to do the same.'

'I would, of course, if I did not have your best interests at heart. But, in all affection, I must tell you of my suspicion.'

'You must?' This was interesting. He would humour her for a moment, discover what she might reveal.

'It grieves me to say so, but I believe you have been duped by your wife.'

'Oh, aye? Tell me why you think so.'

'I believe she has a close friend who is of a lower class.'

'I cannot think what that has to do with me. But since you believe it does, who is it, and why do you think I would even care?'

'It is that woman with the limp who sells cheese. I believe they were acquainted before you met.'

'Would it make a difference if they were?'

'Oh, Joseph, you are too trusting. Can't you see that there is something not above board here? You will not wish to hear it, but I believe that Olive and the cheese maker conspired in some way to catch you.'

'Do you have proof of it? If you do, I would like to hear what it is.'

The trap was neatly set. Come, Hortencia, fall into it and reveal what you are up to.

'It is a feeling only. However, I shall discover what it is, I do promise you I will. On my honour as your closest friend.'

Honour? There was very little of that in Lady Hortencia Clark.

'You are greatly mistaken in thinking so. My closest friend is my wife.'

'So you believe. But tell me, Joseph, why do you only ever kiss each other on the cheek? For a couple in the full embrace of romance, I would expect to see you more enamored of each other.'

'I will not enlighten you on what happens behind our closed chamber doors.'

A respectable woman would blush and drop the conversation; however, this was Hortencia.

'I am not blind, Joseph. Olive does not share your chamber, and you leave hers very early each night.' He wondered if she realized how her smile looked in the moment. Cunning, ugly in spite of its perfection. 'You are being duped.'

'Whatever the state of my marriage, it has nothing to do with you. But back to what you said about the cottager. If my wife was friendly with the woman, it is purely because she is friendly with everyone.'

'I suppose that might be true. Just look how happy she seems with that awkward Curtis girl. It is as well she does not wish to wed, since no man would have her anyway.'

'You cannot be speaking of Vivienne?' It was stunning that his mother had ever wished for him to be bound to this viperous woman. 'She is intelligent and lively. I know many gentlemen who have spoken highly of her.'

In fact, he had not heard them do so, but he ought to have done. She was an engaging woman. Yet it was the lady's sister who seemed to get all the attention.

'You are a guest in my home.' He must try his valiant best to be firm without antagonizing the dragon. 'I would appreciate it if you did not malign the other women. And as for what goes on between my wife and me? It has nothing to do with you. You would be well-advised to turn your attention to other matters.'

'You only say so because you do not see what I see. But I will be patient. When your wife shows her true colours, I will be here. You and I will have the future we were meant to have.'

She went up on her toes as if she intended to kiss his cheek. He stepped back so that her lips only smacked air.

'You cannot put me off forever, Joseph. You have always been meant for me.'

True colours indeed.

So much for his valiant best. He'd stepped on the viper's tail and made her hiss.

Let her then. It remained to be seen who would be the first to strike.

Hortencia struck first.

Until the moment she smiled and buried her fangs into him, it had been a good evening.

Joseph had been at ease during the last dinner of the house party, confident that the visit had been a success and would end well.

With the exception of Hortencia, everyone seemed to approve of his marriage.

In the morning, the guests would be returning to London, so the after dinner gathering in the parlor tonight was especially enjoyable.

Everyone spoke of how they must get together again soon.

Grace sat side by side on the piano bench with Charles. The fellow grinned broadly while she played a lively tune.

Peter caught Hortencia's hand, spinning her about in a playful invitation to dance. Poor man was neatly rebuffed.

Olive twirled in, saving Peter from embarrassment by grasping the hand Hortencia had just slapped away. She filled in the dance step which went wanting.

They were a happy sight, his friend and his wife—

Wife! The endearment that came so naturally had him catching his heart, shoving it back between his ribs.

At any rate, Olive and Peter made everyone smile with their silly, happy dance steps.

After a moment, his father caught the mood. He kissed Mama's hand, then twirled her about the parlor. They laughed together in a way he had never heard them do.

Eleanor and Thomas Curtis joined in, making the parlor dazzle in a whirl of colourful skirts. Laughter added to the music from the piano.

And then it happened. The serpent's tongue flicked. Hortencia clapped her hands in apparent merriment and declared for all to hear, 'Do you know, Joseph, I have never seen you give your bride a proper kiss.'

Grace stopped playing.

The dancers stopped and stared.

Everyone must be wondering if the comment was playful or critical. What they would all know was that it was highly inappropriate. She was getting desperate.

'Hortencia, my friend, you do say the funniest things.' Olive hurried to his side while everyone looked at one another, clearly at a loss to know if they should laugh or not. 'No one can make a jest as well as you can. Now tell me, what sort of kiss is it that you seem to believe my husband is negligent in giving me?'

At that, everyone relaxed, smiled. Everyone except for Vivienne, who looked wide-eyed and offended on their behalf.

Hortencia opened her mouth, closed it…then frowned. 'Well, never mind, perhaps—'

Father cleared his throat. 'Perhaps all of us married men have been negligent in the matter. What do you say? Each of us give our wives a resounding kiss!'

'On the count of three, then,' his mother ordered. 'Married kisses all around.'

Dash it. He was good and trapped. Kissing Olive in the

way which was expected of him was risky. A man could only resist so much temptation. Now here it was and no way out.

Olive whispered so quietly that he could not hear her words, but he read the message well enough.

They would survive this one kiss. She understood what it was and what it was not.

Lord, give him as logical an approach to the matter as Olive seemed to have.

Glancing to the side, he decided to follow the example his parents set.

Hortencia would accept their example as to what made a respectable show of affection.

He and Olive must have both thought the same thing, because they turned as one to look at Lord and Lady Claymore.

Well then…it was not that kiss they could copy.

He had not ever seen his parents kiss that way before. Somehow this visit to the country must have revived the flame in their marriage!

He lifted Olive's chin, deciding the best course was to kiss her a degree cooler than his parents were doing and a degree hotter than the Curtis couple were.

Dipping his head, he felt her breath, hot and quick, on his lips.

'Forgive me,' he whispered against them.

'No,' she breathed, her lips moving on his.

Anyone looking on would imagine they'd exchanged romantic endearments in the instant before kissing.

But 'no'? What did she mean by that? Was it 'no need to', or 'no, I do not'?

Wondering was the only thing which kept him from becoming fully consumed by Olive, caught up in her scent, in her shape as she pressed against him.

'How delightful!' Grace exclaimed. 'I can hardly wait for the day when I may play this game.'

He was aware of conversation and laughter buzzing about the parlor, but dimly.

'No?' he whispered against Olive's ear. 'What does that mean?'

'No more,' she whispered back.

'My, but wasn't this fun? I think we will start a new trend in parlor games.' Joseph heard his mother say. 'Have you seen what you wished to, Hortencia?'

This was not Joseph's first kiss, but it might as well have been. As distracted as he had been during it, a question came to him.

Was this a kiss to build a lifetime on?

'Come with me.' He grabbed Olive's hand, and drew her out of the parlor, down a long hallway, and then into the solarium.

Moonlight shone through the glass. He heard wind huffing around the eaves and Olive's quick breathing.

He needed to know. Now that they were alone, would he still feel the future in her kiss?

If he did, it might be the greatest regret of his life.

A shaft of moonlight etched a path across the solarium floor. Joseph tugged her along, then stopped abruptly beside a small tree.

He jerked her against him, frowning.

She arched her brows in question, because what was this about?

Then he kissed her. Or claimed her. Whichever, she was consumed…possessed.

And then it was over except for the heat. There was not an inch of her which did not sizzle.

Although he took a step back, he did not release her arm. Breathing hard, he looked intently into her eyes. 'No more what?'

She reached up, touched his bicep. It was tense and firm. She felt a tremor race over his skin.

'No more wondering what kissing you would be like without acting being the reason.'

'Now we know.'

'Aye, now we do.' He kissed her again, and she allowed it.

This time the kiss did not have a sense of urgent possession. Rather, it was slow, and she sensed it held a hint of regret.

This intimacy would not happen again. She knew it was true as well as he must.

How sad to put something so wondrous away in the very instant it was acknowledged.

'I cannot be sorry. How can I regret a moment of knowing you?' He made as if to kiss her again, but she shook her head, broke his hold on her arm, then stepped away.

One more taste of the forbidden would make her weep. And she was not sorry for a moment they had shared, either. But grief for what they would be missing might crush her.

'We shall call this…' she waggled her fingers at her heart and then his '…a moment out of time.'

The wonder was, how she had squeezed the words from her throat without weeping.

Society was a beast, keeping people from one another. After his kisses, she knew if things were different, then… Never mind. Things were not different.

'Yes, I suppose that is what it was.' He touched her hair, drew his fingers over the curve of her bottom lip. 'It was a wonderful moment, Olive. I will never forget it.'

Nor would she, and yet remembering was the saddest thing she could imagine.

Olive gave up pacing across her chamber floor and plopped heavily into the chair in the bay of the window.

No matter how hard she tried to, she could not sleep. Not surprisingly, Joseph's first kiss lingered on her lips, as did his last.

She had been too close to confessing she was in love with him. What a grand and heartbreaking mistake that would have been.

She stared out the window. Above the treetops, she saw a pair of smoke columns curling from the cottages below.

Her secret love for Joseph would go with her when she went home. The last thing he needed was to have her confession haunt this house while he tried to make a life with some perfectly lovely and acceptable woman.

For all that she valued truth, sometimes it was better kept to oneself.

Chapter Twelve

Peter Helms and Charles Barlow departed for London after breakfast the next morning.

Joseph regretted seeing them go. Not only because they were men whose company he enjoyed but also because once everyone was gone, Olive would be, too.

Mother, Father, and Hortencia would be here for another week only, which meant his time with Olive was growing short.

Then he would no longer need a wife.

But Olive…would he no longer need her? Her presence seemed as natural as breathing did.

Before all this, he had counted himself lucky to be living at Falcon's Steep by himself.

Look at him now, waving goodbye to Charles and Peter and feeling sad about it…feeling lonely.

If it was this difficult saying goodbye to them, what would it be like when he had to say farewell to Olive?

True, she only lived down the hill. The distance would not be all that great. But there would be a gap between them of another sort. Because of it, she might as well be a hundred miles away. Once she was no longer lady of the manor, she would go back to her old life. He would go back to his.

Provided he had a life to go back to. He feared everything had changed. He still loved the estate and did not wish to live anywhere else, but after Olive, what was he to do with himself?

Perhaps he should wed. The manor needed a mistress.

No, curse it. The manor needed Olive. He needed Olive.

The thought of some lovely stranger taking her place left him feeling odd. It fisted his belly into a knot.

The knot only tightened as the day went on.

A few hours later, Olive stood beside him, giving hugs and wishing the Curtis family a safe trip home.

'Where is Hortencia?' Grace asked. 'One would think she would come and bid us goodbye.'

'Perhaps remorse over her behaviour last night is keeping her indisposed,' Joseph's mother said.

Maybe. Yet her absence made Joseph itchy under the skin.

'Remorse? I rather doubt it,' Vivienne answered while handing up the tripod for her camera to the driver to be stored with the luggage. 'I saw her chatting merrily with a crofter down the hill not an hour ago. They did not give a whit that they frightened away the bird I was trying to photograph. More is the pity. It was quite beautiful.'

Olive went stiff, glanced up at him and whispered, 'Father?'

'It might be anyone,' he answered.

'Let us hope. My father is not known for his discretion.'

He caught her fingers, squeezed them. She squeezed back.

All of a sudden, he wished the week was over. That everyone was back in London with no secrets having been revealed.

As long as he was wishing…

But no. There was no magic lamp that was going to grant his greatest wish.

Throughout dinner, Mama carried the conversation.

Joseph had never been more grateful for her gift of steering talk to pleasant topics. She was a lady born and bred, and it showed even when she presided over a group of five, and four of them family…no, three. Too often lately, he forgot that Olive was not family at all.

Hortencia was stewing, and her mood would have tainted the meal if not for Mama.

The nasty glances she cast at Olive were unusual. Ordinarily, she at least managed a put-on smile.

If Joseph had any doubt that the cottager she had been speaking with was Cedric Augustmore, he no longer did.

Hortencia would have been seeking proof that he and Olive were not wed. She would not have received it from Olive's father. He believed they were. But Cedric couldn't have mentioned his relationship to Olive either, because Hortencia would have crowed about it. They'd been unbelievably lucky—this time.

As soon as dinner was finished, he would whisk Olive away. With any luck, they could avoid Hortencia's accusations for a bit longer.

The second Mama nodded to the footman that dinner was finished, Joseph stood.

'It was a lovely meal,' Olive said, then also stood and grasped his hand.

Clearly she, too, understood the urgency to be away at once.

While they might manage to avoid Hortencia for tonight,

with seven more days before she went back to London, it would be impossible to avoid her altogether.

Only not tonight. It had been a busy and tiring day with all the socializing first and then the goodbyes. When he denied whatever his foe had to say, he would need his wits about him.

Yet there was very little she could do other than accuse. If it came to their word against hers… Olive was the more convincing player.

'Good night, my dears,' Mama said, then slipped her hand into the crook of Father's elbow.

Lady Claymore gave her husband a glance which made him grin. He led her from the dining room at double pace.

Who were these people? Where was the woman who believed that marriage was intended purely for social advancement? That love could not be counted on to endure for a lifetime?

Her attitude about everything seemed so changed, Joseph scarcely knew his own mother. Father knew her, though, and he looked exceptionally pleased.

'Good night, Hortencia,' Olive said. 'My husband and I have had a full day. We shall retire to our chamber.'

'Not just yet.'

Hortencia stood, faced them across the table. She smiled but not in good humour. Once again she looked like a cat with feathers in her sharp little teeth.

It was another ugly image which made the small hairs on the back of his neck leap to attention.

Joseph nodded at the footmen standing beside the door. 'Thank you, Densley… Wilson. You may go.'

Whatever Hortencia had to say, he did not wish for the staff to overhear.

Once they were well out of earshot, Joseph said, 'Speak your mind so that my wife and I might retire to our chamber.'

Hortencia tapped her fingernails on the table.

Click, click, click... Her eyes narrowed, and her smile quirked up at one corner.

'Oh, Joseph, how perfectly wicked.' What was wicked was her giggle. He pressed Olive's shoulder to encourage her...and himself to stand firm.

'When two people are in love, it is what they do. Good night.'

When they were only steps from the doorway, she let her arrow fly. Her point hit square between his shoulder blades.

'I do not doubt that you love the woman, Joseph. But you are not married to her.'

She could not know that for certain. Only Eliza knew the truth, and she would deny it.

'Surely you are not suggesting that Joseph and I are living in sin.' Olive gave a perfectly horrified gasp. 'It is beneath you, Hortencia. A lady would never utter such a lie.'

'Which of us is the true lady, Olive? Show me a wedding gown. Present me with a certificate of marriage. Otherwise, I will assume I am correct.'

Olive closed her eyes, took a breath. He knew what she was doing, had seen her draw deeply into her character on several occasions.

When she opened her eyes, she was so completely mistress of the manor that he nearly believed it to be fact.

'I confess. I am utterly bewildered, Hortencia.' Olive stepped around the table. She clasped her foe's hand. 'Have you feigned our friendship all along?'

The only answer the woman gave was to shrug.

'Oh dear, do not tell me we are not friends? Have I assumed something that is not true?'

Olive dropped Hortencia's hand.

'You are beneath me. Surely you do not think we could ever be friends,' Hortencia spat.

Olive was not beneath anyone! He was about make it clear, but a cool head was called for in that moment, and he did not have one. Olive might not either, but she acted as if she did.

'Dear Hortencia, I believed you to be a lady of quality. I now see that you fall short of the role. I made an incorrect assumption. Just as you have made an incorrect assumption about my marriage to Joseph.'

'Oh, you are good under fire, Olive. Still, I am no fool. I recognize a liar when I see her.'

'Enough, Hortencia!' Anger pulsed under his skin, matching the thud of his heartbeat. 'I am finished with your accusations.'

No matter that they were true, he was finished with Lady Hortencia Clark.

'You have three days to make arrangements to leave my home.'

Of all the reactions he'd expected, it was not to hear her laugh.

'Do I, now?' *Clip, clip* went her shoes on the tile as she walked around the table to him. 'I give you the same three days. You will confess the truth, send this woman back to where she came from and return with me to London. We will be wed at once. I grow weary of waiting for you, Joseph.'

'All you will do is grow wearier, Hortencia. I will never love you.'

'Yes, anyone can see that Olive is the one you love. Not

that I care one way or another. Love whoever you wish to. Marry me.'

'Why, you immoral creature!' Olive had the presence of mind to exclaim this quietly. It would not do to have the household aware of the drama happening in the dining room. 'Leave our home at once! You will not take my husband to London or anywhere else.'

'But I will. In three days. Produce proof of your marriage or I will ruin you, Olive.'

'Come, my love.' He snatched up Olive's hand, kissed her fingers, then tucked her under his arm. 'This is nonsense. She can do nothing to us.'

'How do you think Lord and Lady Claymore will feel about being played the fool?'

Olive went rigid, but she said quite coolly, 'Presumptions will be your downfall.'

Hortencia snorted.

'Come, husband.' Olive's hand trembled. He gripped it tight to keep Hortencia from noticing. 'We shall retire to our chamber.'

The door had not been closed for a full minute when Olive decided what she must do.

Hortencia had run mad if she thought Olive would just hand Joseph over to her.

'Three days, indeed,' she grumbled.

He did not seem to have heard her, or if he did, he did not respond.

Pointing at the bed, he mouthed, 'Bounce.'

When she gave him a blank look, he caught her hand and took her to the bed, where he proceeded to sit and show her, causing the mattress to creak, the bedding to rustle.

She followed his lead but had no idea how this helped with anything. It was amusing, but right now she did not feel that amusement was called for.

Action was. And she had a plan.

'Good,' he whispered. 'Now moan.'

'Why ever would I do that?' she whispered back, her breath coming in huffs from exertion.

'Because Hortencia followed us. She is probably listening at the door. So act as if you are in the throes of passion. We do not wish for her to think we are worried about what she just said.'

'What? Joseph, I have never been in the throes of passion. I have no idea how to sound like it.'

Could she act something she had never experienced? She had read of it, imagined it…so perhaps.

'Very well. I shall try.' Being already breathless was bound to help. So would picturing Joseph without his shirt, his chest glistening because he was emptying a bucket of water slowly over himself… How delightful were those liquid droplets sliding over bare, pebbled muscle?

She made a low sound, added a gasp, and said, 'Oh, Joseph… Joseph…'

With her eyes closed, she bounced and imagined his hair wet, his eyes all smoky desire.

Bit by bit, she became aware that Joseph had stopped bouncing, that in fact, he was no longer sitting on the bed.

When she opened her eyes, she saw him standing, looking down at her. The smoky desire was real and hotter than in her imagination.

Glory fire, but he made her bones go soft. It was difficult to love a man, to see him giving her such a look, and not react by stretching out on the bed and offering herself up to him.

Mentally, she grabbed her heart and gave it a good stiff shake.

She inclined her head toward the chamber door, arching her brows in question. Was Hortencia still snooping outside?

He whispered for her to get beneath the blanket.

While she scrambled under it, he walked toward the door, yanking open his shirt buttons, kicking off his shoes.

He gave her a wink, a grin, and then he bent to curl one sock off his foot.

If Hortencia was on the other side of the door, Olive's show of heaving lust would be convincing…and unfeigned.

Joseph yanked the door open. No eavesdropper had her ear pressed to the keyhole, but footsteps did echo in the hallway, tapping out a quick retreat.

He closed the door, leaned against it, the long toes of one bare foot wriggling.

Scrambling out of the bed, she took a moment to gaze about the grandest bedchamber she had ever seen.

Dark wood gleamed with polish. Velvet drapes of hunter green hung from ceiling to floor, drawn shut over a window which probably took up the better part of one wall.

Olive did not belong here. Not that she had any notion of how she was going to stop being here, especially now.

More than ever, their lie must prevail, and the truth must fail. She had never imagined a more tangled web.

What would Joseph think when she turned it all on its head?

Her idea was easier to come up with than to present. She had no notion of how he would respond.

There was only thing to do if this situation was to come out in their favour.

She loved Joseph, and there was nothing she would not do to protect him from a tragic future.

She respected his parents with all her heart. To have them discover the truth of what they had done was unthinkable.

No amount of explaining would make it acceptable for her and Joseph to have been living together without being married.

There was really no way to say what she needed to gently, so…

'We will wed.'

In the face of his gaping stare, she added, 'You do have experience with arranging marriages in Gretna Green. We will stay in this room tonight and leave at first light. Then we will return home with a licence.'

'It is generous of you to offer to sacrifice yourself for my sake. Only, I cannot accept.'

'You must. Unless you see another way out of this.'

'I do see another way. We shall admit to the truth.'

'And live with the disaster that would follow? I might as well hand you over to Hortencia on a silver platter. No other woman would have you with your reputation so blackened.'

'Aye.' He shook his head, frowning until his brows nearly met. 'Yours would be, too.'

'I would be utterly ruined, an outcast in the place where I was born and raised. Of course, I did expect to be a spinster anyway.'

With his hand working through his hair in clear agitation, Joseph paced to the window and back.

'You would make a terrible spinster.'

'You know I am right about this.'

'I see the wisdom in the idea. But it is not as if we can

seek an annulment afterwards. We have done too good a job of convincing people we are in love.'

Far too good a job. She was utterly, madly in love with him. Not that she was free to admit it.

She owed this man more than she could ever repay. What would have become of Eliza, James, and Laura had it not been for him? Instead of living apart, they were now a family.

Marrying Joseph was small recompense for all he had done.

An easy price to pay.

The difficult part would be carrying on, day by day, without him knowing she was in love with him.

Which she must do so that he could go about his life as he would have done before all this.

He had saved her family from disgrace. Now she would do the same for his.

'Once we have done this thing, we can live separate lives. Me at my cottage and you in your manor house.' She swallowed hard, because this was a wickedly difficult thing to say to the man she loved. 'If you wish.'

If he wished! None of this was what he wished.

To wed the woman he adored and yet live apart from her?

It was madness. Clearly, it was also what she wished.

Cursed awful was what it was going to be…trading one lie for another.

He was not certain he could pretend this was only a convenient marriage. The honest truth was that he was in love with Olive, and he was not certain he could act as if he was not.

'We will not live in separate homes. Separate chambers would do…if you wish,' he said, giving her own words back to her. Not to mock her but only to agree with what she seemed to want.

He could not understand why she would wish such a thing after the way he had kissed her, after the way she had kissed him back.

There was plenty to build a marriage on.

'Olive, I…' He did not understand but he would not pressure her for her reasons. 'May I have my grandmother's ring?'

Blinking, she looked away while she slipped it off her finger and pressed the warm circle of gold into his palm.

Had she misunderstood? Thought he was refusing her?

'Will you look at me, Olive?'

She still did not, so he turned her chin in his fingers. Moisture shimmered in her green eyes. She was hiding herself behind them.

The sight made his gut clench. Here they were, hours from being wed, and she was hiding herself from him. She had never done it before.

All he could think of was that she was sorry for the sacrifice. Even though she was pressing for it, and he did see there was no other way, it was evident she did not wish to wed him.

He couldn't blame her. He had promised this charade would last a week, and now she was to give up a lifetime.

'I will do my best to be a decent husband, Olive. I promise.'

The vow given, he went down on his knee and took her hand.

'Olive Augustmore, will you do me the great honour of becoming my wife?'

He put the ring back on her finger and noticed her hand trembling. So were the corners of her mouth.

It took a moment, but she nodded. 'Yes, Joseph, I will marry you.'

She looked at the ring on her finger, then pressed it to her bosom.

The moisture in her eyes spilled over in a single tear. He wiped it away with the pad of his thumb.

He wished he knew what the tear meant. But then, perhaps it was better he did not.

Chapter Thirteen

The next morning they left for Gretna Green at dawn.

By noon, the minister declared Joseph to be Olive's husband, and Olive to be his wife.

He pledged his love and fidelity to her and wondered if, in spite of the circumstances of their marriage, she had any sense of how deeply he meant that promise.

Standing in this quaint church, his marriage only seconds old, he had the same sense of coming home as he had when he first rode up the drive to Falcon's Steep.

He wished he could tell Olive that he did not regret marrying her, that there was a sense of wonderment to the morning, but he held this tongue.

She would not appreciate knowing…not if she did not feel the same way.

The ceremony ended quickly. It was time to go home.

As they walked down the front steps of the church, a dragonfly buzzed over a silk flower on Olive's hat.

A sign of good days to come? What wouldn't he give to regain the easy way that used to be between them?

Something had happened to change it. Perhaps being the husband she wanted would get it back.

Dash it, though. The husband she seemed to want, which was no proper husband at all, was not the one he wanted to be.

It was a fine line he would walk with Olive Billings, but he would choose no other.

'Olive Billings,' he said, taking his bride's arm and leading her toward their waiting carriage.

'Yes?' She glanced up at him, her expression neutral.

It cut him to see it, because brides were not supposed to be neutral. Typically, they were blushing with joy.

The dragonfly still hovered about. Its wings glistened blue and green in the sunshine. There had not been time for either of them to procure more elegant clothing. The flowers she carried were purchased from a street seller.

The dragonfly, though—to him, it added a little magic to the moment, rescuing it from neutrality.

'I'm just trying out your name, now that it's real.'

'Mrs Billings,' she repeated after him. To his great relief, she smiled and seemed more herself. 'It sounds honest, at least.'

Perhaps now, with the vows spoken and their futures secured, they could once again be the friends they had been.

What he must not do was press her for any more than she was willing to give him. Which was her whole life.

While he could not give her everything he wished to as a husband, he could at least give her his restraint.

The dragonfly alighted on the bodice of Olive's travelling gown. It flexed its wings on a shiny button. Lucky insect.

To his way of seeing it, the insect was a messenger reminding him to be patient, and one day he and Olive would find their way to a true marriage.

She nudged the insect with her finger, but instead of flying off, it crawled on her fingertip. 'Isn't it amazing?'

'Oh, aye. Quite a splendid insect.'

She blew on its wings. It took flight, circled their heads, and then off it went.

'Well, something advantageous has come of the morning,' she said.

'The dragonfly, you mean? A portent of good things to come?'

'A lovely sentiment, of course, but what I mean is that we no longer need to think of a way to end our marriage,' she said.

Ach, no. It was now more about finding a way of carrying on with it.

Home by teatime, Olive sat with Joseph and his parents, eating small sandwiches as if this was a day like any other.

The only difference was that Hortencia was absent. Since Joseph was safely beside her, Olive did not worry over where Hortencia was or what she was doing. It was pleasant not to have to feel anxious about the woman's scheming for an hour.

The rest of the afternoon and evening went much as they always had, each of them doing what they always did. As far as Olive could tell, no one even wondered where they been together this morning.

When it was time to retire, Olive was exhausted. The steps to her chamber seemed a mile high.

Then Joseph looped his arm about her waist, helping her up.

She tried not to lean into his strength. Yes, he was her husband now, but not much had changed except having a piece of paper to say so.

The truth was, she had gone from having a pretend husband to a husband in name only.

It was simply more of the same. To let herself believe otherwise was folly.

Had it not been for the fear of being discovered, she would never have demanded he marry her, and he would not have gone on his knee to propose.

They had spoken the vows required to secure the marriage certificate…no more, no less.

Now they needed to speak of what came next.

This was their wedding night. What would Joseph wish to do with it?

She knew what she wished for, but the last thing she would do was seduce him into her bed. Just because a woman offered her body did not mean she would be loved in return.

Now here they were in front of her chamber. She opened the door to her room, but closed the imaginary one on the pining and sighing from her heart.

Joseph stepped in behind her like he always did in case anyone was watching, and closed the door behind him, like he always had.

The bed was ten feet away, like it always was.

And yet it loomed so much larger tonight, occupying far too much of her attention.

Her tricky imaginary door must still be cracked open an inch, because the bed seemed to pulse with temptation.

She really must grab hold of her emotions…focus on the fact that conjugal bliss was not going to be a part of her marriage.

She knew very well why they had married, and so did he.

'Are you worried that now I'm your husband, I will press you for my rights?'

Glory fire, not that. It was more that she would demand what he was not willing to give!

An honest answer to his question would be that she feared offering her heart only to have it rejected.

Better to keep what was between them as it was… friendly, amicable. Going through life as allies.

'No, Joseph. It is not what we agreed to. I trust you to… to refrain.'

'Good, then, we have that settled. It is late, and I am tired. May I just sit on your bed for a while?'

In the past he had done so without asking…when he was instructing her on how to act like a lady.

'This is your home. You may sit anywhere that suits you.'

With a sigh, he sat on the bed, then flopped onto his back with his knees hanging over the edge.

He waved his fingers for her to join him on the mattress.

When she hesitated, he sat up, then rose from the bed and came to lead her by the hand.

'It is difficult to speak to you when you are standing over there.'

It was not the speaking which concerned her; after all, they had done it many times before. The difference between now and then was that a marriage licence lay between them.

Things that used to be forbidden no longer were…except for the boundaries they set for themselves.

Joseph's boundary was that he would not press his marital rights.

Although he did not know it, her boundary was the same.

He drew her down onto the mattress. Together they lay

back. Like before, his legs dangled over the edge. Hers did, too, only his feet were closer to the floor.

'What do you wish to talk about?' she asked quietly.

'Our friendship. I wish to have it back, like it was before we wed.'

'I do not think it has suffered.'

'Good, then may I hold your hand as we have done in the past?'

'Of course.' He caught her hand, drew it to his chest.

She felt his heart beat hard against her fingers. Odd since they were supposed to be relaxing from their long, weary day.

He turned on his side so that they faced one another. He arched his brows, then grinned.

Instinct warned her that he was about to break their rules. She must be the firm one, then. If she was not, she might admit that she loved him.

Folly, folly, folly! She must not be reckless.

'I've kissed you before, too.' He drew her hand to his mouth, lingered over the kiss he placed on her knuckles.

'Only when people were watching.'

'No…there was the time when they were not.' He moved closer. The mattress squeaked with his weight shifting. 'I think you recall it?'

'We have agreed to a friendly marriage.'

'Kissing is friendly, aye?'

Too friendly and yet… 'Would you want kissing in our marriage? Since we are setting our boundaries, we ought to know what they are.'

'We must try one or two in order to know.'

'Don't we know from before?'

Then, kissing had been nearly more than she could resist. Now that he was her husband, he could take things further if he wished to.

His breath came quick, warm on her cheek. His open palm pressed her closer toward him on the mattress.

'My Olive.' Her name, so softly whispered, branded her heart. The sizzle of the burn went all through her body. It cindered her resolve and blew the ashes of her good sense all over the mattress.

And that was even before he kissed her.

When he did, well…she had no argument. She loved him and would show him with every sigh and moan he drew from her, with every stroke, every touch of every part of her that had been forbidden.

Her brain was fuzzy. Her body was not.

It knew what she wanted and insisted on having its way.

She gave herself over to her husband because surely it was impossible for him to touch her with such loving tenderness unless he did, in fact, love her.

This was right. Joy hummed through her at every kiss. The small sighs and noises his touch drew from her was a love song.

All at once his hands fell away from her. He rolled off her with a muffled curse, then all but leapt from the bed.

'I never meant to…' He backed toward the chamber door, jerking his hand through his hair as he did when he was agitated. 'I got carried away, Olive. Forgive me, it will not happen again.'

Within seconds, she was alone in the room.

There was no mistaking what he'd meant.

Joseph had never meant for her to believe he was in love with her.

Her 'love song' must have shocked him out of the trance

that had led him off course. He'd only wanted their friendship back as it was.

She lay down on the bed again, not a button undone on her gown, not a stocking rolled down, silently weeping.

And alone in her love.

The next afternoon, Olive stood in the centre of the entrance hall of Falcon's Steep. Absently, she plucked a dried frond off a potted fern.

What she ought to do was go home. She could not, of course. This was her new life now. She had chosen it, and there was no going back. It was not as if going home would help with her heartache anyway.

Looking back on events, which was all she was doing, it was fair to admit last night was not completely Joseph's fault. There had been two them sharing embraces on the bed.

She had known better and yet still set good judgement aside. Had she been firm in what she knew to be right, none of it might have happened.

When next she saw him, she would not act as if she resented him.

To resent someone because they did not love you as you loved them would only lead to further heartache. Last night she had shed hours of tears, feeling sorry for herself. She was done with it.

As far as she was concerned, she and Joseph were friends and would continue to be. Only, next time he asked to sit on her bed, she would point him to the chair.

Looking about the grand beauty of her new home, she knew there was only one thing to do, and that was to move on.

The question was, how?

No longer was she acting the part of Lady of Falcon's Steep. She was its true mistress now.

In the past, she had managed by drawing on her fictional self. Acting, though, was quite a different thing from reality.

This sudden turnabout in her life would be challenging. Which was probably what she needed right then. Discovering how to remain who she had been, while becoming who she was required to be, ought to keep her mind busy enough.

No longer was she responsible for a goat herd, whose only requirements were to be fed, milked and sung to. Now she was accountable for a household and the well-being of all those who worked here.

And she was to do all this without pressing Joseph for affections he did not feel for her.

Oh, yes, during their wedding vows, he had promised to love her, but everyone said that. It was a requirement.

In this moment, all she hoped for was to regain the friendship which had blossomed so naturally between them.

Footsteps strode across the tile floor from behind. She recognized whose they were straight away.

She had not seen Joseph since he left her chamber last night and had been nervous about what their first encounter would be like.

Distant? Friendly? Resentful? Forgiving?

He did not speak, but plucked the dried frond from her fingers and placed it back in the pot. He managed to do so without his fingers even grazing hers.

'No need to trim the plants. We have servants to do it.'

As far as she could tell, he was neither distant nor

friendly. Not resentful, nor forgiving, either. The best she could figure was that he was as confused as she was.

'You have staff to do everything. Really, Joseph, no one is going to believe I am a baron's daughter.'

'Olive.' He reached for her hand, but at the last moment drew it back. 'Last night I overstepped. Please do not hate me. I have no excuse except for bad judgement.'

'Mine was as bad. We shall go on as if it did not happen and consider it a lesson learned.'

'Aye,' he said, his expression sombre. 'A lesson learned. I hope you will not hate me for the teaching.'

'I've too much on my mind to cling to misplaced resentment. Going forward we shall respect the boundaries of our marriage.'

'Agreed. Now, tell me what is pressing on your mind?'

'How am I to go from being a goatherd to Lady of Falcon's Steep?'

'You have been doing it already.'

'Acting it.' The same as she was acting as if she was not in love with him.

When she thought about it, she had been acting in one way or another since before she met Joseph. At last she was free to be herself.

The last deception must be settled today, this very hour. It was going to come out at some point if Hortencia kept digging for gossip. Better if it was by confession than discovery.

'We must tell your parents who I am at once.'

'It's true. Even if she found out, Hortencia would have nothing to hold over us then.'

'Let's do it now before we lose our courage.'

He extended his hand to her. 'This is acceptable?'

For her, touching this man in any way was risky. And yet they had done so as friends, and she did wish to have a friendly marriage.

'This will have to be said just right. Once they recover from the surprise, I am sure they will want nothing but our happiness,' Joseph said.

'Will we be happy?' she asked. It was blunt, but she did not regret the asking.

'We were, I think…before.' An endearing frown crossed his brow. 'Olive, I was not the husband I ought to have been last night. From now on I will be.'

Fine, except that the husband he thought she wanted was not the one who'd walked out of her chamber.

It was the other husband, the one who'd kissed away all her good judgement.

There was nothing in Hortencia's attitude to indicate that she had so recently threatened him and Olive. Yet Joseph was not fooled by her pretence of congeniality.

The cheerier the woman seemed, the more it worried him. He had given her three days to make arrangements to leave his home.

This was the morning of that third day. She gave no indication of being ready to travel. But he was still not of a mind to bring out their marriage certificate since the ink was still fresh and the date was proof that she had been correct when she claimed they were not wed.

While she chatted with Mama, he did not get the sense she was saying goodbye.

More than ever, he would need to keep a watchful eye on her, because not only was this her day to leave, but it was the day she had given them to produce proof of their marriage.

He had tried a few times to get his parents alone so that he and Olive could tell them who she really was, but aside from Hortencia clinging to them, they'd spent most of yesterday and this morning visiting friends.

The longer the moments ticked by, the more urgent he felt it was to reveal the truth. Something was not right here, although he could not quite put a finger on it. Except that Hortencia was acting far too congenially.

'There is something different about you, son.' Joseph's father stroked his chin in thought.

Quite a bit more than his father knew. He was not aware that being in love and having to act like he was not, showed!

'Something is different about you, too, Father.'

His father laughed joyously. Mama tapped his arm in clear affection.

He had never seen this loving, playful part of his parents' marriage.

It must be that spending time away from London and society had made them look at one another in a new way… or perhaps an old way.

Whichever it was, it seemed that they had revived their first love. Joseph could not have been happier to see it.

Hortencia stopped conversing with Mama, then went to the window and stared silently out.

Probably she was knocked off centre by Cupid's arrow darting between his parents. With luck she would not notice it going off target where he and Olive were concerned.

All at once, she turned away from the window. She smiled that cat smile she had.

'Lady Amelia, I have invited a guest to join us. I hope you do not mind.'

His mother raised her brows, but Father spoke up. 'Have you met a young man, Hortencia?'

'I have met a man. I didn't realize exactly who he was at first, but now I do. I'm sure he's someone you will be most anxious to meet.'

Hortencia slid a look at Olive, sending her a slow, malicious grin.

Olive's face drained of colour.

Joseph stood.

'What have you done?' he asked with a scowl.

'I have merely invited a charming gentleman for tea.'

Footsteps clicked in the hallway.

'Mr Cedric Augustmore has come to call, sir.' The butler sniffed, bowed at the viscount and then backed out of the parlor.

Olive rose from the couch, she had recovered nicely. She did not appear to be distressed, and he admired her for it. No, he loved her for it.

'Good afternoon, Father.' Olive hurried across the parlor, then gave him a hug.

There was nothing to do but introduce him. This meeting had come before she'd hoped for it to, but now that it was upon her, she must push through.

What a blessing that she did not smell alcohol on her father's breath. The situation might be far worse.

'Lord and Lady Claymore, I would like to introduce you to my father.'

Neither of them spoke. Apparently they were struck dumb, wondering how this man could be the baron they had been told he was. Although Father had worn his best suit for the occasion, it was still patched and out of fashion.

To complete his look of cottage farmer, he held a pair of small bleating goats, one under each arm.

'A gift for you, my lord, my lady.' He extended the kids, adorably speckled, one with brown splotches and one with black. In Father's estimation, this was a grand gift which anyone would appreciate.

Her mother-in-law gave a great blink. What, Olive wondered, was the biggest surprise? The goats or the man she had greeted as her father? He did not resemble a baron in any way.

To her credit, Lady Claymore recovered quickly, hiding her surprise behind a gracious smile.

The viscount took the kids, awkwardly cuddling one in each elbow. 'We haven't owned goats before. Thank you, sir. They are interesting little fellows.'

Interesting and nibbling the shiny buttons on Lord Claymore's sleeve.

'It was kind of you to come all this way to pay us a visit, Mr Augustmore.'

'Oh, but it was not all that far, Lady Amelia,' Hortencia announced. 'Mr Augustmore lives only down the hill… the first cottage you come to on the path. I met him again by happy circumstance when I was out walking earlier today. Once I knew who he was, it only seemed appropriate to invite him to tea.'

Olive uttered a mental curse. She and Joseph had missed their chance to tell his parents who she was and introduce her father to them on their own terms. Now it was Hortencia steering the moment as she wished to.

'I did want to give my best wishes to my daughter and

my new son-in-law. And to make your acquaintances.' Father gave a polite nod to each of them. 'I am pleased to be able to call you family.'

'It is a great pleasure to meet you, Mr Augustmore.' Lady Claymore indicated the tea tray with its assortment of delicate sandwiches. 'We are delighted that you are able to join us.'

Hortencia gasped, probably horrified seeing her scheme turn against her. 'Oh, but I do not think—'

The viscount interrupted her to say, 'Please do stay, Cedric. I hope I may call you that? As you say, we are family now.'

'I thank you kindly, my lord.'

'No more "my lord". We shall be Marshall and Amelia.' Her father-in-law's smile looked so like Joseph's it took her breath for an instant. 'Until we are called Grandfather.'

'And Grandmama!' Lady Claymore exclaimed. 'Hortencia, will you serve tea?'

Knowing she would not be giving these dear people grandchildren made Olive want to weep on the spot.

Hortencia flinched. 'All of a sudden, I do not feel—'

'A word, my dear.' This was not a request but an order given by a viscountess. Hortencia did not dare ignore it.

Lady Claymore walked towards the corner of the room, where she was sure to be out of earshot of the men who chatted easily with one another despite the difference in their social stations.

The conversation was not out of Olive's earshot.

'Hortencia, you have invited a guest. You will now have the courtesy to serve him tea.'

'Of course, Lady Amelia. Forgive me. I do not know what came over me. I feel recovered now.'

Hortencia's words were certainly not genuine, but uttered in order to save face with Viscountess Claymore. It would not do to make an enemy of such a lady of wealth and influence, one whose son she had designs on.

Clearly, she still did not wish to burn the bridge she believed she must cross to get to Joseph.

Once again, the trickster was all gracious smiles, especially to Olive's father.

Olive doubted that her father was aware of what Hortencia was about. Papa would be feeling grand having such a beautiful lady treating him so attentively.

Flirting was what the hussy was doing. To see her father being so used made her sizzle to the tips of her hair.

She was saved from visions of mayhem by Joseph, who finished his conversation with the men and joined her. He led her to the bay of the window, where he could speak and have it appear to be a tender whisper.

'I knew my parents would not change how they felt about you. You may feel more at ease now, aye?'

'Not aye. We are not free of her scheming yet. The wicked besom might still demand to see our certificate of marriage. There is the date to worry about. Your parents are still coming to terms with my low birth. Now to discover we are only recently wed? They would not easily overlook that scandal, I'm sure.'

Joseph nodded, his mouth set and his frown square on Hortencia's back.

'I suppose not.'

Chapter Fourteen

With afternoon tea finished, Olive's father asked her for a word in private, and told her he could not return home without speaking of an important matter.

She took his arm and led him outside. They sat on a bench which gave them a view of the front garden and the driveway.

'Do you mind that I did not marry James?' She might as well get to the heart of it…her defiance of his dictate.

'Ach, no. You did very well for yourself. All is as it should be.'

'You do understand that I would not have wed the baker, no matter how much you insisted. He was Eliza's beau.'

'And now her husband. They have brought Laura home to live with them already.'

'They have? That is wonderful news! Then you are right about all being as it should be. I only pray that no one suspects the truth of who she is.'

'You girls did a good job of keeping the secret.' He caught her hand and held it in both of his. She could not recall the last time he did that. 'I have a confession…and a promise to go with it. Seeing how everything worked out so well for you and your sister made me want to brag about how I succeeded in bringing it all about. Then it was pointed out to me that I had nothing to do with any of it.'

'By Eliza, I suppose.'

'No, by your mother…in a dream. She told me I was high-handed and had nearly ruined everything for her girls.'

'You saw Mama in a dream?' She wished it was true, but he'd probably been drinking.

'As clearly as I see you. She told me to apologize.'

'I accept your apology.' She squeezed his hand, blinked away the moisture gathering in her eyes.

'Ah, I'm glad, then. Now for the other part, the promise. You will recall that your mother was a virtuous woman. Well, she gave me strong words about seeking comfort from a jug. It paid her no honour whatsoever. She made me promise to quit immediately. I have never broken a promise to your mother, and so I sit here beside you, a sober man.'

'This is the best news! But it must have been difficult for you.'

Mama must have come to him, then! He would never have promised to stop drinking otherwise.

'It is odd, but no. The reason I indulged in a wee dram was to ease my sorrow. I missed your mother so. Now that I have seen her, it makes me think she was never gone. Only out of sight, you see?' Olive nodded, because she earnestly wanted to see. 'My good wife gave me a hard scolding. You will recall that she used to, sometimes. She pointed out that I was not the father I ought to have been.'

'Oh, Papa, you were the best you could be. I could burst, I am that proud of you.'

When he smiled, she nearly did burst. Her Papa, the one who had swung her about as a child, told funny stories and tickled her…it was that father's smile she saw now.

'It is good to hear, but lassie, I sorely regret the years I've wasted. I need for you to know it. I promise I will not miss the time with my grandchildren that I did with you and your sister. I suspect that man of yours will do his part to provide plenty of them.'

As true as this was, it was not a thought to indulge in while sitting beside her father.

'I am glad you came to visit. The kids were an adorable gift,' she said in a quick change of subject.

'They were your mother's idea. Your sister said I was daft and should not bring them.'

'If Mama visits you again, you may tell her they were well received.'

'We had a good visit, your mother and I. It was a long dream. She told me she would come to me again as long as I behaved myself.'

The front door opened. A whisper of rustling skirts and the sharp click of shoes on tile announced Hortencia's arrival.

'Ah, there you are, Cedric. I was afraid I had missed giving you a proper goodbye. Please allow me to walk you to the end of the drive.'

Olive wanted to growl. No matter how Hortencia acted the part of a lady, she was not one.

Father stood. Then he bent to kiss Olive's cheek.

'Do not trust her,' Olive whispered.

'Ach, I am fool enough to enjoy her attention but not fool enough to think she means it.'

The day could not end soon enough. Matters might have come out far worse than they had.

They still might.

To add to Joseph's misery, he was once again alone with Olive in her chamber. Echoes of last time came at him from every corner—especially, though, from the bed.

He did not dare even glance that way, let alone think of it.

Olive directed him to sit in the chair beside the window. He settled in and closed his eyes.

Something dropped down onto the mattress. Heaven help him. How would he survive this torture? Had his wife undressed and climbed under the covers?

No, there would not have been time.

'I thought you two would never come upstairs!'

'Eliza?'

Eliza!

Olive gawked at her sister as if she might be a vision and not standing next to the bed, pointing at the valise she had tossed on there. 'What…where did you come from?'

'From behind the curtain, naturally. The pertinent question is, do you know where that awful woman is?'

'Hortencia was in the parlor when we came up,' Joseph answered with a shrug. 'I assume she is still there.'

'It would be a mistake, assuming anything about her.' Eliza opened the latches on the valise. She withdrew the highwayman's costume and tossed it at Olive. 'She is going to the tavern tonight to expose us. You must stop her.'

'She knows?' How could she? Anyone who knew the secret about Laura would take it to the grave. 'Help me with this, Joseph,' Olive said while fumbling with the button of her bodice.

'I suppose it is my fault. I made the mistake of sitting out in the sunshine with Laura on my lap this afternoon when Hortencia walked by with Father after tea. I was kissing her nose and tickling her belly. I may have said something about being her proud Mama, I cannot recall…but as you said. The woman is part hound.'

'How do you know she is on her way to expose us?' Olive asked.

'Hortencia made the mistake of believing I couldn't hear her from the garden. You should have heard her grumbling to herself about what she was going to do tonight. It was fascinating to be privy to what was going on in her mind. And a good thing I did hear it. We must hurry. What sort of vile creature would label a child a bastard in order to gain her own selfish ends? You being her selfish end, Joseph. I heard her say so several times.'

'The woman is daft as well as wicked.' Joseph plucked the red plumed hat off the bed and placed it on Olive's head. 'I will have a horse saddled for you.'

'No time for that,' Eliza said. 'Star is at the edge of the woods already dressed in her costume. I think she is anxious to perform one last time.'

'How do you know she is?' Joseph thought it unlikely.

He was not anxious for this performance. The last thing he wanted was for his wife to go out in the dark and face Hortencia alone.

'Perhaps it is the apple she is anxious for, but she knows that when the gauze goes on, an apple will soon follow,' Olive pointed out while she picked up her sword. She turned it in the lamplight, making the steel glimmer.

'I hope you run her through with it,' Eliza snapped. 'No, never mind. I would not have you commit murder.'

'Joseph and I are now wed,' Olive announced abruptly.

'Well, then. I am happy for it. I am only surprised it took you both so long.'

'You are not stunned?'

Eliza gave a short snort-laugh. 'Any fool can see how much you love one another.'

Olive shot him a stricken look. What did it mean?

There was no time to dwell on it now.

How close was Hortencia to the village? Perhaps she had already arrived.

He would forbid Olive to take this risk if there was any other way. But curse it, his wife was probably the only one who could turn her away from The Shepherd's Keep.

'I will check the stable to see if she has taken a horse. Pray she had not got ahead of us.'

'Joseph,' Olive caught his sleeve and gave it a tug. 'Try and imagine this as an adventure. I find it helps.'

'Adventure, is it? I shall follow behind to make certain it remains one.'

She looked as if she would object, but Eliza cut her off by saying, 'Do not worry. We will stay well-hidden.'

Olive closed her eyes and took a slow, deep breath. He knew the look. She was drawing the highwayman into herself.

'Ho, me lads,' Olive said once she opened her eyes. 'Let us venture out into the storm and slay the wicked plans of our villain. Defend the reputations of the fair Eliza and Laura.'

Her words were playful, but the urgency of the outing could not be overstated.

Luckily, the storm Olive had mentioned did not exist. The villain did.

The three of them went out of the house, as silent as the mouse they frightened on the back stairway.

It could not be denied that there was a splash of adventure to the outing.

More, though, there was risk. Much could go wrong.

Olive waited in her spot under the shadow of the tree. There was no telling when their villain would come along. Joseph had reported that she had not taken a horse, but he had seen her walking towards the stable.

It could only be assumed that she meant to take one, and where else would she be going than where she said she would?

Olive glanced over her shoulder. She did not see Joseph or her sister, but she knew they were there, crouching in dense shrubbery.

Joseph's fears of her, once again, hitting a branch or dashing her head on a rock were unfounded, probably.

Honestly, she did not mind that they were keeping watch.

Ah, just there…a muffled sound. Olive strained to listen. Hooves clopped on the dirt, coming slowly closer.

It was not likely that anyone but Hortencia was riding this particular stretch of the road.

Within seconds, the woman was going to get a fright to last a lifetime.

The ghoul withdrew her sword from its scabbard. The hiss of steel on leather sounded ominous. Flashes of silver in beams of moonlight would give the rider a terrible fright.

Ah, here she came, the hood of her cloak dipping over her face.

The highwayman and her fearful steed stepped out of shadow. Olive gave a shrill, awful wail. Star rose, pawed the air while neighing and showing the whites of her eyes.

How gratifying to know what a wild sight those eyes must be in the darkness.

While Olive had never enjoyed frightening her father, glory fire, she was enjoying this.

Hortencia drew her mount up short, and stared hard as if questioning what had just dissolved out of the darkness to block her way.

Humph…apparently she was not as easily convinced as Father was that she was facing a spectre from the underworld.

A low, creepy moan issued from the shrubbery. Hortencia's mouth went wide at the sound, but no shriek emerged. Her face was as pale as the moon, though.

Clearly her composure was shaken now. She jerked hard on her mount's bridle, probably in an attempt to make him run for home. But Ben was the gentlest horse in the stable and seemed to want nothing more than to stand in place and gaze at Star.

Bless the beast for doing his part.

Star trotted forward, then pranced in in a circle around their 'victim'.

Since Ben understood nothing about highwaymen or phantoms, he offered Star a friendly whicker.

Being well-trained, Star remained in character, snorting and stomping.

The ghoul in Olive grinned. She extended the tip of her sword. Feeling fiendish, the highwayman flicked the hood of Hortencia's cloak with the blade tip.

The hood flipped back on her shoulders. A respectable gash showed in the deep blue velvet.

Ordinarily, Olive would not ruin a perfectly lovely garment, but in this case, it was necessary.

Once the fright was finished, Hortencia must not discount it all as a vision and then decide to go to the village later on.

A high-pitched scream burst from the bushes, then faded to a whimper.

Bless a gust of wind for rusting the leaves overhead just then, and double bless an unseen owl who took that instant to whistle a hoot.

Hortencia jerked, lost her balance, then tumbled off the saddle. She crumpled into a heap on the path and, covering her face with her skirt, she sobbed.

Given how pretty she was, a passerby might think her an angel being accosted by some depraved creature.

Luckily, there were no passersby.

This little stage served as a lesson that one could not always believe what one's eyes saw.

No matter how pretty she looked, this woman was a menace.

But where to go from here?

Olive could not speak a warning for her to turn around. For all that she looked a highwayman, she sounded like Olive… Billings.

There was nothing for it. The sword must do the speaking.

Olive swung it in a circle overhead. It struck a low branch, slicing a shower of leaves down on her.

One of the leaves brushed Hortencia's hand. Her head jerked up.

There was no reason whatsoever Olive should feel regret for the tears tracking Hortencia's cheeks. And yet, she did. Even knowing what the woman intended to do, Olive disliked seeing the terror she'd instilled.

Still, with the sword circling, Olive pointed her other

hand at Ben. Hopefully conveyed the message that she was to mount.

Pointing her sword toward the village, she wagged the weapon, a clear warning not to go that way. Next she nodded, pointed the sharp-looking tip up the hill toward the manor house.

When Hortencia merely blinked up at her, Olive gave the silent signal for Star to roll her eyes.

Ben, sweet horse that he was, nudged his fallen rider.

Without taking her eyes off the phantom highwayman, Hortencia rose shakily from the path. She stood beside Ben for a moment, her gaze sharp on Olive. Then she mounted the saddle.

Swiping tears from her cheek, she turned Ben's head toward home, all the while casting the spectre a speculative frown.

Once she was gone, Joseph and Eliza came out from hiding.

'We must reach home before she does.' Olive slid off the saddle and hurried to undress. She shoved the costume at her sister. 'I did not like the way she looked at me, at the last. I think she suspects.'

'She is a canny thing,' Eliza said. 'You did keep your hat low? No moonlight shone on your face?'

'I was involved in the moment and cannot say for certain where the moon was shining.'

'No hope for it now, if she did recognize you,' Eliza said. 'You and Joseph ride Star to the manor by way of the stream. It is a quicker way back. I will follow, find Star, and bring her home.'

Joseph made a leap onto the saddle, drawing Olive up in front of him. Without a further word, they were off for home.

It took only moments to reach the woods near the stable. Joseph secured the horse out of sight. Then then he grabbed Olive's hand while they ran for the back door of the kitchen.

The door was not quite closed behind them when Olive heard Ben's hooves trotting into the yard.

Joseph looked out the chamber window, watching for Hortencia's arrival.

The excursion had been a success in that Hortencia had not made it to the tavern, but the problem remained. She knew their greatest secret and meant to reveal it.

Olive was stepping into the gown she had discarded at the beginning of this caper, and he was watching that, too.

'Hurry, love. I see her crossing the paddock.'

All at once, Olive ceased fastening buttons and gave him a quizzical look.

Clearly she had not missed his slip of tongue.

Turning from the window, he hurried across the chamber, then finished buttoning up Olive's gown.

And then…then, with his hands on her shoulders, he drew her to him. Kissed her hard, urgently.

Hortencia would be halfway across the meadow by now, so he had no time to explain, even if he knew how. Only this afternoon, he had promised Olive he would be the husband she wished for him to be.

'We must hurry,' was all he said in the face of her astonishment.

They dashed downstairs, rushed through back hallways, passed by the kitchen and at last entered the parlor.

Grimacing, he greeted his parents with a nod. Mama and Father glanced at one another, brows raised.

'Back again?' his father asked. Who could blame him for seeming surprised? They had said their good-nights only an hour ago.

Joseph snatched a book from a shelf on the way to the couch. Pulling Olive down next to him, he opened it.

'*The Migration Patterns of Songbirds*,' Olive read the book title aloud. 'I have always wondered how it works.'

Three paragraphs into discovery, Hortencia burst into the room, breathing hard...but glaring harder.

At Olive.

'My word,' Olive exclaimed. 'You look a fright. Have you encountered some sort of mishap?'

'Indeed, my dear,' Mama said. 'You have ripped the hood of your cloak.'

Hortencia had something curled in her fist. Crossing the room, she let it fall on the open pages of the book.

'I found this in the hallway outside of the kitchen. It is a leaf.'

'I am sure my daughter-in-law will have a word with the housemaids in the morning. Certainly there is no reason to be distraught about a leaf on the floor,' Lady Claymore said.

'This woman is not who you think she is!' Hortencia swirled her cloak off her shoulders, displaying the damage done to the hood even though it had already been noted and commented on. 'She is a deceiver...a trickster! You see what she did with her sword.'

'You are overwrought.' Mama patted the couch, the spot between herself and Father. 'Please do sit down. I will ring for a cup of tea.'

'I was accosted by a phantom...her.' Hortencia pointed her finger at Olive.

'There have been rumours of a highwayman in the area. Although, who would believe it?' Joseph commented, snapping the book closed. The leaf fell on the floor. 'When did this happen?'

'You know very well when. Not twenty minutes ago. That was you howling in the bushes, wasn't it?'

'Really, Hortencia.' Father frowned. 'My heir howling in bushes? I rather doubt it.'

'We shall send for the doctor.' Mama rose. Crossing the room, she looked at Hortencia's face for a moment and then pressed the backs of her fingers to her forehead. Mama used this gesture to ferret out any sort of illness.

'People do take delight in spreading fearful tales,' Mama said.

Joseph wondered if his mother sensed the anger pulsing from her would-be patient.

Even sitting several feel away, he felt it. But it was probably because he knew why she was so angry.

'It is no tale. Olive is the highwayman.'

Mama shrugged, then frowned. 'You are speaking irrationally, although I do not detect a fever.'

Hortencia spun out from under the other woman's touch. She marched jerkily to the hearth, turned her back on them all and hugged her arms around her middle.

A tempest was about to be released in the parlor.

He reached for Olive's hand. Gave it a reassuring squeeze. She gave him one back. There was something very right about touching his wife. He was close to telling her so. Only not now. Later, if he was lucky enough to be allowed in her chamber. After kissing her again, he might not be.

For the moment, Hortencia was silent. The only sound in the room came from her skirt shifting across her hips while she swayed. Damned if it did not bring to mind a cobra in the moment before it strikes. This viper was rising for a final attack.

He prayed that they would all survive her venom.

'No matter how my parents react to this, you remain my wife,' he whispered to Olive. 'We have things to discuss.'

Olive nodded in the second that Hortencia pivoted, her eyes pinpoints of hatred. 'Oh my…isn't that the sweetest thing you have ever seen?'

'Aye, it is. As I have told you before, I love my wife.'

He felt Olive jerk at his words. She might be displeased to hear it was the truth.

'This would all be ever so admirable, so utterly charming…if there was any truth to it.' Hortencia's walked slowly toward his parents.

'What has come over you?' Mama's patience appeared to be at an end. 'Anyone can see how much my son and his wife love one another.'

'Nothing you have to say will change that, Hortencia,' Joseph pointed out, although he did not believe it would deter her from what she was bound to reveal.

It was only that he wished for his wife to know it.

'Dear Lady Amelia.' Hortencia took his mother's hand, her expression suddenly soft and sorrowful. 'I hate to be the one to reveal the truth, but no one else will, and I can no longer see you being taken advantage of.'

'I have no idea what you are going on about. Perhaps we should all retire before I discover what it is.'

'Hortencia does not believe that Olive and I are wed,' Joseph declared, deciding it would be better to lead the charge. Let the accuser be the one to defend herself.

'It is true, Lady Amelia. As I tried to tell you before,

they have been living in sin right under all of our noses. I cannot imagine a worse insult.'

'I see,' Mama said, her voice sounding calmer than it ought to after such a revelation. 'Please tell us why you think he would do so?'

'Our Joseph has been bewitched…clearly ensnared in some sort of enchantment.'

How right she was. At the end of this, Olive was going to know it, too. She might reject him. Regardless, he could no longer lie to her about his feelings.

'You are undone, Hortencia. Olive and I *are* wed. You cannot change it.'

'I would be undone, wouldn't I? Joseph and I are to wed. You, you wicked thing, have trapped him in an immoral liaison.'

'You are wrong,' Joseph stated.

'It must be true. Why else would you dally with a common goatherd when you could marry me?'

'Olive Billings…' he emphasized her new last name, making it clear that she belonged to him and this family '…is the finest lady I know.'

'You see? He is possessed. Surely, Lady Amelia, you will not allow this behaviour to carry on under your own roof. Tell your son to put her away and wed the woman he was intended to wed.'

Hortencia stepped close to Olive, her face a sneer.

In spite of the finger wagging near her nose, Olive appeared unflustered.

No acting the part of a lady, this. Olive was one, no matter her birth.

'I will not allow you to marry my husband.'

'Show me a wife who would?' was Father's comment on

the matter. He sat back on the couch, watching the drama unfold as it would. 'And just to be clear. This is Joseph's roof, not ours. A wedding gift from me and his mother.'

Mama caught Hortencia's finger, drawing it away from Olive's face. 'My dear, kindly act the lady you were brought up to be.'

'I was meant to be the future Lady Claymore.'

'Son, this matter can be cleared up easily enough. Be so good as to fetch your marriage certificate,' Father said, draping one arm across the back of the couch.

'Oh, by all means do that. He would never show it to me!'

'I cannot imagine why he would need to.' Father's casual pose belied his annoyance. Joseph knew the posture well.

'Lord Claymore, you are about to face a ruinous scandal. I will protect you from it by wedding your son, even though his behaviour of late is unforgivable. I will not let your family be brought to shame.'

'If there is shame brought upon us, it will be done by you, not me, Hortencia.' Joseph narrowed a gaze at her, then addressed his father. 'I will bring the certificate.'

Joseph strode the short distance down the hallway to his office and plucked the document out of the desk. He sniffed it. Close up, the ink still smelled fresh. Hopefully no one would notice.

More than that, he hoped his parents did not notice the date in the corner.

If they did, what Hortencia accused them of, living in sin, would appear to have been true for a time.

When he entered the parlor, Father and Mama stood close together.

His mother took the certificate. Father peered over her shoulder.

'This is...' Mama looked up sharply at him. Then she subtly covered the date with her thumb. 'Hortencia, come and have a look. We would appreciate putting this matter behind us.'

Mama gave her three full seconds to study the document before she snatched it away, folded it in quarters and handed it back to Joseph.

'Now that we have that nonsense settled,' Mama declared, 'I am certain you will be anxious to return to London, Hortencia. I have no doubt you miss society. You do seem out of sorts without it.'

'I am not out of sorts. However, you will be. There is something else. I would not normally bring it up as it is so indelicate. However, my hand is forced. I have knowledge of a matter which would ruin this family in society's eyes. You will not be welcomed into a decent home again.'

Mama grew pale. A respectable name was everything to her.

'You know of what I speak, Olive. Give Joseph back to me or I vow, I will tell everyone.'

Chapter Fifteen

When the moment came, it was worse than Olive could have imagined possible.

Seconds ago, she had believed that no matter what, she would never give in to Hortencia.

Joseph was her husband. She would not give him to anyone.

Now here she was, facing a decision. Who was she willing to ruin?

Would it be her sister? Sweet and innocent Laura?

Would it be her husband?

Or would it be the reputation of her new family?

No matter what choice she made, Olive, herself, was ruined, because whichever way she went with this, she could not live with the guilt.

A wave of nausea hit her hard. She pressed her fingers to her middle.

In the moment of stone silence which followed Hortencia's threat, a gust of wind whipped around the eaves, howling and putting her nerves further on edge. Probably everyone else's, too.

Joseph gave her a look which she could not interpret. Fear, perhaps, that she would hand him over to their enemy.

When she'd pledged herself to Joseph in marriage, she'd

meant it. Her life recently had been a series of lies, but those vows had been the truest words she had ever spoken, despite playing a part.

Would she now forsake him? Let no man separate them, the minister had said.

If she did not, Hortencia would rip her sister up without a qualm. In doing so, she would ruin the family only just begun. The damage to Laura would be unspeakable. What kind of twisted soul would label a child a bastard knowing the shame would follow her all her life? Fallen Leaf was a small village. It was not as if they could hide from the scandal. Even Mary and Harlow Strickland would suffer for their part in it.

'You have half a minute more. Then I will reveal the truth.'

'The truth, Hortencia?' Joseph placed a reassuring arm on Olive's shoulder. 'There is nothing you can say which will change the fact that Olive is the woman I chose to marry. Whatever she decides, I will not wed you.'

Strong words, determined ones.

And yet there was more to it. If she truly loved Joseph, and she did, would she allow the Claymore title to be besmirched?

Joseph's parents had accepted Olive, commoner that she was. They took her to their hearts when they might have rejected her. Back in London, her low birth was going to be gossiped about. These good people were willing to risk tainting the family name for her.

The truth that Hortencia threatened to reveal would be another thing all together. To accept a fallen woman as a part of one's family would be unthinkable. Their son's sister-in-law would certainly be a family member.

The truth that Olive had always valued was about to take her around the throat and choke her.

'Joseph,' she gasped, hugging him tight.

He pressed her head to his chest with his wide palm. His fingers curled in her hair, and his heart thumped hard under her ear.

None of this was his doing.

She loved him.

That was the end of it, was it not?

At their beginning, all he'd wanted was to escape this horrid woman who would have ruined his life. No one could fault him for it.

How could she now sacrifice him?

Joseph and his family or Eliza and hers?

No.

She could not.

Either way she went, she could not.

She had the impression Joseph wanted to say something to her but bit it back.

'What do you choose?' Hortencia actually stomped her foot in childish temper. 'I am finished waiting.'

Olive hated what she must do. Lives would be ruined.

She pushed out of Joseph's arms.

How was she to survive this?

'I choose my husband.' Grief for what everyone else would suffer brought tears to her eyes. 'Do what you will, Hortencia.'

'I have heard all I need to,' Lady Amelia declared, then walked to the bell pull and yanked on the cord. Within seconds, a footman entered the parlor. 'Ready the carriage for Lady Hortencia, please. Inform her maid that she will be leaving for London within the hour.'

'Right away, my lady.' The footman spun about and hurried to do as he was bid.

'Oh, but Lady Amelia, you know I only wish the best for this family,' Hortencia said. 'And so I must tell you what I know. It will break my heart, of course. Trust me, though, once you have heard the truth, it is that woman you will put on the coach.'

'Olive, my dear, it is apparent she is going to reveal something that should not be revealed. Would you like to be the one to tell us what it is? I do not trust Hortencia to present this in the most favourable light,' Lady Amelia said gently.

She would not like to, no…it was the very last thing she wished, but she was grateful to be offered the chance.

'Thank you, I—'

'Her sister is a fallen woman! There is no favourable light.'

Hortencia's face looked harsh and unhinged. With her mask off, her genuine character made her pretty face ugly.

Her mother-in-law flinched.

Joseph's mother had overlooked a great deal when it came to Olive, but this…it would be too much to accept.

'I know it is a blow, Lady Amelia,' Hortencia cooed. 'The trollop is the woman who sells us cheese. I can only imagine she gave up her virtue for a penny and got stuck with the unhappy outcome.'

'She's called Eliza,' Olive put in. 'Her daughter's name is Laura.'

'Unhappy outcome?' Joseph snorted, his disapproval palpable. 'You are greatly mistaken. No mother cherishes her child more than Eliza does…or more than her aunt does.'

'Do you believe children to be a blessing, Hortencia?' Lady Amelia's voice was mild, but it was her viscountess voice, so Olive knew better than to believe mild was what she felt.

'Certain children, of course. This one was kept in the care of a neighbour. Can you believe it? Right next door to her disreputable mother. The apple does not fall far from the tree.'

'I believe that to be true…in some cases,' the viscount said, staring at Hortencia in disgust. 'Don't you agree, Amelia?'

'It does seem to be true, although I am sorry to say I did not recognize it until now. I do beg your forgiveness, Joseph.'

'I do not understand what we are talking about.' He lifted his brows, clearly as confused as Olive was.

'They are grateful I spoke up and saved the family from shame…before it all came to light from someone who did not care. We can be together now, Joseph, just as we were meant to be,' Hortencia implored.

'It would be prudent of you not to take this conversation any further than this room.' Lady Amelia leveled her weighty stare at Hortencia.

'It shall be our secret, Mama.'

'You do not seem to understand. I am *not* your mama, not in any sense of the word.'

'But I soon will be…' Lady Claymore shook her head one time, but once was all it took. 'Surely you are not suggesting that you will choose a commoner over me?' Hortencia exclaimed.

'I believe that *is* what she means,' the viscount said.

'Precisely what I mean. Understand this, Hortencia. Although you are a high-ranking lady of society by birth, you will still need to marry well to maintain your respectability.'

Hortencia lifted her perfect little nose, giving an imperious sniff. 'I have every intention of marrying well, with or without you.'

'I am sure you expect to. But let me ask, do you know how long it is between a child's conception and its birth?'

'A foolish question, and not to any point I can think of...but nine months.'

'Surely you are aware that many pregnancies, even in proper old London, are shorter? Some much shorter than others.'

Hortencia blinked, apparently not understanding.

'Our Joseph was a little early,' the viscount announced. Was that a gleam in his eye? Yes...quite clearly, it was a gleam. 'Eight weeks, wasn't it, my dear?'

'Yes, dear, eight and a half.'

'I was—' Joseph gasped, coughed, so Olive patted him helpfully on the back.

'You were a lusty nine pounds when you were born in spite of it.' Lady Amelia smiled at her son, then gave her attention back to Hortencia. 'You do understand what that means?'

'Well, I suppose...it means... I dare not say.'

'Do you not? I shall say it for you then. It is not all that rare for children to be conceived before the vows are spoken. I need for you to understand this before I continue with what I am going to tell you.'

'Very well.' Hortencia rolled her eyes as if saying none of this had to do with her or their present situation.

'To begin, your mother and I were friends, but not terribly close ones.'

'I know that. Everyone does. I do not know what it has to do with—'

'You were born at six months, Hortencia. Your mother conceived you well before she wed.'

'Ah,' the viscount declared with a grin. 'You and young Laura share a bond…being not quite the blessing other babies are, I mean.'

'What a vile thing to suggest! My birth was…it was… My mother was no fallen woman. She was a noble lady.'

'You are fortunate that she was. Because of it, your arrival in the world, at every bit of seven pounds, was remarked upon, but soon it was politely overlooked.'

The footman stepped into the parlor and nodded at Joseph's mother, indicating that the carriage was waiting.

'Well! I will make my escape. To think I nearly allowed myself to be attached this family.' Hortencia gave a smirking smile to each of them. 'I would say I wish you well, but I do not. There is no hope for any of you.'

'Be that as it may, Hortencia, but if you speak a single word against any member of my family, I will remind people of your…unusual birth. Do not think they will not recall it. No proper gentleman will have you.'

Storming towards the hallway, Hortencia cast a glare over her shoulder. 'You are cursed, the lot of you.'

As one, they gazed at the now empty doorway.

'I for one, feel blessed,' her father-in-law announced.

'Greatly,' his wife agreed. 'That woman would have crushed our boy. Olive, my dear, we are so pleased that it is you and not her.'

'And we are anxious to meet your niece.' The viscount grinned at his wife. 'What relation is she to us? Not granddaughter, but surely she is something special.'

'I do not believe there is a term for it, but she is our son's niece, and so we shall simply call her our special girl.'

Olive sat hard on the couch and began to weep. She and Joseph had survived the ordeal. Eliza and her family had as well. There was such relief and joy inside of her that tears were the only way of letting her emotions out.

A weight settled beside her. Motherly arms wrapped her up.

'No one will learn any of what went on here tonight. We may be a family with secrets, but all families have them. Dry your tears now, daughter. All is well.'

'It could not be better, if you ask me,' her father-in-law declared, patting Olive on top of her head. 'I never did trust Hortencia, even as a girl. Too much like her mother. The apple and the tree, and all that.'

'I am sorry to my soul that I pushed her on you, Joseph.' With that, Lady Amelia kissed Olive's forehead, then rose from the couch. She hugged her son about the ribs. 'Please forgive me.'

'Always, Mama,' he said.

'I am quite done in, Marshall.' She sighed. 'Take me upstairs.'

Arms about each other's waists, Lady and Lord Claymore walked towards the doorway.

Without turning, Joseph's mama said, 'Tomorrow we shall discuss your marriage licence...that bit about the date.'

They disappeared down the hallway.

'Just when I thought our troubles were over,' Olive said.

'A small skirmish, that's all.'

Joseph wondered what would Olive do when they reached her chamber door.

Now that Hortencia was no longer a threat, there was no reason for her to invite him in.

No one else to be fooled…no more lessons to be learned.

She reached for the doorknob, but he caught her hand.

'May I come in? I wish to have a word.'

'It would probably not be wise.' She slipped her fingers out of his, opened the door and stepped into the room.

She pushed it closed, but he caught it with his hand. 'I am done being wise, Olive.'

'I am not sure what you mean but…' She let go of the door and stepped aside to let him in.

Good so far, but it was not her chamber he wished to be in. It was her heart.

How to get there, though? What words were there to open that door?

None.

He cupped her cheeks, lifted her face, then bent his head to kiss her. Actions were better than words. He might stumble over finding the right ones, but it was his heart speaking.

She did not struggle against him, so that was hopeful. But dash it, she did not lean in and give herself over to him, either.

'I have something to say to you, Olive. If it makes you unhappy, I will not stop you from going.'

'Going where?'

'Home.'

'Humph.' She pushed against his chest, freeing herself of his embrace, although she did not step away. 'And where do you suppose home is?'

'At the cottage, with your family?'

'I say this in friendship, but you are a fool, Joseph Billings. We shall discuss it further after you explain why you are toying with me by continuing to kiss me when you have made it perfectly clear that—'

'That I love you.'

'You...' Her cheeks flushed, and her eyes shimmered. 'I do not believe you. Only last night, you ran from—'

'Aye, love, I was a fool.'

'Maybe this is you being a fool again.' She crossed her arms over her chest, narrowed her eyes.

'Put me to the test. See if I flee or I stay.'

'How do you know I will not be the one to flee this time?'

'All I know is that I love you. If you do not love me, too, you may tell me to go at any time, and I will. But if we are together at the end of it, then we will have gained the world.'

'At the end of what?'

'Our conversation.'

He took her by the shoulders and backed her toward the bed.

The mattress made all sorts of creaking sounds when he tumbled down onto it, drawing her on top of him.

He kissed her again. This time she warmed to it but cautiously.

'This is not talking, Joseph.'

'It is, love, only without tricky words to get in the way.'

'I need to hear the tricky words. Last time we spoke without them, I thought certain things, and then...well, I was wrong about them.'

'You were not wrong. I was.' He picked the pins from her hair. It tumbled over his face in a soft tangle. 'I was wrong about how I felt, wrong about how you felt.'

She squirmed on top of him as if shuffling out of her slippers, one then the other.

'I never told you how I felt, Joseph.'

'Oh, aye, love. You've told me many times.'

She lifted up on her hands, shook her head. With her

hair falling all around, it seemed as if they were enclosed in a silky tunnel.

'When?'

Since she was lifted up, he took the opportunity to free the buttons of her bodice.

'There was the time you came to me that windy night and agreed to help me.'

'I did not say I loved you then. I only agreed that we could help one another.'

Ah, things were looking up now, as she began unfastening his shirt buttons.

'Then you will recall the time when you tried to leave me wearing only your shift?'

'I do not know how you can take that as saying I loved you, either.'

'I can, because you stayed.' With her gown open, he discovered a delicate blue bow holding her chemise closed. He tugged it open. 'Then there was the time you knocked me off the log and urged me to ravage you. That was love.'

'No, it was protecting you from a viper.' She undid a button on his trousers. Words were working better than he'd expected.

She rolled off him so that they lay facing one another.

'Truly, love, I knew it when you chose to save me.'

'Oh...' She touched his cheek, drew her fingers across his lips. 'Well then, you were not wrong.'

'I need to hear the tricky words, too.' Joseph looked vulnerable all at once. Her heart rolled all over itself. 'That night, the reason I left your bed was that I thought you did not want me to love you.'

'But I did.' She kissed him softly on his lips, then moved

so it was easier for him to get her arms out of her gown. 'I do now… Joseph, I love you. You hold my heart.'

'Aye, and you hold mine. It will always be in the palm of your capable little hand.' He kissed her fingers. 'Now, we must put our words to the test, aye? If neither of us flees the bed, we have our proof.'

'The suspense will be too much.'

'Not to fear, I will assure you as we go.'

Olive closed her eyes, feeling reassurance in each touch. When she opened her eyes, she saw love reflected back at her.

The last thing she intended to do was flee. She meant to have this spot beside him, and in his heart, for the rest of her life.

The night went on speaking in tender touches. For the longest time, they did not even need words at all.

At last, when the first bird began to sing, Joseph said, 'Here we are then. Neither of us fled.'

'But I wonder, maybe we should give it another hour or so, just to be sure?'

Three hours later, Olive watched her husband busy at the shaving bowl. His back moved with each stroke of the razor.

What a fine, strong back it was. She had reason to know.

She sighed, not bothering to hide the sound. She did not bother to hide anything from Joseph now.

'What?' he asked, turning to look at her with white froth covering half of his jaw.

'I was just thinking how good it is to look at a finely made naked man and know he is yours.'

'Oh, aye? You think me finely made?' He grinned through

the shaving cream. 'I am not naked, though. There's the towel.'

'In my mind you are.'

'Ah.' He loosened the towel and let it drop. 'You do my ego a great deal of good.'

'What do you think, Joseph? Did we start a child last night?'

He grinned, nodded, wiped his face and then strode towards the bed. 'We were rather diligent in our efforts. But just in case, we really ought to give it another go.'

'Are you certain you are not saying that simply to avoid facing your parents this morning?'

'A grandchild would go a good way towards them looking kindly on the date of our marriage.'

Olive sat up, reaching for Joseph's trousers, which were in the exact spot he had dropped them last night. 'Put them on. We must face our comeuppance.'

'I don't regret what we did, love, no matter how it looks to anyone else.'

Nor did she. Life was coming about as nicely as if it were a book which she'd written with her own hand.

Chapter Sixteen

All during breakfast the next morning, Joseph expected to be called to account for the discrepancy of when his parents had believed him and Olive to be wed and the actual date on their marriage licence.

It never did come up, but something else did.

Between his last chew of ham and his first bite of toast, his mother asked, 'Would it be appropriate for us to take a walk to the village and meet your sister-in-law and her family?'

'We are anxious to get acquainted with little Laura,' Father said. 'We have not had a child in the family since our boy was small. Will your sister mind if we come by?'

'She will be over the moon, I am certain. No one in Fallen Leaf has ever had a visit from a viscount and viscountess.'

Which was the point of the visit, Joseph suspected. If there was anyone in the village who questioned Laura's sudden adoption by Eliza and James, or speculated about her birth, a visit from peers of the realm would forever validate her.

To be accepted by Lord and Lady Claymore would place Eliza's family above reproach.

'Isn't this the day James bakes our favourite bread?' Going to the village seemed a fine outing. 'It is worth every step of the walk just to smell it baking.'

Once along the way, he noticed his mother looking at the swathe of pure blue sky visible beyond the treetops.

'It is no wonder you love it here, Joseph. The weather is lovely. I can nearly taste autumn coming.'

'We will miss it here, son.' Father breathed in a deep, dramatic breath of crisp air. 'But we must return home. Lady Green has her autumn ball in two weeks. Everyone in society will be there. Also, it would be wise for us to keep an eye on Hortencia for a while.'

'It would not hurt to find her a husband.' Mama stooped and picked up a leaf whose edges were beginning to turn yellow. She twirled it in her fingers, looking thoughtful.

Thoughtful about last night, Joseph suspected, and wondering why Hortencia had put so much focus on a leaf.

'Ah, I pity the poor fellow, though.' His father shook his head. 'Tell us, son, why is your wedding certificate dated after you claimed to be wed?'

'There is a good reason for it.' Hopefully his parents would think so. He might be a man grown, but still, their approval was important to him. 'I was desperate to avoid Hortencia. I knew she meant to compromise me. It would not have been so difficult to do here with so few people around.'

'And at the same time, there was my father,' Olive said. 'He had it in his mind that as the oldest daughter, I would wed first. He was insisting I marry James, who was Eliza's true love. I could not have done it, naturally.'

'It only made sense for us to pretend we were wed… We meant to go our own ways once everyone went home.'

'A sensible plan,' Father said with a nod. 'But how would you have explained going your own ways?'

'We never did come up with an explanation.' He grinned at Olive. 'It's why we wed.'

'He is making that up. We had to wed because Hortencia suspected we were not.'

'Are you claiming you were forced to wed against your will? If so, I do not believe you,' Mama said archly.

'Forced, yes...but glad for it,' he answered in all truth.

'It is not for me to pry, or to judge, and yet...' He had never seen his mother blush, but she did it now. 'Joseph, you... How do I say this?'

'We did not share a chamber until after we wed.' Olive blushed as deeply as his mother did.

'Only the once,' Joseph amended truthfully, thinking of the night before their wedding.

'Heaven help me,' Mama muttered. 'And you, dear Olive. I believe you will need what help you can get.'

'Nothing untoward happened that night.' His bride cast him a frown. Not a terribly annoyed one, though.

'It is true. But it did make it clear that we wanted something untoward to happen. So when Hortencia forced the issue, we were well and gone, past willing.' He and his father shared a grin.

'Men...incorrigible, the lot of them, no matter their age.'

Olive slipped her hand into the crook of her new mother's arm while they walked, Joseph and his father a step behind.

High up, tree limbs on each side of the road met, making a canopy and giving the path a pretty dappled look. All around, leaves rustled and whispered.

'Joseph makes it sound as if he was a rogue. The truth is, you raised your son well. He was always respectful.'

'I am not one to judge in any case.'

'That is not our job, is it…to judge?' Olive said. 'Ours is to forgive. I hope you forgive us for tricking you.'

'Oh, quite.' Mama patted Olive's fingers. 'I trust there are no more secrets.'

'I do not see how there could be.' Father laughed when he said so.

Joseph took a long step, bringing him alongside Olive. He gave her a wink and a grin. She shrugged…nodded.

Taking his elbow, she drew him back a step. 'From now on, I am going to live a strictly honest life. I do not wish to take part in any more schemes.'

'Agreed.'

His parents turned, probably wondering what the whispering was about.

'There is just one more thing.'

'Will I require a fainting couch, son?'

'I think not, Mama…only… You have heard of the fearful highwayman ghoul?'

Both his parents blinked, silent and clearly puzzled.

'The one with the fire-eyed horse…sprung from the underworld?' he clarified.

Father's brows nearly touched. 'Oh, that one. Indeed we have.'

'Aye, well…it was Olive.'

Two weeks after Joseph's parents returned to London, Eliza invited Olive and Joseph to dinner, along with the sisters' father.

It proved to be a happy time which dissolved the last of her concerns that the lives of a viscount and a cottager would not mesh.

She ought to have known it would be this way between

the families since it had always been so between her and Joseph.

Even in the times when her mind warned her they could never be together, her heart knew the truth. She and Joseph were destined for one another. How else would they have overcome what obstacles society had placed between them?

While they ate, laughed, and talked about everything from making cheese to the proper way to hold a dance partner, it became clear that they, all of them, high born and common, were family.

She'd got a sense of kinship taking root on the day they had walked to the village with Joseph's parents so that they could meet Eliza, James and Laura.

Tonight, before the meal was finished, she no longer recognized a separation of class, only people coming together to celebrate.

It was after sunset when she and Joseph walked her father home. In the west, lightning glittered over the hilltop. Cooling air smelled damp with a coming storm.

Father had no sooner waved them goodbye and closed the cottage door when rain hit hard.

If they ran for home, they would get drenched. If they took shelter in the cottage, they would not be alone.

'The stable.' Joseph snatched her hand. They dashed around to the back of the cottage, then along a short path.

Olive drew open the stable doors, breathing in the mingled scents of goat and fresh straw. She loved living in the manor house, but she also loved it here. One more illustration, she thought, of how the two sides of her life could meld.

She did not need to choose one over the other. Because Joseph was hers, both lives were as well.

'What is behind that pretty smile, love?'

'Well…it's love.'

Gilroy rose from his straw bed, gave a bleat and then nudged Olive's hand to be petted.

'Looks like I am not the only one in love with you.'

Olive stroked the goat between his ears. Gilroy leaned against her, clearly content.

'He misses me, I suppose.' Although she did visit the flock nearly every afternoon. 'I used to sing to them in the morning.'

'Can't blame the poor fellow. I'd miss it if you did not sing to me.'

'When do I sing to you?'

'You don't know?' His eyes warmed, and his mouth quirked up at one corner. He touched her lips with his thumb then drew it down her throat in slow circles.

When he kissed her, she sighed, gave a little moan.

'Aye, just so.'

'That is not singing,' she protested.

'But it is, the sweetest love song a man could hear.' All of a sudden, Joseph jerked and spun about, swiping at the seat of his trousers.

'Gilroy! You little beast! You should be ashamed.' But then she grabbed her middle and laughed.

The sight of the goat placidly chewing a torn piece of Joseph's trousers was too much. The humour could not be ignored.

Not by her, at any rate.

'Curse the beast!' Joseph plucked the shredded threads of the hole Gilroy ate in the wool.

'And to think, that at this very moment we could be attending the Autumn Ball,' she said.

They had been invited to the grand event but had promptly declined the honour.

Not that Olive wasn't curious about that side of her husband's life. One day she would be required to be a part of it.

Not yet, though. For now, they did not wish to share each other's company with anyone.

'I do not mind missing it any more than you do,' he said while brushing a curious kid away from the hem of his trousers.

Joseph took her by one hand, twirling her in a circle. 'We shall enjoy a private ball, right here among our four-legged friends. See how they enjoy our skilful steps.'

He waltzed her over bits of straw on the stone floor. Star whinnied when they whirled by her stall. Olive did enjoy dancing this way, the steps so smooth and elegant. A day was coming when she would wear a fine gown and spin about a crowded ballroom, but it could not be as lovely as this moment.

No orchestra would match the soft bleats of the kids, the whicker and stomping of hooves…the rush of Joseph's breathing.

Joseph changed the pace of the dance. Slower, then slower still, until they were simply standing and swaying…looking at one another in a language which went beyond words.

She touched his chest, tapped her fingers on one button of his shirt. Her message was clear…she wanted him… quite impatiently.

When he pressed his big hands on her waist and drew her tight against his hips, she supposed it was his answer. She would have him…and he would have her.

'That ladder,' he whispered. 'Is it solid, and where does it lead to?'

'Solid.' She lifted her chin, indicating the top of the ladder. 'We keep fresh straw up there…and blankets.' The loft was her favourite place to read.

'Come then, love.' With his fingers pressing her waist, he walked her backward, step by slow, sultry step. 'I wish to hear you sing.'

Epilogue

Claymore House, London,
December, one year later

'Are you nervous?' Joseph murmured.

Olive nodded. 'Does the trembling show?'

Members of proper society were beginning to enter the grand parlor. She and Joseph stood beside his parents, her father, then Eliza and James next to them.

Lady Amelia had promised this would be a comfortable evening at home with some of their dearest friends stopping by to meet the newest members of the family.

She was certain introducing one's country kin to society was not usual, but having country kin was not usual either.

She admired her new parents for being so comfortable in their social position that they did not fear doing so. To Olive's way of thinking, they set the trends which others would imitate. Hopefully, they would. If they did not, she would follow Lord and Lady Claymore's example and not be troubled by it.

As it turned out, a few of Viscount and Viscountess Claymore's dearest friends made up a large crowd. In fact, they would add up to more than the population of Fallen Leaf.

Olive could only wonder what her father thought about

being stuffed into black formal wear and glossy shoes. He did look wonderful.

While he was so fine and dapper, his own goats would run from him, not recognizing who he was.

Olive scarcely recognized him either. The change in her father made her soul sing in gratitude. He had kept his promise to Mama and gone all this time without drinking. She had every hope he would continue that way. These days when he went to The Shepherd's Keep, it was to visit friends and puff out his chest over who his new relatives were.

More voices came from outside. She must have shivered or gasped or done something to alert Joseph she was nervous.

'Draw on a character, the way you used to do,' Joseph suggested softly. 'It will settle you.'

'No, I cannot. I am standing here as myself. People will accept me or not. I will not present a false character.'

'Good then. I like you fine as you are. Everyone else will, too.'

'They will pretend to, anyway, for your parents' sake.'

'It's true. All my life I have had to puzzle over who is a friend and who only pretends to be.' He squeezed her hand. As always, his strong presence calmed her. 'We will be home soon, and it will not matter. Let us muddle on.'

'You do not need to muddle, Joseph. You were born knowing what to do.'

His gaze grew suddenly warm with the expression she knew quite intimately. 'I know what I want to do.'

She did, too, and longed to run away upstairs with him.

'Later.' She jumped when he discreetly tickled her ribs. 'But look who has just made their entrance, the Curtis family. Your mother says that Grace is betrothed.'

Olive watched the sisters walking side by side. One Curtis girl had the fair good looks and proper attitude which society adored. The other Curtis girl was taller than most ladies, and slim, with eyes a deep shade of warm brown.

To Olive's way of thinking, Vivienne was lovely, even if she was not society's prescribed beauty.

'I do like Vivienne,' she remarked. 'I hope she gets what she wants from life, even if it is not a husband.'

'It is different for daughters of a lord. They wed for advantage. Same as first-born sons do.' He gave her a wink and a grin. 'I wed for great advantage.'

'Our daughters will wed as they wish. They will have the futures they want to have. We shall see to it.'

'So we shall. But if we have a son, he will be born to obligation.'

'Such nonsense you speak, Joseph. You have the life you chose.'

'By some miraculous good fortune, I do. I wonder if good fortune can be passed from father to son. I will say it can and believe our boy will be as happy as I am. But so far, we do not have a son or a daughter.'

'I hear an orchestra beginning to play. Dance with me.'

Waltzing with Joseph was rather like floating on a delightful cloud. For those few moments with her feet not touching the earth, everything was perfect.

'I've had news,' Joseph said, grinning in the mischievous way he had.

'Good news, I hope.'

'Depends upon who you are. For us, it is.'

'Then who is it not good for?'

'Hortencia.' He gave her a quick spin. 'It seems that she has fallen into her own trap. She set her cap for a marquis's son. Meant to trap him in the dark where she would compromise him.'

'As she enjoys doing.'

'It did not end well for her, though. Seems the wrong fellow came by and fell into it, a second cousin to the fellow she wanted. A good man, but not of the highest ranking. Well, she pounced upon him. Then, when her chaperone discovered them, as they had arranged for her to do, Hortencia was in the embrace of the wrong man. They are to wed next week.'

'Poor fellow.'

Olive was kept from laughing aloud when her sister walked past.

'Will her babe wait until the party is over to be born, do you think?' Joseph asked, his eyes going wide at his sister-in-law's large, cumbersome form.

'She has a bit of time yet, she thinks.'

'She also says her children need cousins.' He waggled a brow at her. 'All children need cousins. Makes life happier.'

A cold December breeze blew in through an open garden door, fluttering her skirts and ruffling Joseph's coat sleeves. The air was refreshing, and she took a deep breath to savour it.

'Come to the garden with me,' she said, leading him out of the door and ignoring his warning that it was too chilly outside.

With all the talk of cousins, time alone was called for. The house so full of people that she would need the privacy of the garden.

Joseph sat on a bench, drawing her down beside him. With a sigh, she snuggled close, as content as she had ever been in her life.

How could she have ever doubted that life would be easy between them, despite their birth?

Only a few people strolled in the garden. Some of them nodded, and others stopped only long enough to offer their congratulations.

London was not as bad as she had imagined it would be. The people of high society seemed polite and gracious for the most part.

Still, she would be glad to go home. There was much to get ready before spring came.

Olive snuggled deeper into Joseph's side. How delightfully big and warm he was. 'I am so happy I could burst.'

She said this as a clue for him to follow…a crumb to a puzzle's end.

'I'm so cold I could shiver.'

He lifted her chin with one knuckle, then kissed her.

'Hmm, you are cold; that was certainly an icy kiss.'

'I reckon you will need to warm me up. You know how.' What a wonderfully suggestive grin it was, given in the most inappropriate location.

Still, she could not resist kissing him over and over again. He was correct about it being cold outside. However, she needed a bit more time out here.

Eventually, light in the garden grew dim. Distant voices grew fainter. The guests must be going inside.

'We should join them before we turn to ice statues.'

'Soon. Just… I am so happy I really could burst,' she repeated.

'I'd just as well have you whole, if it is all the same to you.'

'Very, very whole, then,' she said, but he was still not catching on. 'Immensely whole.'

'Can you be immensely whole indoors, please?'

He tugged her up from the bench, curled his big body around her and rocked back and forth for a minute.

His breath felt wonderfully warm on her hair.

'It is more that I will be immensely whole, late next spring.'

He cocked his head. 'You are speaking in riddles, love. Tell me directly what is on your mind so we can go back in. Your lips are turning blue, and I think I just saw a snowflake.'

She could do that, but this was so much more fun. In spite of the weather, she wanted to drag out her fun for as long as she could.

Not his fun, she thought, since he was beginning to frown. He would cheer up when she got to the end of it.

'Do you recall a few moments ago when you said that Eliza's children ought to have a cousin?'

A light flashed in Joseph's eyes. Comprehension, she hoped.

'And you are about to burst in the late spring…with the cousin?'

'With your son or daughter.'

'Ah, my sweet Olive. You make me a grateful man, a thousand times over. You will be the loveliest bursting woman come spring. I cannot wait to see it.'

Snow began to fall in earnest now. It seemed to wrap them in a blanket of white, silent velvet.

'It is as if we are alone in London,' she murmured.

'Not so alone, aye?' He pressed his hand to her only slightly rounded stomach.

'I think I felt it move.'

'Not yet. That must have been me shivering…or you.'

'Must be me since now I'm shivering with joy. But let's go inside before our wee baby freezes.'

They were steps from the door when Joseph stopped short.

'Did you see it?'

'See what?'

'Just there, a flash in the shrubbery near the door.'

Oh, dear, she ought to have let him come inside sooner. Now he was imagining things. She peered into the bush, though, just to humour him.

But then…she squinted her eyes at something, its blue and green wings fluttering gently.

'It's a dragonfly! But I can scarce believe it. It is long past their season.'

'Like the one from our wedding day. It was on your finger. I took it then as a hopeful omen.'

The insect flew away and disappeared among the snowflakes.

They blinked at one another.

Olive was the first to recover her voice. 'Did we really see what we thought we did?'

'Maybe…or maybe not. Except it was both of us seeing it.'

Olive took his hand, leading him inside, where a rush of warmth wrapped them up.

'Do you think that was the point? To remind us of that day…that it's the two of us, always.'

'Maybe so. I like the romance of it.' Then he kissed her for a long time. 'The thing of it is, I do not need an insect to remind me. You do it every day.'

'When do I do that? I do not recall saying so.'

'But you do. When you smile at me…when we laugh together, and when you snuggle up to me during the night… especially then.'

He kissed her yet again, a long, slow, forever sort of kiss.

'And when you make those sweet little sighs and moans like you did just now. Oh, aye, love. There is good fortune and forever in it.'

Something mysterious bubbled deep inside her belly, a sweet private tickle.

Good fortune, wonderful blessings.

* * * * *

If you enjoyed this story, be sure to check out these stand-alone historical romances from Carol Arens:

Meeting Her Promised Viscount
The Gentleman's Cinderella Bride

Or let yourself get swept up in her charming The Rivenhall Weddings miniseries

Inherited as the Gentleman's Bride
In Search of a Viscountess
A Family for the Reclusive Baron